OLD FLOATING CLOUD

Can Xue

OLD FLOATING CLOUD

Two Novellas

TRANSLATED BY RONALD R. JANSSEN AND JIAN ZHANG
WITH A FOREWORD BY CHARLOTTE INNES

Northwestern University Press   Evanston, Illinois

Northwestern University Press
Evanston, Illinois 60201

English translations of *Yellow Mud Street* and *Old Floating Cloud*
© 1991 by Northwestern University Press. Foreword © 1991 by
Northwestern University Press. All rights reserved.

This translation was partially funded by the National Endowment
for the Arts.

First printing, 1991

Printed in the United States of America

Library of Congress Cataloging-in-Publication Data

Ts' an-hsüeh, 1953–
    [Ts' ang lao ti fu yün. English]
    Old floating cloud : two novellas / Can Xue ; translated by Ronald
R. Janssen and Jian Zhang ; with a foreword by Charlotte Innes.
        p. cm.
    Translated from Chinese.
    "Yellow mud street": p.
    ISBN 0-8101-0974-3. — ISBN 0-8101-0988-3 (pbk.)
    1. Ts' an-hsüeh, 1953—Translations into English. I. Ts' an
-hsüeh, 1953– Huang ni chieh. English. 1991. II. Title.
PL2912.A5174T7513   1991
    895.1'352—dc20
                                                            91-19942
                                                                CIP

The paper used in this publication meets the minimum
requirements of American National Standard for Information
Sciences—Permanence of Paper for Printed Library Materials,
ANSI Z39.48-1984.

To Xu Ying and Fern Janssen

Contents

Can Xue is an anomaly in Chinese Literature. In fact, her surreal, innovative writing is so different from traditional Chinese realism that some of her fellow Chinese writers seem quite bemused by it. As Michael A. Duke observes in his introduction to *Modern Chinese Women Writers,* Can Xue is "currently the most non-traditional and modernistic Chinese woman writer . . . all of whose works of fiction are radically non-representational, even to the extent that some serious [Chinese] critics believe that she is genuinely unreadable or that she is not writing 'Chinese literature' at all." In the West, Can Xue has been hailed as one of the best modern writers to come out of China. Of course, literary taste is always subject to cultural bias. But, on the evidence of *Dialogues in Paradise,* Can Xue's first book of short stories to be translated and published here, and now the two novellas, *Yellow Mud Street* and *Old Floating Cloud,* there can be no doubt that by Chinese literary standards Can Xue is revolutionary. By any standards, she is one of the most interesting and original Chinese writers to appear before a Western audience in years.

To understand Can Xue's uniqueness it is important to know something of recent literary developments in China. In 1985, Jeffrey

C. Kinkley wrote that Chinese literature had developed "more or less in a desert" in the last three decades, and that the Western reader must be prepared to find most works wonderfully naive. Kinkley was talking about the bulk of recent Chinese writing, which is still based on the socialist-realist precepts espoused by Mao Zedong in 1942. A typical example to appear in translation here is *Old Well* by Zheng Yi, a love story set against the struggle to find water in China's arid north. This tale contains many fascinating details about rural Chinese life, but the characters are two-dimensional and the language flat. Even the best modern works to be translated—such as *The Ark* by Zhang Jie or *At Middle Age* by Shen Rong, two moving novellas about the plight of professional women in China—appear melodramatic and unsophisticated by Western standards.

Nevertheless, as far back as 1978, two years after the death of Mao, Premier Deng Xiaoping had called for "the emancipation of thought." The Chinese people were permitted to sample Western culture (music, literature, and art) in generous doses. Many Chinese writers cast off the chains of self-censorship and began to write critically of the past. In the magazine *Today,* edited by Bei Dao, one of China's foremost poets, and his colleague Mang Ke, fiction began to appear that revealed a search for new ways of thinking and for more complex literary forms. Within a year, however, the government's crackdown on artistic freedom had begun. There followed a growing rebelliousness on the part of students and intellectuals which culminated in the terrible massacre in Tiananmen Square on 4 June 1989.

Traditionally, literature that lacks resolution or fails to end on an upbeat note has been viewed with suspicion by Chinese officialdom as an attempt to undermine socialism, even if that were not the author's intent. That anyone ever had the courage to write in this manner in China is astonishing, given the numerous crackdowns on intellectuals and the very few occasions on which free thought has been allowed to blossom. In the past two years, millions of books, magazines, and videos considered "unhealthy" have been destroyed. Dealing in "pornography"—a vague term which may cover work disapproved of by the government, although no one knows for sure—could bring with it a sentence of life imprisonment or even the death penalty. Writers, who in China receive a salary from the government and are therefore vulnerable to political pressure, are once again being asked to return to the literary forms and themes advocated by Mao. Several of the new writers, including Bei Dao, are in exile.

Nevertheless, the new writing has survived in China and even flourished throughout the more recent difficult time—indeed, some say because of it. Can Xue began writing fiction seriously in 1983, in the middle of the government's so-called anti-spiritual pollution campaign, and she has continued to write throughout a period of increasingly severe anti-intellectual activity by the government. Clearly, whatever the true nature of the present upheavals—and it is always hard for Westerners, schooled in Western-style democracy, to understand changes within the context of Communist China—feelings of confusion, disillusionment, and rising moral indignation are widespread, and writers express an urge to describe their experience unconstrained by socialist dogma. Some critics complain about the lack of readability of the new writing; others call it a sign of literary health. At a 1989 panel on Chinese writing held by PEN in New York, the critic Li Tuo declared that new novels by writers such as Yu Hua, Ye Zhaoyan, Sun Ganlu, Li Rui, and Liu Heng are "expanding the country's cultural sophistication." Young people, he said, are trying to write like Joyce or Proust, rather than Sidney Sheldon—that is, they want to write *literature* rather than the politically informed tales of earlier decades.

At the same time, Li Tuo and others have pointed out that the new writing may also act as a shield against condemnation by officialdom. To what degree writers such as Can Xue are being intentionally obscure is unclear. Can Xue has written that she "deliberately" makes her stories "run counter to reality"—although this seems to be more a matter of personal taste, a response to what she calls her "attacks of madness." Whatever her motives, "unreadability" does seem to have its benefits: the government is slower to condemn what it doesn't understand.

Fortunately, Western readers have sharper cultural tools with which to appreciate this "exploring" fiction, as it has been called in China. From our exposure to a range of literary styles, we know that good innovative writing has its own crazed logic. Though it may *seem* remote from everyday events, it is always rooted, like any writing, in the author's social, cultural, and personal experiences. Can Xue, at the forefront of the new literary trends and at the center of the debate about them, is no exception.

Part political allegory, part poetry, part literary allusion, and part analysis of real human conflict that ranges from somber to playful, *Yellow Mud Street* and *Old Floating Cloud* are far removed from typical Chinese social realism, having more in common with European and American surrealism and with classical Chinese literature. Can Xue's writing reveals an eclectic taste in reading. Her stories have a sense of menace and a fear of petty officialdom that many readers will associate with Kafka, and the absurd, illogical, despair-informed humor typical of Beckett. *Yellow Mud Street,* with its chorus of alternating voices and its attention to seasonal and poetic rhythms, contains echoes of Virginia Woolf's *The Waves,* first published in China in the early 1980s. And her dream symbolism surely draws on Freud. At her most satirical, however, she sounds more like Lu Xun in *The True Story of Ah Q,* and in her interweaving of reality and illusion, she harks back to *The Dream of the Red Chamber,* the great Chinese novel of the eighteenth century. Yet there are moments, especially in *Old Floating Cloud,* when Can Xue appears closest to, and is as lyrical and allusive as, the eighth-century poet

Tu Fu. Like Tu Fu, who was disillusioned with Confucianism and feared the looming threat of war, Can Xue reflects despair with the current disintegrating order. Concrete realities—poverty, political oppression, family bickering and sexual desire—rub shoulders with more metaphysical questioning. And while readers will sense warmth, empathy, and humor, they will also be aware of that teetering on the brink of madness which comes when everything around one seems on the verge of chaos—or when reality, as everyone else sees it, runs counter to one's own internal sense of reality.

Can Xue's stories have their roots in poetry or even painting, in imagery that suggests rather than states. In *Yellow Mud Street,* the narrative is carried forward by a series of mood changes related to shifts in the weather rather than by the event-filled drama of a conventional plot. The shape of *Old Floating Cloud* is defined by the seasonal changes of the paper mulberry tree. Incidental scene-setting description (a man losing an ear, mad dogs entering a factory, armies of demon rats) is of the sort that appears only in nightmares or in the paintings of Salvador Dali. It is a credit to the translators that, even in English, Can Xue's poetic prose moves forward with a wonderfully smooth insistent rhythm, that her images seem evocative and fresh, if sometimes painful, that her earthy humor can make the Western reader laugh, and that all these strands are woven together to make an original and powerful whole.

Yellow Mud Street is the story of a street, its people, and a strange event that happens there. It may be seen as the more political of the two novellas, yet the state of affairs it describes is both universal and Chinese. Thus we read of people's capacity for self-deception and for accepting dreadful conditions with only the vague hope of improvement to keep them going; of the underdog's pride in a connection with power, and of the eternal Chinese fear of foreign influence or invasion. The word "yellow" (the essential Chinese color) in the title suggests China, and "mud," rural China—impoverished home to seventy percent of the population, their lives informed by paranoia, suspicion, and the superstitions of the past.

"At the edge of the city was a byway called Yellow Mud Street." From the opening words, the story is placed at a distance from the intellectual and social ferment of the cities. The street is dilapidated, though it had once seen better times. The air is always polluted. There is garbage everywhere—at times, excrement literally flows through the street—and the residents suffer from a range of ailments. The "S" Machinery Factory, "the only thing that might raise the value of Yellow Mud Street in people's minds," is in fact rusty and decaying, though it once ran day and night, producing steel balls—for what, no one knows. People still deceive themselves into thinking this factory is a fine place, the envy of "foreign devils," and an important connection with "the authorities," through which one day "skilled people like us will all have private cars to take us in and out of Yellow Mud Street." Yet on the first page we read of the narrator's difficulty in finding the street, of people staring at her with "dead-fish eyes," and of a beggar who remembers only that "there used to be a spiderweb on a broken doorframe." It's clear that we are also venturing into the land of imagination and dreams.

The thread that binds the story together is the appearance of "a thing" which people call Wang Zi-guang. No one is sure if it is a person, a flash of light, or a cloud of will-o'-the-wisp. Its appearance becomes a focus of discussion, rumor, and superstition, and prompts the spouting of political slogans and an investigation by the authorities. (In fact, it is possible that Wang Zi-guang *is* an authority.) In a wonderfully ironic passage, Can Xue describes the boast of an old man, Old Sun:

> "The image of Wang Zi-guang is an ideal for us Yellow Mud Street people. Our life will be greatly changed from now on." . . .
>
> He was a crafty old scoundrel, a wily fox with good vision.

His words had revealed the truth. Truth is often a tiny, dim star enveloped in thick layers of cloud and fog, quite beyond recognition by ordinary eyes. Only sophisticated yet simple and sincere creatures can "discover" it in meditation. Old Sun belonged to this kind of creature.

Can Xue seems to be mocking not only the tendency of Chinese leaders to idealize the lives of peasants, but also the idea of a single truth and the axiom that one must work hard to find it; she is also making a statement about her work: look and you will find what you want—it's not that difficult.

While the authorities investigate the will-o'-the-wisp, the inhabitants become concerned with solving the "problem" of Yellow Mud Street, and paranoia mounts. A sinister barber threatens to murder people; an old lady sees spies everywhere; there is endless talk of plots; and a character called Yang San wonders if "a yellow weasel" has something to do with it. Woven throughout the narrative are the details of everyday life. Families crammed together in rickety houses nag each other to death. Rain comes in a flood. Roaches run over the food. Rats kill a cat. And the general sense of dislocation worsens. Every event is endlessly chewed over in conversations in which the participants are not really communicating but voicing their personal obsessions. Like the mutterings of a madhouse, the same crazy preoccupations wind in and out of the story, a series of refrains that build to a screaming frenzy—and then quite suddenly subside.

From the beginning, however, there is a hint of something other than hopelessness—"some fragile, tiny orchid, strange and alien," grew in the dust"—still flourishing despite corruption and decay. In a passage of lyrical power at the end, Can Xue suggests that the search for Yellow Mud Street is the survival of hope in an untenable situation. Or it may be the search for China, an elusive, perhaps indefinable place that lingers in the imagination like a delicately brushed watercolor, as an idea of tantalizing beauty.

Although it shares the same absurd humor, *Old Floating Cloud* is bleaker, more lyrical, and more hallucinatory than *Yellow Mud Street*. It is the story of a man, Geng Shan-Wu, who has an affair with his neighbor's wife, Xu Ru-hua. Within that frame, Can Xue describes the damage people do to each other, their obsessions, their lack of connection, and their attempts to exert power over one another. Ruthlessly unsentimental, she scorns her characters' nostalgia for the past. The affair between Shan-wu and Ru-hua is made to seem quite pathetic, as is Shan-wu's toadying to and subsequent humiliation by his bosses at work. Like *Yellow Mud Street,* this novella teems with insects and excrement, descriptions of none-too-attractive bodies, and other distasteful images to emphasize our earthbound state. A typical example is of Shan-wu's deteriorating relationship with his wife, Mu-lan, and his teenage daughter:

> For lunch Shan-wu chomped on a lump of cartilage.
> "Great, great!" Mu-lan said in appreciation. Her Adam's apple bobbed. She gulped a mouthful of sour soup.
> The daughter followed their example, chomping and gulping.
> The meal was over. Shan-wu stood up, wiping the soup from his mouth. Picking his teeth with his fingernail, he addressed himself to no one in particular: "The spider on the window frame has been trying to catch mosquitoes for more than an hour, but how can it?"
> "During the workbreak exercise Old Lin emptied his bowels in his trousers," Mu-lan reported. A hiccup brought up a stream of sour soup. She swallowed it again.
> "The ribs we had today were not thoroughly cooked."
> "But you had tenderloin." She glanced at him in surprise.
> "I had tenderloin," he said, still fixing his eyes on the spider. "I mean the ribs."
> "Ah!" Mu-lan made a face. "You're tormenting me again."

Next door, Xu Ru-hua's relationship with her husband, Old Kuang, is also degenerating. They are watched obsessively by Mu-lan, who has positioned a mirror in which the neighbors' doings are reflected. Xu Ru-hua eats pickles and pats her belly all the time, which infuriates her husband. Finally, he leaves her to go back to live with his domineering mother, who "always had an iron club in her hand" with which she is often to be found "exorcising evil spirits." Later she sits at home and collects her saliva in order to undergo "a thorough cleansing of the soul," while Old Kuang dedicates his life to quotations. In a key passage which suggests Can Xue's distaste for dogma, Old Kuang lies by his window, where sometimes "he saw floating clouds vanish from the sky. He felt deeply touched, even moved to tears. 'Keep on learning as long as you live,' he muttered to himself, happy to be able to use this set phrase to describe his feelings." Old Kuang's addiction to political quotations gives him purpose in life. But it is a flimsy prop, for when his mother abandons him, he falls apart spiritually—as the other characters deteriorate physically—and the story descends into nightmare.

In Can Xue's work the reader must play an interpretive role. It would be a mistake to say that close readings of *Yellow Mud Street* and *Old Floating Cloud* yield a literal description of current events in China. To read Can Xue is more like falling asleep over a history book and *dreaming* a horribly distorted version of what you've just read. Nevertheless, though her world may seem nightmarish, remote, and impressionistic, the reader should remember that the people in it behave much as they would anywhere. They scheme, fall in love, irritate each other, deceive themselves, suffer, and still hope for better things. Can Xue is intriguing not simply because she is writing about China, but also because she presents people in a new and interesting way. Readers need only set their imaginations free. Even if they do not always understand Can Xue, they will invariably be challenged, fascinated, and provoked.

Charlotte Innes
Los Angeles, 1990

Translators' Note

These translations are based on photocopied manuscripts provided by the author and delivered to us by Jon Solomon, a student at Cornell University.

Yellow Mud Street has been published three times in Chinese in three different countries, and these publications represent two different states of the text. The work first appeared in November 1986 in the mainland journal *Chinese Monthly of Literature*. The text was reduced by the editors to about half its original length. This same text was followed when the novella was included along with six other works by Can Xue in a volume Jon Solomon published through Taiwan's Yuanshen Publishing House in September 1987.

The original text of the story is that represented in Liang Heng's New York-based journal *Chinese Intellectual* in Spring 1987, though it had been written four years earlier, in the spring of 1983, and acquired by the editor sometime in 1984. In late 1983, the author began rewriting the story, a task she had not finished at the time of Liang's visit to China. She later made an effort to send him a copy of the revised text, but it seems to have disappeared en route.

The present translation, the first in English, is based on that late

1983 unpublished revision of the text. This version differs from all other texts by including the section entitled "A Significant Event Which Changed Attitudes toward Life." It differs from the mainland and Taiwan publications by including "The Days When the Sun Was in the Sky" and by expanding "The Torrential Rain" from three to five parts and "The Sun Shines on Yellow Mud Street" from four to five parts. The version of *Yellow Mud Street* that appeared in *Chinese Intellectual* had as its penultimate section a chapter entitled "A Child without an Asshole" and ended with a short chapter called "The Sun Shines on Yellow Mud Street," which is retained in the present text as part five of the chapter of the same title. In the *Chinese Intellectual* text "S" Factory was called "Xin-wu" Factory.

Old Floating Cloud was first published in the People's Republic in *China Monthly of Literature* for May 1986 and was included in Solomon's Taiwan volume of 1987. Like *Yellow Mud Street*, it appears here for the first time in English translation.

YELLOW
MUD
STREET

YELLOW MUD STREET

At the edge of the city was a byway called Yellow Mud Street. I remember it very well. But everyone says no such street ever existed.

So I set out to find it. Passing through the yellow dust, passing among human shapes covered with the dust, I searched for Yellow Mud Street.

I asked every one I met, "Is this Yellow Mud Street?" They only stared at me with their dead-fish eyes. Nobody answered my question.

My bodily form moved aimlessly along the steaming asphalt road. The sun was so hot that my eyeballs stuck in their dried-up sockets like two glass balls. I suppose my eyes, too, looked like those of a dead fish, but still I tried hard to identify my surroundings.

I came to a street where all the houses were ruined and beggars lay along the way. I remembered there used to be a spiderweb on a broken doorframe. But one old beggar said, "A red spider? What year is this?" A green-headed fly as big as a scarab fell out of his hair.

Black ash poured down from the sky like garbage. It tasted salty, a bit like sulfanilamide pills. A little boy ran toward me. Digging the dust from his nostrils, he said, "Two cancer patients have died over there."

I followed him to a rusty iron door. A row of crows perched on the iron barbs. The sickening smell of rotting corpses filled the air.

The beggars had fallen asleep, smacking their lips while licking the salty ash in their dreams.

There was a dream. The dream was a green snake. It hung from my shoulders, soft and cool.

ABOUT YELLOW MUD STREET AND THE "S" MACHINERY FACTORY

Yellow Mud Street was long and narrow. Both sides were jammed with a variety of dwarf houses, all tilted and slanting: houses with brick walls or board walls; with straw roofs or tile roofs; with three windows or two windows; with doors facing the street or facing away from the street; houses with or without front stoops, with or without yards, and so on. Every house had its special name, such as "Xiao's Wineshop," "Luo's Incenseshop," "Cheng's Grand Teahouse," "Wang's Petite Noodlehouse," and such. From these names one could guess that the residents on Yellow Mud Street had once enjoyed a certain status. However, the memory of the inhabitants of those houses now was as dilapidated and decadent as the structures themselves. Nobody could remember the good old times.

Yellow Mud Street was blanketed with soot. It came from nowhere. It seemed to fall every minute, all year round. Even the raindrops were black. The dwarf houses looked as if they had grown out of the earth. They were so thoroughly covered with mud and dirt that one couldn't tell windows from walls. Passersby would look for shelter from the falling soot. Most of the residents on Yellow Mud Street suffered from festering red eyes and a chronic cough.

The people on Yellow Mud Street had never noticed that the color of the sky could be classified into navy blue, indigo, silver gray, flame red and so on. The small patch of sky above them was always only one color: yellowish gray, resembling the color of aged sails.

The people on Yellow Mud Street had never seen the magnificence of a sunrise, nor the glory of a sunset. In their tiny dim eyes, the sun was nothing but a small, yellow ball, going up and coming down, never changing. They said only "There's sun today"; "There's no sun today"; "The sun's very strong today"; "The sun's not very strong today" or similar remarks. But when summer came, a raging flame burned outside, and the insides of the houses became steamers. The people would mutter in rage, "The maggots are steamed out of me."

One favorite activity on Yellow Mud Street was the selling of rotten fruit. For some reason, fruit went rotten as soon as it was put on the market: rotten apples, rotten pears, rotten oranges, rotten peaches, rotten tangerines, rotten grapes. The people sold everything they could get. The street was filled with the tempting odors of the rotten fruits, sweet and savory, stirring up the appetite of the passersby. But in ordinary times, the residents of Yellow Mud Street could not afford the fruit, even the rotten ones. When a child made a tearful appeal for fruit, the adults would frighten him by saying, "Rotten fruit causes cancer!" Despite the fear of cancer, however, once in a while, people would buy a couple of rotten fruits to satisfy their craving.

Wherever you find a lot of families, you find a lot of garbage. The same was true of Yellow Mud Street. In the past, the garbage was dumped in the river. The current was so swift that the garbage disappeared as soon as it entered the water. One day during a downpour an old woman dumped a pail of coal-ash at the doorway of the restaurant. She said, "Coal-ash won't hurt anything." Her deed was soon discovered, and a second person, then a third and a fourth tried the same trick. Each did it without being noticed by the others, but they always ended up being discovered. The garbage piled up higher and higher until it formed a hill. It started with ash, but then rotten vegetables, worn-out shoes, broken bottles, baby's excrement and many other things were added. When rain came, the black stinking water ran across the street and up to somebody's door. This person let loose a torrent of abuse: "So my house is being used as a garbage dump. What a sneaky way to kill me without spilling my blood! Very well! Tomorrow I'll file a charge with the municipal committee." But how could he ever find the time? Every day he was too busy, so the idea of lodging a complaint was soon forgotten and replaced by daily routine. It was not remembered again till the next rain. Of course, at that time, again, no complaint was made owing to some other trifles.

The people on Yellow Mud Street were all chicken-hearted. Besides, they were haunted by nightmares. Every day, they would complain to others about what dreams they had, how scary they were, what strange sounds they heard, what omens the dreams implied. . . . They talked and talked until they were pale with fear. Their eyes almost fell out of their sockets. It's said that once a man had a nightmare, and he talked about it for several days. The last time he was talking about it, he suddenly fell down in a heap and stopped breathing. According to the autopsy, his gallbladder had burst. "Never swallow anything and keep it to yourself!" the old busybodies warned, raising a finger. "It's better to speak up."

The people of Yellow Mud Street loved to set "traps." They were supposedly meant for catching thieves, but the "traps" always ended up hurting their owners. One example was old lady Qi, who always hung a huge kettle of boiling water above the door frame. Once when she opened the door, the water poured down on her and left a big scar on her foot.

The animals on Yellow Mud Street were crazy. Whether cat or dog, they went crazy while growing up. These animals would jump and run madly and bite everyone they met. Whenever a cat or a dog went crazy, every door was closed. Nobody dared walk on the street. But the beast always dashed out from the least imaginable place and did something violent. One day, a mad dog killed two men at once as they stood side by side, their legs touching.

The people on Yellow Mud Street preferred to wear thick clothing. They often wore their cotton-padded coats even in summer, believing that unlined garments were "too buoyant," making the heart "unsteady." They thought people needed "macerating lest some disease attack." Even with a disease, "a macerating" would help. One summer, an old man suddenly felt a terrible itching on his back. When he peeled off his coat for inspection, he found a mass of wriggling worms "macerated" in the cotton. As a result, that old man lived to more than eighty. When the little ones felt hot and tried to take off their cotton-padded coats, adults would scold, "Court death! You've lived long enough, eh?"

The people on Yellow Mud Street seldom went to the city. Some of them never did. It's said that there used to be no city, but only this Yellow Mud Street. Therefore, most of the residents were born and raised on the street and had nothing to do with the city. Take Old Hu San. He had never been to the city in all his life. When people asked about this, his aged brown eyes became murky. Rubbing sleep from them, he would proclaim, as if in a dream, "Long ago, all kinds of good things fell from the sky. Fat chunks of meat lay in the gutters. Pick them up and they were yours! Every house raised huge roaches that ate rice at the table like a person . . . Why ask me? What's your opinion of the prospects for the rebels?"

The residents of Yellow Mud Street were always sleeping. Nobody knew how many years they'd been asleep. They never opened their doors till the sun was high. They rubbed their tiny sleepy eyes, opened their mouths alarmingly wide, and gave out a long yawn: "Ahhhhhhh. . . . " If an acquaintance passed by, they greeted him half asleep: "You're so early today. Morning! Good sleep . . . ," all as if talking in a dream. They were still asleep while having breakfast; their heads fell, rose, fell again, very rhythmically. They read crumbling ancient classic books, but before long, their eyes felt heavy, and the books fell down. So it was better not to read at all but just snore instead. Even going to the toilet, people stole a doze. The nap was over when the shit was done. Standing in line to buy steamed buns, a person would slump toward the one ahead of him, then suddenly start awake and stand up straight again. A shrewish woman shouting in the street would fail to hold back a yawn, then a second and a third. She'd continue her abuse, accompanying every word with a stamp of the feet and a dozen yawns.

How could people not feel sleepy? It was because of the sunlit and enchanting scenery of spring, or the charming autumn scenery, or the short summer night, or the good-for-nothing winter weather. Every season provided its own excuse for being sleepy. And besides, it was better to sleep till noon to save a meal. The lower the energy drain, the less reason for eating.

So, from one end of the street to the other, in the little houses or outside, man or woman, old or young, everyone bumped into everyone else; everyone staggered and doddered. Before they knew it, the day had passed. People sighed, "It goes so fast!" And true enough, the sun again dropped behind Wang Si-ma's shabby straw roof. How could it be that the days in Yellow Mud Street flew by so fast? Only the blink of an eye! No time even to think about it! It seemed that in the space of a nap, one season was over.

Hopelessly, Yellow Mud Street would go to sleep again. Every door was closed. Some families left a yellow light on; others left only pitch-black windows. By nine o'clock every light was out. When the whole street had closed its last tiny eye, it seemed to disappear completely from the edge of the city, nowhere to be found.

At the end of Yellow Mud Street, right after the houses, stood the "S" Machinery Factory.

"S" Machinery Factory was the only offspring of Yellow Mud Street.

"S" Machinery Factory was the only thing that might raise the value of Yellow Mud Street in people's minds.

There were about five or six hundred workers in the factory, most of whom were residents of Yellow Mud Street.

What products did the "S" Machinery Factory turn out? "Steel balls," the people would answer. Every half a month, several dozen cases of black things were carried from the factory. What was the use of these steel balls? Nobody could say. Pursue the inquiry and people would look you up and down suspiciously and ask, "Are you sent by somebody higher up?" If you didn't leave at once, they would continue, "What do you think of rationalized management? Should the tradition of the old revolutionary base area be kept up?" They wouldn't stop their questioning until your mind was dizzy with puzzles and you turned to flee.

No one could tell the history of the "S" Machinery Factory. It stood at the end of Yellow Mud Street. It had been there from the very beginning. It was born with Yellow Mud Street.

Whenever the inhabitants raised the topic of "S," they would say something like: "Our 'S' is a piece of good, fat meat. The foreign devils dream of swallowing it down. Our 'S' has been connected with the authorities since long ago. Skilled people like us will all have private cars to take us in and out of Yellow Mud Street. Our 'S' is extraordinary; its six huge workshops are full of grandeur. Once an old granny was frightened to death by the sound of our double-housing planer. Someone is digging a tunnel from the city to destroy the foundation of our 'S'" and so on and so forth.

In reality, the "S" Factory, which was locked up behind a rusty gate, was hardly worth seeing. There was only one recently built office building, and even that was already covered with black dirt and filled with spiderwebs. It stank like a toilet. The six workshops were all dim and black. They used to be ordinary houses with small, low windows like the eyes of ghosts. Beside the windows stretched some ropes with strings of dirt hanging from them. When the machines started to roar, shaking the surrounding air, the strings of dirt would fall like willow catkins or poplar leaves.

In front of the factory lay a pond. People called it "Pure Water Pond," but in fact the water was anything but pure. It was ink-black with a scum of engine oil floating on its surface. Stench filled the air. Alongside the pond, the waste of cotton yarn and iron slag overflowed from the pond itself. No one had ever seen any fish living in this body of dead water. Not even mosquito larvae could survive there. There were always some dead cats and birds floating in the pond. No one had seen them fall in. They seemed to come from nowhere. Whenever a dead cat or bird appeared in the pond, people from "S" would gather to give their comments until they began to peer around and feel scared. Then someone would say loudly, "This damned weather! There must be something wrong!" as if to boost his own courage. After that, everyone would find a reason to hurry away.

At the back gate were several mounds. It was said that this used to be a garden, but now there was no flower to be seen, nor even a tree. Only a pile of broken tiles and bricks covered with moss lay there, and some wastepaper and garbage danced in the wind. Once in a while, sparrows stopped, but they never stayed for long. Even today, people can recognize a big pit filled with mud under the mounds. A skeleton was buried there, and ever after, for some reason, people saw a huge ball of will-o'-the-wisp floating over the mounds. Pure green and extraordinarily bright, it lit up the mounds as if a person were prowling around with a lantern. Naturally, nobody dared pass by the mounds at night. Liu Tie-chui once bet five yuan with someone, but he turned back in fear on his way to the mounds.

Outside the workshops were heaps of things carelessly thrown away. They were forgotten as soon as they were discarded. These included a rusty, useless tool, a machine base with air holes, a pile of rusty steel balls, several pairs of broken pliers, a heap of pig-iron bits, and so on, all crusted over with a thick coat of rust. Some of this junk was half buried in the ground. Eroded by wind and heat, it had melted into the mud. People thought all this would eventually turn completely into mud, so they never bothered to clean it up.

For a time, the "S" Machinery Factory was stoked and roaring day and night, pouring out those strange-looking steel balls. The residents of Yellow Mud Street passed their days muddleheadedly amidst the roar. Year in and year out, they began to consider this roar something natural. They would certainly feel upset and restless if they ever woke up without hearing that muffled roar.

So, once upon a time there was a place called Yellow Mud Street.

And on the street, a place called "S" Machinery Factory.

All year round there was dirt everywhere, and some fragile, tiny orchid, strange and alien, grew in the dust.

There were rows of roofs resembling ruined umbrellas. Flocks of bats flew back and forth in the setting sun.

Oh, Yellow Mud Street, Yellow Mud Street. I have some dreams, dreams so dear, so melancholy, so incoherent. In these dreams there is always a strange-looking iron gate, a dirty, yellow, tiny sun. From this gate a row of barbs juts up menacingly. The tiny sun hangs in one corner of the gray, dusty sky forever, giving out the metallic light of death.

Oh, Yellow Mud Street, Yellow Mud Street. Maybe you exist only in my dreams? Maybe you are only a shade, quivering with a touch of sadness?

Oh, Yellow Mud Street, Yellow Mud Street . . .

A SIGNIFICANT
EVENT WHICH CHANGED
ATTITUDES TOWARD LIFE

Everyone on this street remembers that long, long ago there came a thing called Wang Zi-guang. Why should he be called a "thing?" Because no one knew for sure if Wang Zi-guang was a human being or not. It may be better to consider him a flash of light or a cloud of will-o'-the-wisp. This flash of light or will-o'-the-wisp, fallen from those dark green eaves, lightened the narrow, dim hearts of the Yellow Mud Street people, caused them all manner of confusing fantasies, and sank them into an inescapable alternation of agony and excitement for a long time.

It was in the small hours of June 21 when old lady Qi, going to the toilet, first discovered a flash of mysterious light flickering on the Gentlemen's side. According to her, those grayish white stars fell suddenly from above the roof. The tiles clattered madly as if something were running across them. She meant to raise her head to have a look, but her neck had become as soft as cotton. Involuntarily she sat down beside the toilet. Then she sank into an artistic reverie in which numerous black dogs attacked each other, and the sun stood level with a clump of winter grass. With her eyes closed, she dreamed for a whole morning. When people found her, she was pulling off her shoes to string them with ropes and hang them from her ears while running around the toilet.

At the same moment, a man with whiskers, Wang Si-ma, hung a large manure bucket on the chinaberry tree in front of his door. Then he climbed the tree and sat in the bucket to swing. He swung until noon, when the rope finally wore out and the bucket banged to the ground. Wang broke a leg in the fall, so he decided not to get up. Instead, he started to snore under the tree. His snore was as loud as the bombardment from a distant cannon. It shook the hearts of the residents of the whole street, making them sneeze by the dozens.

Later on, Wang Si-ma recalled that a headless corpse had knocked on his back door before he climbed the tree. He knew a good thing had come as soon as he heard the knocking. That was why he set himself in the bucket. Once in his bucket, he heard firecrackers going off outside and saw gunsmoke rolling above his head. Afterward, in his dream, he sucked on a huge peach and unconsciously called out that rosy red name: "*Wang Zi-guang?*" This is where the first comments about Wang Zi-guang came from. It was a mysterious and obscure experience, impossible to grasp and ever-changing. Some people believed it was some kind of reflection, a rhapsody, an adhesive, a magic mirror . . . Old Sun even boasted in public, "The image of Wang Zi-guang is an ideal for us Yellow Mud Street people. Our life will be greatly changed from now on." While talking, he slapped a fly that had landed on his leg.

He was a crafty old scoundrel, a wily fox with good vision. His words had revealed the truth. Truth is often a tiny, dim star enveloped in thick layers of cloud and fog, quite beyond recognition by ordinary eyes. Only sophisticated yet simple and sincere creatures can "discover" it in meditation. Old Sun belonged to this kind of creature. He was a man without a home. If the Yellow Mud Street residents peeped out their windows at midnight, they could see a large black shape hanging from the dead tree in front of the inn. It looked like an ape, but it was Old Sun.

Old Sun never slept deeply, nor did he wake up completely. He worked as the doorkeeper for "S" factory. He had never made any errors, though he let mad dogs into the factory every day. They snapped and barked while Sun circled the factory clapping his hands and whistling to excite them and spur them on. Strangely enough, those dogs never bit him. Sometimes, when no dog came for a couple of days, he would search far and wide and fall sick if he couldn't find one. His face would turn yellow and weary; he would doze off with a wet towel on his head, complaining, "What a terrible headache. Better to die fast."

After the spirit of Wang Zi-guang appeared on Yellow Mud Street, Old Sun threw away his dirty, ragged, cotton-padded coat and bared his body in public. His eyes shone with high spirit, and his face looked noble and dignified. He got an air gun from somewhere and every day he shot at the dead tree in front of the inn. The second day, he found a new trick. He hung colorful balloons on the tree and shot them down one by one. He also carried a bucket of dishwater to the attic and waited for a chance. When the plan went off well, he would pour the water on the head of a passerby.

"Sparkling red star, shining bright,"* he told every customer of the inn. His face lit up with his talk, and a small boil erupted on his nose. In order to display his great spiritual changes, he persisted in eating a rotten pear every day. In front of others, he would bite right into the spot where the insect holes showed. With a crunch, he took a full bite. After eating, he would tell his admiring watchers, "I've already found certain traces of Wang Zi-guang." This had "a direct relationship with a kind of cat bearing tiger stripes." The reality was "unimaginable," and so on.

---

*Title song from the popular mid-1970s revolutionary film *Sparkling Red Star*.—TRANS.

Without things like Wang Zi-guang, our Yellow Mud Street would have been a tiny, gray, lightless street forever, a lifeless street, burned quietly by the dim yellow sun. Nothing memorable would ever have happened, nor would a couple of great heroes have appeared to shake the world.

However, at the instant when old lady Qi entered her dream of the sun and the winter grass beside the toilet, everything on Yellow Mud Street changed. The small dilapidated straw huts started to wiggle, shining in the sun with a queer liveliness. It resembled the sudden spurt of activity prior to collapse in one's old age. Even the dried-up thatch on the roofs nodded to passersby as if injected with a certain juice of life. Yellow Mud Street had gained new life.

To celebrate this rebirth, the people applied two round plasters to their foreheads, and tried hard to hold back the jubilation in their hearts. They suddenly turned into a group of gentle and polite people. If someone asked, "Any new tendency in the weather?" the answer would be as subtle as "From the newly rain-dampened soil, intelligent little creatures like earthworms are wiggling out. What a pleasant scene for both the eye and the mind of the observer!" They also put all kinds of slogans on the walls. On red paper, green paper, and yellow paper, the following statements were written: "Darkness has already passed, and brightness is coming!"; "A real man has lofty aspirations in all directions!"; "Cultivate the civilized habit of drinking boiled water!" and so on.*

Finally, one noon, old lady Yuan Si appeared on the street. She had a piece of bloodred silk around her waist. When she started running, armies of demon rats, big and small, dashed down to-

---

*Popular Communist slogan from before 1949 Liberation; popular Communist slogan of the 1950s and 1960s to encourage service in remote areas; slogan often found in public places.—TRANS.

ward the street from the mountain. Their footsteps clattered like stones. People in the small huts peeped out with black eyeshades on. They tilted their heads to listen closely. All at once, they started to weep, "Wuwuwuwu—" Their whimpering rose high into the heavens.

THE DAYS WHEN
THE SUN WAS IN THE SKY

1

When the sun is up, everything goes rotten, everywhere.

The vegetable mound in front of the market steamed in the sun. Its yellow drainage ran to the corner of the street.

Every household hung last year's rotten fish and meat in the sun. White maggots crawled all over.

Tap water became undrinkable, also. It was said that a decomposing corpse had blocked the pump. For days, people had been drinking "corpse water." They feared it might cause an epidemic.

Stinking water oozed from the aged putrid ulcers on their shanks. Several people almost a hundred years old rolled their pants high to display their wounds at the doorway, letting passersby enjoy the cracked red flesh.

A postal vehicle paused in Yellow Mud Street for only half an hour before one of its tires decomposed. When they checked, they found the inner tube had turned to a lump of paste.

One day Wang Si-ma, who lived at the corner of the street, suddenly lost one ear. When people asked him where his ear had gone, he treated them to a supercilious look and said, "Of course it rotted off during the night. It's as simple as that." Looking at his "ear"—a naked and almost invisible little hole running with yellowish pus—people felt uncomfortable, afraid their own ears might rot off. What would they do if that happened?

In this weather even iron could rot. And sure enough, the rust on the "S" factory gate gradually peeled off. Eventually, an iron bar rusted through. Nobody, least of all the people inside the iron gate, could remember how long the scorching, white-thorned little sun had been hanging in the top corner of the rust-colored sky. It seemed it had always been there. And since it had been there all the time, nobody really paid any attention to it.

The "S" factory people never watched the sun, though they could smell the weather, their noses being very sensitive indeed. When there was a breeze, they hunched their shoulders and complained, "It's getting cold." When the sun dimmed even a little, they said, "A chill is in my bones." Pointing at their heads, they explained, "The dampness settles here." They waved their hands at the same time, as if the "dampness" were coming out and they wanted to drive it away. When the sun became scorching, they were annoyed again, saying, "One degree higher today. Someone might die."

In people's memories, the sun had been high for a long time. For that reason, the four to five hundred people inside the iron gate had been sleeping for a long time. They were confused because their gummy eyelids stuck tight. They felt so comfortable that they smacked their mouths and let the saliva dribble out. All kinds of dreams—warm dreams, sweaty dreams—rose from the messy pile of rotten lumber and greasy boxes to form a web of dreams. These were accompanied by a host of snores resembling animal howls. It was simply grand! In such a good sun, even mosquitoes and flies dreamed. Weren't there several green-headed flies dreaming on the ulcer on Yan Lao-wu's shank? A half-awakened fly even stumbled into his gaping, dribbling mouth.

In a trance the doorkeeper Old Sun spoke to others after a dream. "The Son of Heaven will appear. Something strange will happen. But first of all, it should be said that the situation is excellent . . .* Isn't there a principle from above called 'very good'? It has to do with patriotism. What does 'very good' mean? The situation at present is very good! The instructions given by the authorities are very good! I mean, don't close both eyes in sleep. Keep one eye open. Something strange is going to happen."

The sun lay on the brick wall. The wall creaked, echoing Old Sun's words. His voice dropped, leading to a belch, which led to a yawn. In sudden realization, the listeners agreed. Their eyelids dropped, and before long they all dozed off.

Nobody paid much attention to Old Sun's comments. Yet his prophecies showed their power very soon.

A barber came bearing a greasy shoulder pole full of oils and a shining razor in his hand. He banged his equipment down right in front of the "S" factory gate and shouted, "Heads shaved!"

Everyone inside learned back against the wall shaking their tiny, frightened heads.

"Has it come?"

"It's come, ah?"

"Heads shaved!" came the man's shout again. His eyes were bulging and bloodshot. Everyone could feel the two beams of cold light from his eyeballs.

It was time. Hadn't the bloodred color dyed the world between the sky and the earth? Wasn't there a big spot of bright light lingering on the west wall? It was as red as fresh blood.

---

*Allusion to Chairman Mao's remark during the Cultural Revolution that "the revolutionary situation is excellent."—TRANS.

"A dead cat floats in the pond." Old lady Song lowered her voice. She was sneaking along the wall like a rat, not looking at any one.

"Oh, fart! No, there's no dead cat at all." Old lady Qi grabbed the short woman. She pondered for a while, then suddenly remembered something. Raising her head, she clapped her hands and queried with a flushed face, "Thousands of heads will roll?"*

"A dead cat is again floating in the pond."

"Ghost shaving. . ."

"Thousands of human heads . . . "

"Disaster of bloody light . . . "

Everyone was gossiping while looking with fear at the bloodred light on the west wall.

"Crack, crack, somewhere heads are being chopped off," Zhang Mie-zi was telling the others confusedly, stretching his eyes until the whites showed.

Everyone was startled and their faces turned pale. Raising their heads, they wondered why the sun was so bright, so white. The light was obviously false. There must be a plot behind it. Weren't the dogs barking now? And the iron gate, it clanged without anybody's touching it.

"Thousands of heads will roll!" Old lady Qi was running around madly in the factory, baring her teeth. She stopped before everyone she met and chopped her hand through the air with force, mumbling, "Every one of them will fall to the ground."

The "S" factory people paced back and forth nervously. Repeatedly they sneaked a look at the dazzling bloody spot of light on the west wall. Then they made a scrutinizing face with brows furrowed and eyes narrowed. Yet nothing came of the scrutiny. Finally, they gave a sigh. They wanted to go to sleep, but dared not. Even their voices changed. Everyone whispered hoarsely.

*Set phrase from the Cultural Revolution referring to Lin Biao's Russian connection.
—TRANS.

"But the weather is fine." They looked for some topic to talk about.

Everyone waited.

At long last, something turned up.

A dog barked on Yellow Mud Street. The butchers selling rotten meat shouted. The shrews screeched. The new sound seemed to have traveled long distances before reaching "S" factory. "Hummm . . . hummm . . . " It sounded like a swarm of bees humming around their ears. The people inside were puffed up like quilts hung in the sun and befuddled by the heat. One shake would cause a cracking sound, and one pat would send up a cloud of dust. Good weather!

"Heads shaved!" Bulging Eyes was again at the door, waving something shiny in his hand. His eyes shot out cold beams.

Aroused, the people hurried to the workshop to escape.

"Comrades, a document has come from above." Old Yue dashed in, stretching his bony arms high. "Malignant poisonous sore . . . . A thief is forever glaring at me. There's a plot lately! I hear a crackling sound. I turn left and right, but the sound is everywhere. What the hell is it?"

Something is desperately wrong!

The iron gate of "S" factory had been clanged shut by Old Sun. Everybody looked like a ghost. They frowned and hid from each other. They muttered irrelevancies and harbored sinister thoughts in their hearts.

No more sleepiness.

"The poisonous sore is on the back," Old Yue announced with immense pride.

"Who is it?" the "S" factory people asked each other in trembling voices as they searched the sky. Then they fell to pondering and searching, beset by fear. After their hunt they were still staring, still asking the same question: "Who?"

No one could tell the meaning of the document or who would be investigated and prosecuted. Besides, the Yellow Mud Street people were all solid, cultivated citizens, not those monsters in the habit of digging into everything. Investigation meant investigation. If someone pushed hard, and there was no answer forthcoming, people would widen their eyes, take a deep breath, and give a loud shout: "Idiot!" This would frighten the questioner half to death.

The investigation went on and on, but without result. People started to doubt themselves: "It can't be me, can it?" So they turned their thoughts over and even touched their own backs to make sure there was no sore. Next, they flared their nostrils and popped their noses up close to each other. They sniffed and sniffed and sucked in so much dust that the rims of their noses turned black.

The weather got hotter day by day. It was June, and the sun was getting stronger. Following the old custom, the Yellow Mud Street people still wore their cotton-padded coats. Normally, they would perspire slightly, but now they were under such tension that they were soaked with sweat. They smelled terribly in the sun, but dared not take off their coats lest they catch cold.

The investigation did not seem to affect Old Sun a bit. Each day he stood at the gate preaching to everyone, "The current situation is excellent!"

One day Yang San-dianzi declared in public that he had found the culprit. However, it turned out to be not a person, but a lizard. He claimed the lizard could be found on the wall of Wang Si-ma's house. That morning when he passed the wall, he tried to hook the lizard down. The animal spat on him in retaliation. At first, people were quite interested in his story. They they remembered that a lizard couldn't possibly cause a poisonous sore. What's more, this insane man had not even mentioned the sore. This proved his story was sheer nonsense. He was merely having some after-meal entertainment.

Then more gossip started to the effect that the one who had the sore was not a human being at all, but a ghost—a drowned person turned into a drowned ghost. The vast majority of "S" factory people had seen that ghost, though they had never seen its face. Every time it visited "S" factory, it had a piece of black cloth over its face. Even in the extreme heat, it never removed the cloth. The ghost looked weak and thin with its back bent low. It appeared poor and pitiful and tried hard to avoid people. It made rustling sounds. Sometimes it hid in a dark corner to eat the garbage it had picked up.

"The ghost is a Liu ghost, I believe," Liu Tie-chui said. "What?" Old lady Qi jumped up. "What Liu ghost? I think it's our Qi ghost. This morning a gust of chilly wind swept into my house. I could smell it. I even said on the spot, 'Good Lord, it's coming!' Who else can it be but him?"

"Rubbish, you old devil!"

"Don't lose your temper for selfish reasons," old lady Song intervened. "When can we end this investigation? With sweat like this, my back will scab up and become a shell."

Old Sun spat and added, "The current situation is excellent!"

"It may be an owl," Yang San-dianzi offered a new explanation. "Something drums on my roof every night. Whenever that happens, I dream of an owl."

After two days, Old Yue came, all smiles. In his hand was a document. "Comrades, what's your reaction to the spirit of the higher authorities? The weather looks like that on the eve of a big plague. Large numbers of dead pigs are floating down the river. The stink is so bad I can't eat my breakfast. That reminds me of something important: There's a plot lately! A thief waits outside my door all night. What kind of threat is this?"

After the second document came out, "S" factory people began to walk with their bodies turned sideways as if they all suffered from paralysis. They dared not remain still even when sitting down. They tried to hide from each other even when asleep. No one dared start an open conversation. They carried on all dialogue at great distance and with half-hidden faces. Their fear reduced the possibility of finding more clues. People would think in silence for a long time, focusing their eyes toward the sky. But from their mouths only the old threatening word leapt forth: "Who?" This was followed by a nervous sweep of the eyes. Their hearts beat fast with anxiety.

One afternoon, Old Sun woke from his long nap under the rotten lumber pile. He patted his thigh and cried out, "Is it possible there's no such problem as the poisonous sore? The current situation is very good!"

"True," Zhang Mie-zi agreed. "The iron gate has been clanging all day. Can it be the wind? I feel so nervous whenever I think of the iron gate. Maybe it's not caused by the iron gate, but by the dogs on the street. They make my heart beat fast. Lately there's an increase of mad dogs. They often bite passersby to death."

"Exactly." Yang San joined them, yawning. "The owl appears in my dream so much recently. Always the same owl. I just don't understand it. Why not a yellow weasel?"

That day the sun was particularly bright. The iron gate was clanging. The investigators appeared unexpectedly.

It was Old Sun they took away. Who could have expected that!

"What a danger! Danger! Danger!" Old lady Qi ran madly through the factory shouting, "Schemer! Spy! Thousands of human heads will fall to the ground!" After her shouting, she knelt down to take a bit of mud and swallow it. In no time a hole soon appeared in the ground. She was a ferocious woman and could swallow iron.

A green-headed fly as big as a scarab landed at the center of the bloodred spot of light on the west wall.

"Something is floating in the pond again." Old lady Song dashed through like a rat.

"Someone is plotting to grab Old Sun's post!" Yang San-dianzi started up as something passed through his mind.

"Comrades!" Old lady Qi spat out some muddy water. She shouted as she ran, "What's your expectation about the question of thousands of heads rolling? Ah? Ha! Close your windows at night! Beware of spies!"

But most people were not excited. They focused their empty white eyes on the patch of yellow sky, thinking of something. In the midst of their scrutiny, they would speak up loudly. "Old Sun? Mm, used to be one. Ha!"

Several slugs grew under the washbasin. A crowd surrounded the basin. Some sprinkled pipe tobacco around; others suggested pouring boiling water on them. The final decision was to do nothing for now, but to leave them there for further observation.

A crack appeared in the yard wall. Again a crowd surrounded it. Some suspected there was something good hidden inside the wall. So they found several iron bars to dig with. After a whole day's work, the crack was much widened. Finally, they decided the treasure must be hidden underground. Therefore, dropping the bars, they went back to sleep.

A yawn spreads quickly. If one person starts, no one around can keep his mouth closed. The whole of "S" factory was yawning. And once the yawning starts, there's no way to keep the eyes open. And dreams follow. How tiring! The sun is great!

Dirty clouds gathered like cotton. The weather was still too warm. "S" factory dreamed in the sun and the dust. Sometimes there were meetings. As the meetings proceeded, the whole audience went to dreamland, leaving the chairman alone shouting like a longhorned beetle, "Rustling, rustling . . . " People dreamed of sweat, dreamed of the white thorns on the sun, dreamed of growing maggots, partly because of the humming of the beetle.

Old Sun had been taken prisoner. Nobody remembered this any more, except Sun Xiao-long.

One day, Sun Xiao-long waved Old Sun's quilt in front of everybody, glaring and swaggering. The quilt was new and white.

"Damn it! What the hell is he to Old Sun?" Old lady Song was the first to recover her senses.

People stared at Sun Xiao-long's back and thought hard. Suddenly it dawned on them that Old Sun was no longer there. Where had the old man gone?

Then old lady Qi took over the doorkeeping job. "S" factory echoed with her broken-gong voice from morning till night: "Beware of thousands of heads rolling!" After shouting thus, she clanged the iron gate so loud she startled everyone, making their ears ring for a long time.

"A toad demon is in the latrine . . . " Yuan Si's wife said in her dream. The dream was full of wasps. She couldn't drive them away. Her whole body was swollen.

"Why not a yellow weasel? Eh?" Yang San mumbled in a daze from the pile of rotten lumber. He looked restless as if something were troubling him.

Mad dogs barked on Yellow Mud Street.

Old lady Qi paced here and there, making noise with the iron gate. Sometimes she went in a vigorous stride, dashing into a remote corner and peering around with her aged eyes open wide. When she was sure no one was around, she would kneel down for a bite of mud, making a kind of squeaky chewing sound.

Once there was an Old Sun. Then he disappeared.

How did Old Sun disappear? No one could remember.

The dreams were endless.

The sun hung forever high in the yellow sky.

2

The hot spell was followed by damp weather. Not surprisingly, many tiny creatures were cooked out. They screamed and whined and bumped against one another. The ones with wings flew up and down, circling in the sun like a fleet of helicopters. The whole space of "S" factory was occupied by them. In the shade, in all the dark corners, those without wings rolled and jammed together in small clumps. How could it happen that so many creatures grew out of nowhere? Nobody could explain it. One possibility was that the air in "S" factory was different from anywhere else. It was much damper and heavier than outside. Heaviness always encourages growth, no matter what. These creatures were both fat and active. Under the eaves of the latrine, the snails grew first, one row after another; then out popped a huge colorful moth as big as a bat. It made a whistling sound when it flew. The whole mob from the forging shop, led by Old Yue, the head of the shop, joined in the battle to catch it. They ran around the shop again and again until they knocked it down. But when they got closer, they could find nothing at all on the ground. The powder drifting down, however, blurred many people's eyes. The result was an epidemic of pinkeye. People drew the lesson that newly grown creatures should not be harmed. Only peaceful coexistence could lead to good health.

Gradually, something began to grow in people's abdomens. For a long time, some had had an odd rumbling sound in their bellies and felt bloated. The irritating feeling then crept into their bones, and their bones seemed to be bursting. When such fits came over them, people punched at the wall and stamped on the ground. If the feeling worsened, they would beat themselves blindly, spitting and screaming, "The ghost of the plague is on me! It's squeezing me everywhere. Can I survive?"

What was growing inside them? No one knew. A couple of believers in modern science went to the hospital to get X-rayed. But even after repeated X rays nothing could be found. After some useless diagnoses, it was suggested that their bellies be opened. But how could one's belly be cut open? The doctor was thought to be mad. This proved that even science was unbelievable.

"A bearded old man in the city was pregnant. After ten months, he gave birth to a pair of twins . . . " Yang San related.

"What twins? Twins are nothing! To tell you the truth, I'm worried about snakes! A few days ago, I went to the city. A woman gave birth to a big python. As soon as it was born, it bit the midwife to death. Things like that . . . " Old lady Song's face changed color as she spoke. She hunched her back and shrank into a ball. She looked like a handful of bones wrapped in a black cloth, cracking inside from trembling.

At night there was a shower. When the sun came up, the ground steamed, and the tiny creatures in the sky hummed in the steam. People shaded their eyes from the bright light with their hands while looking at the sky. They shook their heads.

"'Brightness at the four corners indicates rain. Brightness at the top indicates no rain.'* Again we'll have fine sunny days."

"Oh, this weather could steam an old sow to death."

"Steam a dog to death."

"Steam a chicken to death."

"Even a man could be steamed to death!"

"The belly is like a steamed bun ready to explode. When will we get a change of weather?"

During the day, they puffed, sweated, watched the weather, jabbered, listened to the rumbling of their stomachs, and waited for the sun to go down. Then the second day came, and again they puffed, they sweated . . . —an endless round.

Old Yue entered the iron gate. He was greeted by purple tongues everywhere. More than a dozen spitting people surrounded an anthill under the tree.

"Hello, how are you doing today?" He smiled mysteriously. "A thief knocked at my door all night. A red-eyed dog broke into my house. When the dog barked, centipedes dropped from my eyes.

---

*Chinese proverb from the countryside.—TRANS.

Doctors told me I'm suffering from lung cancer. What do you think? Will I die?"

At his question, people stopped spitting. They strained hard to recall, showing the whites of their eyes.

"This weather is a bit of something . . . ," Qi Er-gou replied hesitantly. Peeling off his rubber shoes, he scratched his toes. The harder he scratched, the more they itched.

"Exactly." Everyone breathed out in relief and said, "What dreadful weather. Damn it!"

"Weather for maggots!"

"In this weather, a stinking fart can spread two miles!"

"Under my bed nests of worms have been steamed!"

"I salted a jar of fish. This morning when I opened the lid, I found no fish left at all—they'd all been eaten by the maggots!"

"Wait a minute, Comrades." Old lady Song, who was stealing along the wall, whispered, "The street is full of dead dogs. The pond is again floating with . . . What does this mean?"

That day, "S" factory was particularly quiet. Everyone was holding his breath and listening intently. Something invisible was wandering around, bumping into this, clanging against that, making everybody restless.

"It's only the wind," Zhang Mie-zi said, gathering his courage. But he hunched his shoulders as soon as he finished as if cold. "The weather seems a bit damp."

"What noise?" Qi Er-gou reassured them. "It's nothing at all. It's only your imagination. The problem lies in the river. It's said that this morning a gigantic queer-looking fish was floating there. I smelled it early this morning. At the time I mistook it for the smell of dead dogs."

"Something went by horizontally." Wang Qiang came up, his cheeks puffed up, gasping for breath. "I didn't see it clearly. Could it be a monkey?"

"A monkey?"

"I think it's *that thing* coming again."

"Disastrous. Didn't it come one other year? That time dead fish fell from the sky. They punched my roof full of holes. I thought I could preserve them if I couldn't eat them all in time. Who could tell it would start a plague? Comrades, never, never eat dead fish!"

"The ghost is cutting off the chickens' feathers! Early this morning, all the chicks in the street had their feathers cut."

"Kill! What are you waiting for?"

"A mad dog was running in the street. Someone was chasing it. Oh, I hope it won't come here."

"A mad dog is nothing. I was bitten once. I didn't beat the creature, nor did I get hydrophobia. This shows that not everyone gets the disease once bitten. I've never had any trouble."

"If you're soaked with sweat from beating the dog, then catch a cold, how can you expect to survive? The man is exaggerating his ability!"

"This fucking weather. Sooner or later, we'll all be steamed to death."

"Once bitten, one should die by oneself. Why should he beat the dog? To gain attention?"

Rapid footsteps were heard. It was Old Yue.

"Damned Wang Si-ma. He's disappeared."

Everything was strangely quiet—there wasn't even a mosquito flying or an insect crawling. Wang Si-ma? What Wang Si-ma? Everyone was sweating all over and trying to understand. They glanced at each other and turned their heads around and around like millstones. But they couldn't understand anything. So they put on a nonchalant air and paced back and forth, staring at the sun with narrowed eyes and spitting saliva.

"Is Wang Si-ma a real person?" Zhang Mie-zi suddenly spoke up in a terrified tone. He was so startled by his own voice that his ears hummed.

The mob seemed to have understood something, or nothing.

They felt that Wang Si-ma should be a real person. At the same time, Wang Si-ma might not be a real person. How could a real person disappear? Something was wrong here? Was it some delusion caused by the befuddling heat? What was wrong with the iron gate?

"Have you heard of 'the ghost cutting off chicken feathers'?" Old Yue asked slyly.

"Damned ears! Ah—!" Zhang Mie-zi threw himself against the wall. "Something's biting me inside. It's killing me! Killing me!"

"What's the relationship between 'the ghost cutting feathers' and the case of Wang Si-ma?" Old Yue sneered.

The latrine was jammed with people. Everyone had diarrhea. Those on the toilet refused to get up, and the ones waiting were in such a hurry that they shit right in their pants. They all jabbered while moving their bowels.

"How many times have you taken a shit?"

"This is the third. To hell with it!"

"This is my eighth time! Think I ought to have an X ray?"

"Don't do that! When you have nothing left to shit, you'll be OK."

"This plague is worse than usual. I suggested long ago that garbage not be dumped in front of the restaurant. Nobody listened. There wouldn't have been this much weird trouble if we had dumped the garbage in the river and let it be carried away by the water as we used to do."

"Public moral standards are getting worse and worse."

"My belly is bursting."

"Hold on a while. It won't take long."

"I can't hold on any more. Let me shit here in the corner. It doesn't matter."

"We've never had to wait so long for a toilet. You could always find an empty toilet and take a shit immediately."

"Wang Si-ma's ear didn't really rot off. It was obviously shaved."

"It's said that Wang Si-ma fled because he was too ashamed of the maggots in his ears."

The hair all over their bodies felt like it would explode when they squatted too long. The collars of their cotton-padded coats were soaked. Everyone was wondering, "Why is it getting hot so fast today? How time flies! It's possible that we can't even wear our cotton-padded coats tomorrow. Too bad! The iron gate keeps clanging. We can't even shit in peace."

"What do you think? Doesn't this problem call for deep thought?" Qi Er-gou's voice could be heard outside. "I've never thought Terramycin could cure nerves."

All kinds of heads, sweating and stinking, were gathered together. Because of the concentration of too many glances, Qi Er-gou's chapped thumb began to swell. It expanded to several times its normal size. Some moving thing could be dimly seen on the fingernail. Some sound could be heard also. But when people looked carefully, they could see only black dirt. After their inspection, people nodded meaningfully to each other; smiles gradually played across their faces.

"Comrades, this problem is very serious."

"Pay attention if an owl perches on the wall."

"A gigantic weird fish is floating down the river."

"The big clock in the city has been striking madly the whole night. My wife became so upset that she broke our bowls. She broke twenty-three in a row."

"Never take medicine when you have a cold. Be careful not to poison your nerves."

The sun was as warm as a stove. The "S" factory people were thinking that if the sun were not so hot there would be fewer flies. Usually, the hotter the sun, the more flies there were. Flies love sun. Rain was better. So people hoped for rain. But the sun was as strong as before, and the flies were as many as before. There was no promise of rain. The earth had become an oven. Everywhere there was a cracking sound. The flies disturbed people's sleep at night. Rolling over in bed, one would feel something cool at the waist— some tiny creatures that had been crushed. Turning on the light, one found several corpses of flies. White maggots crawled out from the round broken belly. It was disgusting. Too many fly bites under the sun caused sores. It occurred everywhere, yellow fluid running from the sores. One old woman's eyeballs fell out because of the rotten sores on her eyes.

Sores even began to appear on the walls. Were they caused by fly bites also? This started when the wall surrounding "S" factory swelled into a big lump. In the sun it gave off an unbearable stink. Facing the big swelling, Old Yue, his face long and blue, looked at his watch. It was 7:30.

"Comrades, let's have a good discussion," he said.

"Please keep your windows closed at night!" Old lady Qi dashed in and out, nodding affirmatively to every one.

"There's a dead dog behind the latrine." Zhang Mie-zi ran in. "I'm worried that something unexpected might happen. Its belly is full of flies. Yellow fluid is running everywhere."

Old Yue looked at his watch again: still 7:30.

"Hey," he said. "What's your opinion on using Terramycin? Eh? I heard that all the drugstores have sold out of it. This proves a lot, doesn't it?"

"The heat is killing!"

"Damned maggots everywhere. When I pick up my bowl in the morning, I wonder if it will have maggots in it. Pah, ppp!"

"Lately, a lot of nerve-poisoning drugs are for sale in the drugstores."

"The investigation has confirmed that there are altogether eight whores on Yellow Mud Street."

"I cover my head tightly with my quilt, but the striking of the clock still sneaks into my ears. When the striking starts, my wife begins breaking bowls."

"Wait a minute. What's that sound?"

It turned out to be a sizzling sound from the swelling on the wall. Before they could listen carefully, everything on earth seemed to start sizzling. Small golden worms swam in the yellow sky. A huge fly descended like a helicopter. People felt their eyelids itching. As they rubbed their eyes, the yawns began. And dreams followed the yawns, long, endless dreams. Everything in the dreams was queer. Dogs, centipedes, owls, houses, trees, everything was sizzling. And from the sound, a thin gummy substance oozed out and stuck to the edges of their eyelids.

That day Old Yue stood stock-still under the wall, his face ghastly pale. He looked at his watch all day.

When the sun set, the mad dogs started barking again.

"So the poisonous sore is located inside the farthole." Qi Er-gou rolled over, rubbing his tiny eyes open. "Skeletons are hanging in the peach tree. The ground is covered with footprints."

"Why not a yellow weasel? Eh?" Yang San said quietly. "I believe it could very well be a yellow weasel."

"I simply can't close my eyes. I'm afraid of that dead dog. Where is that dog from? Why should it die suddenly behind the latrine? Don't you feel the sun is like a golden cherry?"

"A name bothers me all the time. Yesterday when I was having supper, the name suddenly came out of my mouth. I was frightened. The whole night I was listless. Never form the habit of talking to yourself."

"Some black mushrooms fell from the cracks in old Hu San's ceiling again."

"I haven't had any dreams for three days. Is something wrong with me?"

"All fancy ideas are caused by the heat."

One afternoon, the big clock in the city struck two. Old Yue woke up from his daydreaming. He remembered Wang Si-ma again. He still called it angrily the "Wang Si-ma Case." He explained to the public for a long time, including the description of a monkey that could make noodles like a human being, or even better than a human being. "Isn't it a miracle? What do you think?" he asked seriously.

Wang Si-ma thus disappeared like a shadow. "S" factory people could never decide if there had ever been a Wang Si-ma. Such a problem was too complicated, and took too much energy to clarify. Besides, there were so many problems to think about. For example, the latrine was collapsing again. Excrement and urine spilled from the broken hole. Maggots grew everywhere. There seemed no way to stop it all. Wherever the flies bit, there were maggots. A thief wandered about the factory, scaring everybody. Nobody could get a peaceful sleep. As soon as their diarrhea stopped, the endless sores began . . . and so on.

WANG ZI-GUANG ENTERS YELLOW MUD STREET

1

The sun grew more fierce each day, making everything crack and sizzle. There was always something humming, humming in the air. The dull, prolonged hums lasted whole days. Nobody knew where the sound came from. Many tried to spot the source by shading their eyes with their hands. But nothing could be detected. Some said the sound came from mosquitoes, some said it was from the roof tiles, and still others said it had to do with their own ears.

The days entered and left "S" factory through a gap in the wall. They seemed meaningless, and yet they also seemed to contain some unexpressed significance.

Along the corridors, under the eaves, everywhere, one met sleepy eyes and large, gaping mouths the color of pig's liver. Green-headed flies crawled across people's faces; mosquitoes moaned around them. Often Old Yue's hoarse voice broke their fanciful dreams: "Meeting time now."

This woke everyone up. Smoothing their clothes, they entered the meeting room. They managed to stay awake for the first few minutes, but after they listened a while their eyes clouded and their bodies relaxed. Then one man would slouch against his neighbor, and the man leaned on in turn leaned toward the next. Eventually, groups of five, six, seven, or eight were snoring like thunder.

This would last until the leader began to lecture about such important things as, "Someone in this audience is raising an owl!" or "The case of the bat must be thoroughly investigated!" or "A bloodstain has become visible on the wall," and so on. Then people were startled awake. They nudged the bodies leaning against them, and those people in turn started awake. Sitting erect, muttering and complaining, they rubbed their eyes. And they listened, their tiny, round eyes open. But in less than half a minute, their eyes turned lightless again. How could one punish them? Even "lightning will not strike the sleepy."

The flood came in a dream.

Old Hu San was sunbathing as he sat on his night stool, his bony legs stretched out before him. He saw the yellow water stream in like a flock of lake ducks. Narrowing his wrinkled eyes, he watched for a while, then said, "Ha!" Raising his huge body, he entered his house, bolted the door, and lay on his bed. Flies fell onto his mosquito net from a crack in the ceiling, where a variety of other things grew: flies, moths, even some tiny black mushrooms. Every day his daughter would dash in with a sprayer and shoot DDT at the ceiling. Old Hu San lay there a while. He was about to have a dream when the water flooded into the room through the door, bringing along a fishy smell. Turning over with difficulty, he said "Ha" again and wondered, "Why is the back of the scarab red?"

The sun looked like an egg yolk floating on the muddy yellow foam. Steeped in water, the small huts on the street resembled an army of black beetles. Across the street a female corpse lay in the water, soaked like a sponge.

The barber stood in the water naked from the waist up. He was slitting the throat of a cat; his body was stained with blood.

"The river water is slippery. It feels like the dirty water after a bath."

"Lumps grow like boils on the walls, and the walls crack in the night."

"Floods always cause death."

"The water smells like feces. I think a plague will break out. Every time the water smells like feces, there's a plague."

"My ears rang all night. This morning with a nail I dug out a flea and a bunch of flea eggs."

Everyone was outside looking for something to eat. People were searching around full of hope, dipping into the water with their hands, believing they would finally find something. The water was hot. Searching again and again, they found a dead pig and several dead chickens bloated from the water. Dead things are not edible, yet someone insisted on eating them, saying it would be wasteful to throw them away. So, with Zhang Mie-zi taking the lead, people started to eat. They told themselves that these animals had not died of plague, but had drowned. The river water was clean; therefore, the animals were clean and edible. Once they started, there was no stopping them. People went out looking for things to eat every day, and they ate everything they could find.

The whole street suffered an epidemic. All the chickens died, and several cats went mad, howling day and night on the rooftops. People dared not go outdoors, but they couldn't stay indoors, either. The floors were flooded with stinking water that had seeped in, and the walls were covered with slugs that fell down your neck if you didn't pay attention. One day, old lady Yuan Si discovered in the cupboard a nest of poisonous snake eggs, which she almost ate as chicken eggs. After that day, people moved to their attics to live. When they needed to shit and couldn't wait to get down, they cut a hole in the floor and dumped directly into the water.

When Wang Zi-guang came in a little boat, people on Yellow Mud Street were jammed into their attics, gazing into the distance, shading their eyes with their hands. After a while someone started to chuckle. They pushed each other and pounded their chests or stamped their feet in joy. They fell to the floor and rolled back and forth. The sound they made resembled drumming.

The little boat looked like a beetle. It approached very fast. The man poling the boat had no head; at least, because he was bent over and had his rear end pointed toward Yellow Mud Street, he looked headless to the people.

"Wang Zi-guang has a black briefcase with him," someone shouted from one of the attics.

"Wang Zi-guang has a black briefcase with him," people whispered to each other, stretching out their necks like a row of ducks on a fence.

Wang Zi-guang arrived at the first door. He kicked it open and yelled, "Have you heard about the ghost that clips the feathers off chickens? Hey?" Then he stepped inside. His long rubber boots splashed through the water. The room was dark as a cave. He could feel innumerable little creatures flicking and biting, making faint noises. After a long time, Wang Zi-guang discovered a tiny spot of light. Through a small hole in the ceiling he could see the tiles of the roof. Something dropped from the hole. He examined it for a long time before concluding that it was a lump of excrement.

"Something wrong with this room," he said, shivering.

"This house is obviously uninhabited," the man poling the boat said. Without anyone's notice, he had climbed up the staircase leading to the attic. Now he was sliding down the handrail. As soon as he reached the bottom, he climbed up and slid down again. He repeated this over and over, whistling cheerily and stirring enough dust to choke a person.

"Stop it!" Wang Zi-guang ordered. He felt his neck swell as if a cold draft had blown in. "A draft has occupied my neck," he thought. He felt proud for his meaningful use of the word "occupy." It sounded like a formal document in which the word "occupy" had to be used.

"Every attic is crowded with heads. How can this house be uninhabited? Now I notify you formally that there are countless people on the street! What is your response to the question of political outlook? You pestilential chick!" He was not sure why he cursed the man as a "pestilential chick." It just slipped out. He didn't feel at all satisfied after the scolding.

The boat man concentrated on sliding down the rail. He was getting ever more skillful at it. His bottom made a pleasant squeaking sound. "Someone is shitting through the hole," he commented while sliding. "It stinks!"

"So this fellow is deaf," Wang Zi-guang thought. He waded outside, and kicked open the second door.

"Xu Zi-hu!" He shouted out the first name he thought of at random. This time, he was more skillful. He dashed up the stairs without waiting for an answer. He searched around, but nobody was there. Half-finished rice and other dishes sat on the table. Several fat rats were having a feast. They stared at him without concern.

"Have you heard about the ghost clipping off chicken feathers?" He gave a sudden cry as he felt the land slide and the ground sink around him. It turned out that one of his feet had stepped into a hole, and his entire leg was slipping downward. When he pulled up his leg with the help of his hands, he saw that his pants were covered with excrement. It seemed the hole was used by the family to shit in. Wang Zi-guang remembered the same kind of hole in the first house. This hole was also the only outlet for air because there was no window to be found in the attic. Several rays of light seeped through the cracks of the tiles. He ran down the staircase in confusion. He stepped on something soft. Raising his head, he saw a huge black shadow approaching.

"The question of political lines is a cardinal question of right or wrong." The black shadow suddenly opened its mouth. It turned out to be the boat man. God knows when he had sneaked in. He was still sliding down the rail, making his squeaking sound. What Wang had just stepped on was his hand on the staircase. "You've hurt my hand!"

"Hurry, take me out," Wang Zi-guang said weakly. He felt fungus and grass growing in his lungs.

The dried-up legs of the boat man tapped on the floor as he dropped from the rail. He put his hands under Wang Zi-guang's armpits. The hands felt like two icicles. A cold draft reached Wang's lungs.

The night stool of Old Hu San was situated in the yellow water under the eaves. He sat on the stool barefoot. With deep concentration he pinched his nose tightly and blew hard. From between his fingers a yellow filament swung in the air.

"Have you heard about the ghost clipping the chickens? Ha?" Wang Zi-guang smiled strangely, patting Hu San's back.

Hu San's spine made a humming resonance. A swarm of bees bumped about blindly inside him. Like an old turtle, he stared fixedly with his tiny shining eyes and said warmly, "The creeping wood sorrel is growing luxuriantly on the roof of the hut. The Song family next door is again eating flies. Go investigate. Hurry . . . Some people say the force of the rebels is irresistible. What do you think?"

"Is there any association between the ghost that clips chickens and the case of Wang Si-ma?" Wang Zi-guang was laughing again. He laughed so hard that he hiccuped.

"This room stinks. And there are so many flies."

"Ha, ha . . . "

"One more black mushroom has dropped from the crack in the ceiling. Isn't this the third one?"

"Ha, ha . . . "

The next day was a fine day.

Zhang Mie-zi had died quietly. He had certainly chosen a good day! When he was carried out by the others, he had turned charcoal black, his back swollen like the hump of a camel.

A mad cat howled on the roof of the hut. The creeping wood sorrel had blossomed in little purple flowers, one bunch after another, shining in the sun.

"The stink will last tens of thousands of years! The stink will last tens of thousands of years!" Old Yue was shaking his tiny yellow pearlike head.

"If only I'd been told earlier, there might have been a remedy." Old lady Song tapped her shriveled chest. "This Zhang Mie-zi, he was too concerned about saving face, even at the cost of death."

"Zhang Mie-zi had a lot of problems, in fact," old lady Qi said angrily. "He was too simpleminded when dealing with the world. Besides, he was too greedy. He ate spoiled food every day. When talking, his mouth always gave off an unbearable smell of sour rice." As she spoke, she poked the hump on the back of the corpse with a stick. At her light jab a stream of black water poured from the hump, giving off an irritating stink.

"Be careful of the water. It's poisoned. Don't drink well water; don't take a bath," old lady Song said in a low voice. Then she sneaked away from the crowd like a rat.

"Seven-forty." Old Yue looked at his watch. His face was blue. For three days running, Old Yue had been coping with those damned slugs. They kept crawling onto the floor of the attic, and always through that shithole. He had tried awls, hooks, salty water, just about everything. But in one movement, the slugs were up again, slippery, grayish white, leaving strings of tracks everywhere they crept. The strings shone in the dim blue light.

"The sickle moon is high in the sky. The old landlady is making her rounds of the soldiers' beds at night." The radio was broadcasting a song which had been on all morning, making people nervous.

"Our street is full of weird things." Stretching his neck, Old Yue said to Qi-gou, "There's a rumor that Wang Zi-guang is Wang Si-ma's younger brother. What does the death of Zhang Mie-zi show us? Eh?"

"Is Wang Zi-guang a real person or not?" Secretary Zhu was perched like a sparrow on the rail of the attic across the street. He joined the conversation hastily. "It's said that he was here once, but he stopped coming. The problem is, no one really saw him. How can you believe such a man came? It's possible the person who came was not Wang Zi-guang, but only a beggar passing by, or worse still, a monkey or something else. I think the reason people believe Wang Zi-guang exists, sent by higher authorities, is their own inner fear. They create a rumor about the coming of Wang Zi-guang, and pretend to believe his name is Wang Zi-guang, and everyone has seen him. But in reality, nobody can draw any conclusion about the existence of Wang Zi-guang, or whether the person who came was Wang Zi-guang, or even whether anyone at all has really been here. I plan to prepare a case study of this matter and present it to the committee for discussion. I can see there's a hidden trouble inside. It may result in a big mistake if treated improperly. Don't you feel it? The sky looks dim since yesterday. The big clock in the city is striking day and night. Can it have something to do with the death of Zhang Mie-zi? All night I stood in the closet with my wife trying to sleep. My legs are still swollen, even now."

"This morning five rats swam across the street," Qi Er-gou said. He was leaning on the rail. He felt he had to say something. He had a feeling of approaching disaster. After long thought, he squeezed out one sentence from the newspaper: "The current major task is to catch a handful of class enemies." Then he spat out a mouthful of yellow sputum, feeling at ease and justified.

"A bloody ball has rolled across my eyes." Old Yue glared at him and said, word by word, "I have experimented with hammering a long nail into the eye of a dog. The dog did not die. Isn't that a miracle?"

"Something's going to happen." Qi Er-gou lowered his eyes in utter fear. In an effort of bravado he spat again and then coughed repeatedly as if his lungs were clogged with thick sputum.

"I plan to write a detailed record about Wang Zi-guang. I need to collect even the smallest clues." Secretary Zhu flashed with excitement. "Because it may cause some big mistake. For example, the case of Wang Si-ma has already become a big mistake. We were so sure at the time, but now we can't even confirm whether or not he was a real person. In the past, he was thought to be an old resident of Yellow Mud Street. It sounded like a fact. But false impressions are very likely to occur, particularly false impressions shared by many people. This is more terrible. I believe the first thing to ascertain is what kind of clothes Wang Zi-guang wore when he came to Yellow Mud Street. After this is clarified, other questions will take care of themselves. If there has never been such a man, no clothes would have been worn. This is number one. Number two, what is the relationship between Wang Zi-guang and Yellow Mud Street? Was he really a higher-up, or only the younger brother of Wang Si-ma? In my opinion this second point is the most complicated, and it concerns the lives of the residents on this whole street. I want to ask the authorities to send an investigation team. Such problems cannot be solved by local efforts." At this point, he jumped down lightly like a sparrow from the rail, rubbing his fingers joyfully. "When I was trying to sleep in the closet last night, a series of questions bothered me. I was sleepless the whole night, tossing and turning. I was thinking. Finally, I reached the above conclusion. What's more, there's another question: was Zhang Mie-zi's death caused by the mad cat?" He stretched his neck toward the street.

Old Yue and Qi Er-gou followed him in stretching out their necks.

But the mad cat on the roof of Zhang Mie-zi's hut had disappeared. Not even a sparrow could be seen. The purple wood sorrel blossoms shone brightly.

The sun was as red as a pig's lungs. The sky was dusty. Gray ash fell like snowflakes. People said a comet was going to collide with the earth. The end of the world was coming. Every family was cooking good things. Rumor spread that their days were numbered. Eat now or never. Then people felt bloated from overeating. Bloated stomachs in turn led to the shouting of insults in the street. Across the street, across the yellow water, people cursed each other, stamping their feet and shitting at the same time. One man cursed while trying to hold up his pants. At the height of their enthusiasm, they would raise a night stool full of shit and hurl it toward the opposite attic. This action was reciprocated immediately by those across the way. Of course, no excrement really landed on anyone. This was only a way of boosting morale.

Several days passed in such hubbub. But then people fell into moaning and complaining again.

"When Wang Zi-guang came, he had a black briefcase with him."

"Wang Zi-guang was only here once. Now he's stopped coming."

"There's no hope for Yellow Mud Street."

Why had Wang Zi-guang come, then refused to come again? People remained perplexed despite much thought. Was it because he had detected that the resistance in Yellow Mud Street was too great? Hadn't he talked with Old Hu San? Or had he lost heart in the future of Yellow Mud Street? Why had he reached such a pessimistic opinion about Yellow Mud Street?

Finally old lady Qi one day told people excitedly, "Wang Zi-guang is far from a distinguished person. You're all crazy! He's a buyer and seller for the salvage station. This is completely reliable news, because he's a relative of my sister-in-law. Besides that, we've even been mistaken about his name, which is really He Zi-guang."

At this, people felt relieved of a great burden. At the same time, they felt disappointed: so Wang Zi-guang was only a functionary for the salvage station!

At that period, Secretary Zhu worked late into the night, busy with his investigative report. He finally finished it. After working out more than fifty topics, the last one he chose was: The Horrifying Death of Zhang Mie-zi and the Case of Wang Zi-guang.

At sunset Secretary Zhu sent his report to the district by boat.

2

After Wang Zi-guang formed this pessimistic opinion about Yellow Mud Street, everybody felt dejected. People lost interest in going outdoors and could accomplish nothing. When meeting each other, they no longer exchanged conventional greetings. Instead there was always only one remark: "There's no hope for Yellow Mud Street." This was followed by a gesture to show the meaninglessness of life: a dropping of the eyelids, a yawn, and a reluctance to open the mouth again. Even Wang Zi-guang had lost heart! Though he was no more than a functionary of the salvage station, a relative of old lady Qi's, Yellow Mud Street people all had foresight and sagacity. They could see the significance of Wang Zi-guang's pessimistic opinion.

They believed this thing of importance deserved deep thought and thorough understanding. As a result, people went about in a trance every day, feeling world-weary. Nobody could go to work. Rubbing their chests, they complained that without a thorough study of such a question, people's lives were in danger. Who could work in such a mood? Consequently, "S" factory was officially closed.

When people entered their houses they bolted their doors and refused to open them again. The little ones got an angry beating if they cried to go out. After such a beating, the parents would climb breathlessly to the attic and peep out through the cracks. They would even make some noise meant to test any reactions from the outside.

"What a year for weird things," old men sighed, shaking their white heads. Despite the suffocating heat inside the houses, no one opened their doors for fresh air. Every household knew that at midnight an old woman dressed in black sneaked along the outer wall. She jerked her head left and right to look around. Rustling about, she would make a racket either by knocking something over or by throwing a rock into the water. Then she sneaked away immediately. When the old woman was about, the lights in the houses would flash dramatically before going completely dark.

Old Hu San continued to sit on his night stool under the eaves day and night. With his eyes closed, he mumbled, "Rebel . . . Good! I was counting the mushrooms over my bed when a black shadow appeared outside the window, getting ready for murder . . . There's a black shadow! Comrades, be on your guard!"

One day, his daughter poured a stoolful of urine down his neck and spat on him hatefully. Old Hu San's body shrank inside the wet clothes, as if his flesh had melted and his belly had shriveled up.

"Scarab and yellow weasel," he said dully. "What does the case of Wang Zi-guang show us? I sit here keeping watch every day, my eyes wide open. Yet I've never seen anyone called Wang Zi-guang. They say it's hopeless. Somebody's always doing mischief. Hasn't the sun dripped blood? I saw it. Nothing can escape my aged eyes. Black mushrooms grow in the ceiling cracks. Cook them for me to eat." He slumped over and snored like a cat.

Gradually, the yellow water on the tarred street turned boiling hot. During the day, the street was impossible to stand on. Everything became dazzling with white light like splinters of glass in flame. The tiny sun hung motionless in one corner of the gray sky.

Once in a while, a slice of dreamlike cloud would stop and hide the sun. Then people let out a long breath, saying, "Now it's good." But soon the cloud would move on and the earth burned once again with white flames.

In the sunlight Yellow Mud Street looked like a big dirty rag full of black holes. These holes emitted clouds of greasy odors together with swarms of green-headed flies and poisonous mosquitoes with speckled legs. In the attics of the small dark huts, the citizens drowsed. They drove away the flies with lazy motions of their flyswatters. Sometimes they would raise the swatters high and yell at the rats crawling toward the table, "I haven't died yet!" Occasionally the loudspeaker on the street started up, shaking the air and shattering their eardrums. At such times, they would stumble outside in confusion, shuffling along in their worn-down shoes, shading their eyes from the light with huge cattail-leaf fans. Though they listened attentively, they could understand nothing. Vaguely, they heard something about "an entire nation in arms," about corns on the feet, about achieving eternity by taking glossy ganoderma fungus, about the patent for inventing the compass, and so on. After the news broadcasts, people decided none of it concerned them and shuffled back to their attics, still clutching their fans.

"Wang Zi-guang has arrived in town!" old lady Song shouted in the street, clapping her hands.

"Good Lord! What?" Everyone clattered hurriedly out of their huts, bareheaded in the sun, forgetting their cattail-leaf fans.

"Wang Zi-guang has reached the town," old lady Song said. She was sweating and foaming. "That means there is a Wang Zi-guang. He's not a functionary from the salvage station. According to the others, his real identification is still under investigation."

"Real identification? Bah!" Old lady Qi spat out some mud. Walking over, she bumped Biddy Song with her hipbone. Old lady Song staggered from the blow.

"Arrived in town," old lady Song said while retreating. "But now he's dead. He jumped like a carp from a third-floor window. He's still lying in the street. His face is completely destroyed and his legs are gone. Where can his legs be? I searched for a long time, but in vain."

"So he's dead already? And his legs can't be found? How can that happen?" Everyone stared at the old gossip, refusing to give up until they got more.

"Dead. There was a big crowd there. I couldn't see clearly." She spread out her palms, as if telling everybody that was all.

That midnight, the head of the district came unannounced to Yellow Mud Street. He found that only the house of Secretary Zhu at the end of the street had a light on. It looked like a firefly.

The district head banged on the door loudly, but there was no answer. "Bang, bang, bang!" He drummed the door with force. Yet nothing could be heard inside. The district head circled the house and pressed his brandy nose against the window trying to see inside. But he failed—the dirt on the glass was so thick that nothing could penetrate it. Then he had a brainstorm. He took out a small knife and poked at the crack around the door. After some effort, the crack widened and more light leaked out. Peeping in, he saw only a vague cloud of steam. When the crack was about three inches wide, he spat a big glob of sputum inside. Immediately, he heard the squishy sound of rubber boots, and the door opened slightly.

Secretary Zhu's head poked out like a bald broom. "Fifteen versus thirteen. Is there much hope?" he asked, his eyeballs protruding. He held the door, preventing the district head from entering.

"The situation is changing for the better. Open the door, you thief!" The district head barely restrained his rage. He was about to force his way in. Unfortunately, Secretary Zhu held the door tightly and left only a very narrow opening. At the same time, his neck between the door and the frame became very thin, resembling a flat leech.

"Fifteen versus thirteen. Is there much hope?" He was still bugging his eyes and asking the question coldly. Suddenly he twisted his body. Instantly a beam of light shot from above his head toward the darkness outside. "Oh, District Head!" His face paled when he recognized the man outside. The door was wide open now.

By the time the district head splashed inside, Secretary Zhu had already jumped onto the middle rungs of a ladder leading to the top of a big wardrobe in the room. The top of the wardrobe was very spacious. A lamp rested there like a firefly, and piles of documents and papers littered the whole space. The tallest piles seemed about to crack through the ceiling.

"Since the flood, I have moved on top of this wardrobe. Please follow me up, but watch your step." He took the hand of the district head, leading him onto the wardrobe. "I've been busy all night putting together the records of the Wang Zi-guang Case. I mean to send an investigative group to his ancestral home. Do you have any instructions to give?" He was pushing the piles of documents aside with all his strength and stacking them up, sweat running down his face. Finally he succeeded in making a small space. The two men squeezed in and sat down close to one another.

"Fifteen versus thirteen, is this a secret code?" The district head inquired. Suddenly his shining eyes looked directly into Zhu's.

"It's only the volleyball score in yesterday's movie," Secretary Zhu answered, embarrassed. "Please move over here a little, will you? Roaches keep sneaking out of that crack. Yesterday I sat on one and killed it." He dragged the district head toward him. By now the head was actually sitting on Zhu's lap. He could feel that Zhu's legs were perspiring, and he found it uncomfortable to sit on sweaty legs.

"All night, I've been busy preparing the records for the Wang Zi-guang Case. It's been going on for half a month now. Just look." He pointed at a thick pile of papers covered with black dirt. An unidentified insect skittered across it. He laid his cheek on the pile emotionally, saying, "I've already written one million two hundred thousand words." He pulled several pages from the pile and presented them to the district head.

The district head popped the tip of his nose to the paper and sniffed it for some time. Suddenly he said in a frightened voice, "Why is the wardrobe shaking? I can feel it swinging."

"Absolutely!" Secretary Zhu said cheerfully. "Did you notice the ropes on the wardrobe? My wife and my son are pulling these ropes from the back room, so the wardrobe is moving. It's like a little boat floating in the room. You should know there are always people spying on this house from every direction. I have to change directions constantly. This is my brainstorm. Now nobody can do anything to me."

Someone was digging quietly beyond the window. The sound got louder and louder and eventually became irksome.

"Who can that be?" The district head was indignant. "How can you allow such things to go on?"

Secretary Zhu yawned. He looked as if he were going to doze off. His eyes blurred. "That's old lady Qi," he replied sluggishly. "She holds a different opinion about the Wang Zi-guang Case. Every night she comes to sabotage my files. Because of her interference, my job is endless. I have the feeling she's going to succeed in this matter. This woman is like a piece of steel cable. We can't triumph over her. I often think that since she's determined to set herself against me, maybe it's better for me to give up. What do you think?"

"I think I'm going to have a heart attack!" The district head said angrily, clutching his chest.

Two nostrils appeared against the windowpane. The woman beat on the window frame threateningly.

"When she knocks like this, I lose my will to prepare the file,"

Secretary Zhu said in a discouraged tone. "Her aim is to drag the writing on and on. Say, have you ever tried to make wine from soaked roaches?" His eyes immediately turned warm. He moved his legs. This movement made sitting even more uncomfortable for the district head. He felt he was going to slip down Zhu's legs. Accordingly, he held onto Zhu's back to keep his balance. "When I get pimples on my body, I apply the wine, and they disappear instantly. I've kept one bottle at the bottom of the wardrobe. You may have it if you ever need it."

Secretary Zhu started to snore quietly. He had fallen asleep on the district head's shoulder. The district head also felt extremely tired, as if he had climbed several big mountains. He forced himself free of Zhu's legs and collapsed on the pile of documents. Secretary Zhu was completely unconscious of this movement. Deep in sleep, he rested against the district head's chest and clamped his legs around the man's waist, forcing the breath out of him. The district head tried to resist, but he found his neck gripped tightly by Zhu's hand. They struggled like this for some time. Finally the district head was completely exhausted and fell into sleep, the two of them entwined.

Before dawn, the district head was awakened by a strange noise from outside. Someone was making a hullabaloo, and others were banging on the door, which was about to break open. But Secretary Zhu was still snoring like a pig. It was impossible to wake him because he seemed to be neither asleep nor awake. His eyes were open, and he was laughing to himself, laughing and snoring. The district head was terror-stricken. Pushing aside Zhu's legs with all his might, he concealed himself at the other end of the wardrobe, holding his breath. He realized he had fallen into a dilemma. He sat there for a long time in grief and regret.

Then he crawled over and whispered into Zhu's ear, "Five versus thirteen, win!" This was definitely an effective measure. Secretary Zhu yawned and sat up at once.

Zhu listened carefully for a while then climbed down the ladder and went to the door. As he'd done yesterday, he opened the door just a crack, held it firmly, and stretched out his neck. Another uproar, followed by a burst of laughter, could be heard. Secretary Zhu gave four or five big yawns. Then everything fell quiet.

"They've left for the town to see Wang Zi-guang. Isn't it an art to control the mood of the masses?" Secretary Zhu closed the door, looking treacherous. The next moment, he fell into a trance. After a long time, he soliloquized, "Is Wang Zi-guang a real person? The whole truth may come to light this time."

The crowd started out full of confidence. Along the way, they joked and fought with each other, whistling and spitting, falling into the water joyfully and rolling about like a ball.

Thus they arrived at the town. According to old lady Song, the accident had happened on Glory Street. "A big black door. On the eaves, a poisonous spider was spinning a huge web." She was trying hard to recall, swallowing foam from the corner of her mouth.

When they reached Glory Street, they began the search. Then she admitted she couldn't really remember. It might have been Red Guard Road? But they had already passed Red Guard Road. So they retraced the mile to Red Guard Road.

"A big black door. A poisonous spider spinning a huge web," old lady Song said.

Red Guard Road was completely empty, showing no sign of any recent big event. The whole mob was streaming with sweat. They might all get heatstroke if they continued like this. The sun was high overhead. The water was hot enough to blister their feet. Large bubbles of black foam floated on the water. Swarms of mosquitoes danced on the foam. Many people were panting like dogs, their tongues hanging out. Bugging out their eyes, they all glared at old lady Song, wishing they could swallow her down in one mouthful.

"What's the matter?" old lady Song said. She wiped her small, wrinkled forehead, trying to keep cool. "Maybe Wang Zi-guang really isn't a human being?"

"Stink-corpse!"

"Deadly piggy biddy!"

"Pestilent piggy biddy!"

"Making tricks from overeating. Racking her brains to perpetrate a fraud."

"Killing with a soft knife!"

Wiping the sweat from their faces, the mob blew up. Every fine hair was exploding. Their scalps itched so miserably that they wished they could peel them off. They grew furious at the idea that the old woman had the vicious heart to trick them and that they would allow such an idiot to fool them into walking such a long distance.

"That old dame gets up at midnight to eat flies," Liu Tie-chui muttered to the others. "She has a trap for catching flies. I've seen her take flies out of that trap and eat them as if she were eating sunflower seeds. She peels them in her mouth and spits out the wings and the head."

"There's a big spiderweb at the doorway," old lady Song was still trying hard to find the place. She rattled on and on, licking the foam from the corner of her mouth. "A wild cat dashed by. There were big obstacles. Yellow Mud Street is hopeless. Wang Zi-guang's opinion is based on a very reliable source."

When they returned to Yellow Mud Street, they saw the district head and Secretary Zhu lying on top of Zhang Mie-zi's hut, clinging to each other. The sun fell on their hips, and steam rose from their bodies. Each of them had two large wrinkled patches across their rumps.

"The district head is snoring," someone whispered delightedly.

"Notice the patches on their rears, comrades. Those are from the old revolutionary base area . . . "

"Hush. Don't make so much noise. I suggest we stand by the

wall to listen to the district head's snoring. Let's see if we can learn anything from it."

"A brilliant idea!"

People threw themselves against the wall madly. They squeezed and pushed, making loud noises. They whistled, spat, and fussed for a long time. Finally everyone reluctantly settled down. They all craned their necks toward the eaves.

Suddenly the snoring stopped. They heard Secretary Zhu yawn and talk in his dream: "How to decide the nature of the problem in Yellow Mud Street?"

Then the district head climbed down the ladder like an ape. He was facing upward with his neck stretched high. He did not notice the people hiding against the wall. Turning the corner, he walked toward the toilet at the back of the house.

"The district head is going to take a shit," the people said respectfully. After a while, they could smell the stink of fresh excrement.

They had already forgotten about Wang Zi-guang, but they remembered clearly what was to be done today, that is, to "find out something" from the district head. A warm desire grew vaguely in the hearts of the people, and they felt faintly that what they waited for was of vital importance.

However, once the district head entered the toilet, he refused to come out.

"The district head has been shitting for half an hour already."

"The district head is worn out from hard work."

"What kind of instructions can the district head give?"

"Secretary Zhu is still not awake. He hasn't had any sleep for a month now. I see his little light every midnight."

"I heard that Secretary Zhu can't continue his file work because someone is sabotaging it."

"Secretary Zhu is a good man, almost as good as the district head."

When old Yue looked at his watch again, the district head had been shitting for an hour. There was no sound from the toilet. The black curtain flapped in the wind, giving out suspicious sounds.

People held an emergency meeting on the spot, and decided to send a representative to meet the district head in the toilet. When the representative cautiously opened the curtain, he discovered the toilet was empty.

"The district head has already returned to the district," Secretary Zhu declared indifferently to the mob. He stretched sluggishly.

In fact the district head had not returned to the district. He had pretended to go for a shit, but instead ducked into the little hut of Secretary Zhu through the back door. Climbing onto the wardrobe, he fell into sleep again. Secretary Zhu knew of the district head's trick, so he had a strange expression on his face when he said, "The district head has returned to the district." He looked as if he were both satisfied and fed up. Then he also pretended to go to the toilet and sneaked into his hut through the back door. Climbing onto the wardrobe, he fell asleep next to the district head.

They both slept until the next morning.

THE TORRENTIAL RAIN

1

Old Hu San was asleep under the eaves.

It was particularly hot that day. Early in the morning Hu San had a dream in which a red spider with a huge belly and long, hairy legs kept crawling onto the tip of his nose. He whisked it off five times, but it crawled back a sixth time. He was about to whisk it off again when a loud tap woke him up. Opening his eyes, he found a big water drop hanging from the tip of his nose.

Lying still, Old Hu San listened to the rain. It beat on the tarred street like popping beans. Streams of black water poured from the eaves. The rain soaked his clothes, then flooded onto the step where he lay. His whole back was immersed. "The rain this year is a little sticky, and a little salty, too," he thought. "Very similar to human sweat." He recalled the year when there was a rain of dead fish. The rainwater then was also salty. He had even salted two big fish.

The water kept rising. By dusk, Old Hu San's whole body was

steeped in water. Many tiny insects gathered in his hair and crawled toward his face. He continued his dream of the red spider creeping onto the tip of his nose, its huge, cold belly blocking his nostrils, making breathing difficult. He intended to whisk it away, but his hand was unbearably sore.

"Eat!" His daughter's violent stomping woke him up. She shoved a big bowl of rice mixed with flies at the doorway.

Old Hu San propped himself up and took the bowl. He started eating in the rain, all along giving out stinking hiccups. While eating, he tasted something strange, so he stopped and studied the bowl carefully. Suddenly, he realized the vicious intentions of his family: at the bottom of the bowl they had buried a huge steamed spider. A sound like a cock's crow came from Hu San's throat. Then he felt a tickling on his neck. Touching himself, he discovered that long, tough hair had sprouted there.

"What's the meaning of being alive? A hell of a life," the daughter said through the window. She was staring at him.

"Old Hu San, bah!" his grandson also called through the window.

A few days before, his daughter had told him the room smelled terrible. There was a strange stink throughout the house. "The sun has cooked maggots out of everything," she'd said, creasing her eyebrows in anger. "Wherever you sit, you crush a couple of maggots. The grapes in the graveyard are as big as a dead man's eyeballs. Ha!"

After that, Hu San moved out and lived under the eaves. It was so damp there that one of his arms was always aching. He stopped thinking about his arms, and concentrated on dreaming. Lately his dreams had increased, more than in all his lifetime. In these dreams there were always spiders, scarabs, rats, and so on. Everything except human beings.

At evening, a lump of something soft and white floated to his feet. He observed it for a long time but couldn't see what it was. So he felt it with his hand. He probed it this way and that. All of a sudden it dawned on him that it was a human arm. At one pinch, water oozed from the flesh with a sound resembling sawing.

"How can a man live for more than eighty years? This is unthinkable," the daughter was saying inside.

Gradually Hu San calmed down. His dim old eyes wide in terror, he saw something drop from the eaves with a tapping sound.

"Have the rebels grabbed power?" he mumbled, grinding his loose front teeth.

From the darkness, two bloodred bulging eyes glared at him. The barber was standing in the rain, the blade of his knife flickering in the lightning.

A chill shot through Old Hu San. After some hesitation, he asked, "Who is dead?"

"That arm? I cut it off yesterday."

"Something called Wang Zi-guang was once here."

"Whose arm is it? Isn't it shocking?"

"This rain. The flood is knee-high. Can there be leeches in the water? I'm frightened. Sleeping in the water, I always dream of leeches sneaking into my hair to suck my brain. Please tell me your opinion. Is there much hope for the rebels?"

"Since you're so afraid of leeches, let me shave your head."

"Little insects are hiding in my hair. It's so itchy. They must have mistaken my hair for grass or something. They wouldn't have squeezed in here if they had known this was a human being. I almost ate a poisonous spider just now . . . Ah—ah!"

The barber yawned and disappeared in the rain with his shoulder pole.

Old Hu San was still deep in thought. "Is there much hope for the rebels?"

The wall of Zhang Mic-zi's little hut across the street was flashing in a beam of white light. Whispering could be heard from the pitch-black window. The sound buzzed on and on in the ear. It was accompanied by strange laughter.

When dawn came, the rain was still falling. A crowd with umbrellas surrounded old Hu San. He was drenched. Several slugs hung from his short hair like decorations. His hands and feet were snow-white from soaking in the water and were covered with black spots.

"What the hell are you watching for?" he demanded. "I'm counting mushrooms. In the crack in the ceiling of my room a variety of delicate, smooth, black mushroom grows. One of them has just fallen. That's the seventh this month. Last night, I thought about a single question all night."

"We should set up a shelter for the old man."

Old Yu nodded and continued, "This problem will be dealt with. There's a lot of bacteria in the rain water. Steeping in it for too long will cause paralysis. I will raise this issue with the Committee." He acted as if he were in the middle of something urgent and left in a hurry.

"Committee, the hell with it!" Old lady Song stretched out her tiny sharp foot and scratched Hu San's belly. "Take setting up a shelter, for example. The water will still run in, won't it? Let him make his own shelter! Hey, Comrade Hu San, what's your hope for this problem? Can you give us your opinion briefly?"

"I'm counting mushrooms. 'Tap,' the seventh is down. So exciting. What are you wrangling here for? I'd like to hear a sound."

"A sound?" Something flashed by old lady Song's tiny eyes. "What sound?"

"The sound of the rain." Old Hu San dropped his head.

People had been expecting to hear something from Old Hu San. They couldn't imagine he would doze off. So they felt both annoyed and lonely.

"What's the matter with this rain? It's been going on for a day and a night. Just now when I went to wash my hands, the excrement from the latrine was overflowing into the street."

"The cicadas cry without stop. How annoying! I would have slept for a month if I'd known the rain would last so long."

"They say a woman is dead. Her arms were chopped off and thrown by the riverside. I rushed over there for a look this morning, but they were nowhere to be found. Someone must have spread a rumor."

"How scary! There's no end to this rain. I simply can't sleep well. I always hear some noise in my dream. It's quieter to have the sun."

"The foundation of the street is damaged. Will the ground sink?"

"They say it always rains like this before an earthquake. The color of the sky is not right. The raindrops are so black. It's even darker than the year of dead-fish rain."

Old Hu San stood up weakly. He shook his head, and several slugs fell out along with the raindrops. He intended to look for something outside. Therefore, he went out into the rain.

"Comrade Hu San, don't lose heart! Don't feel pessimistic!" Old lady Song was shouting at the old man as she followed him. "I'd love to discuss your opinion about this! Hey, do you hear me?"

2

On that rainy day, the rats in old lady Qi's storage room bit a cat to death.

Early in the morning, old lady Qi was awakened by the popping-bean sound of the rain. She picked up a slipper as soon as she got up. Her hair still uncombed, she rushed into the kitchen to kill roaches. The kitchen was flooded. She splashed about in the water. Raising her slipper high, she jumped here and there and slammed it down hard. The fallen roaches floated in the water, struggling to turn their bodies around. She flipped over the cutting board, and more than a dozen roaches appeared. She leaped forward and killed them. Roaches reproduce very fast. Everything in the kitchen—oil, rice, vegetables—had been tasted by the roaches. Their droppings were everywhere. Some young roaches even hid in the seam around the lid of the wok. When she cooked vegetables in the wok, roaches would fall inside.

Old lady Qi killed roaches every morning. While smashing them, she would curse and gnash her teeth. Her blows were ruthless and accurate. She crushed the dead roaches so hard that they released an odor in the whole room. Sometimes she preferred not to sweep up the dead roaches at once, but to leave them on the floor. Roaches had piled up into a thick layer on the floor. Every time she went into the kitchen, several would stick to her shoes. When she discovered dead roaches on her soles, old lady Qi would make a fuss of taking off her shoes and knocking them together, making an earthshaking noise. It didn't take her long to break one of her shoes in this way.

With a great deal of noise, her husband was making rattraps in the inner room. He made one rattrap every day and baited it with a slice of poisoned meat. Rats ran freely in their storage room. They were huge and cunning. They never touched the meat in the trap.

"Sooner or later we'll be eaten," old lady Qi once said in annoyance.

As if to testify to her words, one day a big rat crawled into their bed and bit her husband's ear. It was then that he started making traps. He worked every morning and put his product in the storage room. He would go and check the next day. If there was no rat in the trap, he would take it back, disassemble it, and make a new one out of it. One night he heard the horrifying yowl of a cat. The next morning when he went to check the trap, he found the cat dead. It was covered with blood. Its throat was cut, and its intestines were bitten through. The husband removed the trap and muttered something. The piece of meat fell out. "On rainy days rats are more ferocious than usual," he thought.

"My good lord!" Old lady Qi appeared at the door of the storage room. "What a year this is! Rats like these could eat a human being. Such rats, they are no longer rats . . . " Something occurred to her while she was rattling on. She dropped the topic of rats immediately and went to Yang San's house. She stepped into his house and sat down on a cracked bamboo chair. She shouted, "Have you studied the newspaper editorial? Ha! The sky is threateningly dark!"

"What editorial?" A voice responded from the pitch-black mosquito net. The owner of the house was not yet up.

"'Catching the Small Handful inside the Party,'* of course." She approached the net and whispered inside, "The rats in my house have bitten a cat to death. It's beyond me to figure out what the matter is. Hey, what do you think about it? I've been arguing with Secretary Zhu for one month now about the case of Wang Zi-guang. I've made an unexpected discovery—a hole in his wall. It's right below the eaves, at the corner of the window."

"A hole?"

"Yes, an out-and-out hole! As big as a soybean. Ever since I discovered it, I've been patrolling around his house every night, knocking on his window in warning. This has worn me out. I have the feeling the hole was used by somebody. In such a situation, the confidentiality of the filing work is practically nonexistent. For this reason, I believe the work should be stopped completely! Think about it and you'll understand. How can rats kill a cat?"

"Is there any new hope for the situation?" Yang San's sleep-encrusted face poked out of the net. "Oh, the rain. It's pouring down as dark as Chinese ink."

"This rain is as dark as the one with the dead fish. Don't you

---

*Slogan from the Anti-Rightist Campaign of 1957.—TRANS.

know why the district head has returned to the district? I can't help feeling disappointed and depressed when I think of it. I don't even want to work. Please recall how he patted his hip and left. This shows that he saw through Yellow Mud Street! All these days I've been thinking about his talk concerning the tradition of the old revolutionary base area. Sometimes, lost in thought, I start mimicking his voice. I believe the solution to the problems in Yellow Mud Street lies in one word: chop!" With a bang, she chopped her hand down on the greasy table.

"Chop what?" Yang San trembled inside the net.

"Chop the legs. This is as clear as day. You don't need to worry about the hole in the wall. I've already blocked it with mud. However, there's no reason whatsoever to continue the filing work."

"I can't get my thoughts straight about this problem. Why can't it be a yellow weasel? It could very well have been a yellow weasel! I've been thinking so hard about it that my head is swollen. I've been sleeping poorly these days. Don't you think my head looks like a steamed bun?"

"The evidence shows the nature of the problem. We don't have room for the doctrine of the mean!" old lady Qi threatened and left the house in anger.

It drizzled gloomily. Old lady Qi had gone some distance when she suddenly turned back and sneaked under Yang San's window. She took out a penknife and started prying. After a long time, she finally pried the window open a narrow crack. Holding her breath, she peeped in with dissatisfaction. She watched for a while, then stood up with a sigh and walked toward Qi Er-gou's house.

"Have you studied the newspaper editorial?" she yelled. The instant she opened her mouth, she smelled the stink from yesterday.

Qi Er-gou stood in the middle of the room, his heels turned in. Stretching his arms forcefully, he gave a big yawn and said, "Such weather. What weather. Rain and rain . . . Good morning. The rain is really annoying." He remembered something all of a sudden. Stepping toward old lady Qi, he whispered into her ear, "Old lady Song next door raised hell all night."

"About what?" said old lady Qi, startled.

"About eating flies. She was caught by her husband. He threatened to drive her out. Then they started fighting."

"Mad dogs run in the streets lately. Be sure to close your windows tight."

"Her husband threw her flytrap into the street. Yesterday, I saw leeches in the rain. They were creeping everywhere. I thought closing the door would help. But they still crept in. Hey, never walk barefooted."

"I've made an unexpected discovery. There's a hole in the wall of Secretary Zhu's house. All in all, the confidentiality of his filing work is lost completely. Early this morning the rats in my storage room bit a cat to death. My husband has been making rattraps. This is the fifty-fourth. The rain is pouring. Such weather is killing. Of course, you don't need to worry about the hole in the wall. I've blocked it with mud."

"How could the district head go back to the district like that? What kind of problem does Yellow Mud Street have? I think if we had only been a little more assertive and stopped the district head for details, we would have better information now and no wild guessing would be necessary. Everybody is complaining that there's no reason to live. Some can't figure out what's going on, so they fall sick. Take me, for example. I've been lying here ever since the district head's visit. After lying in bed so long, I feel the dullest thing is to live in this world. God knows how I've survived. Yesterday, Old Yue was mobilizing us to catch roaches, but we were all in low spirits. As a result, no one has taken any action yet.

"Someone is resorting to demagoguery . . . I've been thinking about the district head's speech. Often I mistake myself for the district head. Last night when I was sleeping, I mimicked the voice of the district head. I talked and talked. My talk concerned the problems in the Party, including Wang Zi-guang. I could see much evidence indicating the nature of the problem."

"The Song family next door . . . Oh, you're leaving now?"

"Close your windows at night. Centipedes grow everywhere on rainy days."

Under the eaves, the twisted figure of Old Yue could be seen through the screen of rain. Rain drops banged on an oilcloth umbrella. The sky was dark again as if dawn had never come.

"How's everything?" the approaching figure asked quietly.

"Hurry up. The sky is dark as night. My eyelids have been quivering since morning! No matter what, there's no hope for Yellow Mud Street."

"Last night, I dreamed of centipedes again. I felt we were living in a hole underground. Centipedes and slugs and many other things kept growing. Oh, the thunder, it intends to kill something. My knees feel like jelly when the thunder comes."

"I've finally figured out what the district head meant. I've been thinking this way and that, and now I've thought it through. Let me tell you the great secret in my heart. Swear not to tell others. The night the district head disappeared, he was in fact sleeping on top of Secretary Zhu's wardrobe. There's a soybean-size hole in the wall of Secretary Zhu's house. I'm the only one who knows the secret. I saw them through that hole. Of course, I've now blocked the hole, and no trace is left. When I saw the district head sleeping, I was both surprised and overjoyed! So the district head used a strategy. Don't tell the others about this, because it affects the confidentiality of the filing work . . . "

"It's pitch-black now. I wish I had a flashlight. Something keeps sneaking into my rubber boots. I hope it's not poisonous snakes. Have you heard the story about how the god of thunder stamps characters on people? There are so many rumors lately. My wife is so scared that she squeezes under the bed at night, saying that someone might come to murder us. They say that mad dogs have killed large numbers of people in the city. Have you noticed the light in old lady Song's house?"

"Light?"

"Yesterday the light was on all night. I was wandering outside her house the whole time. I even threw several pebbles in from behind her house. Of course, no one knew I did it. They thought it was the wind blowing."

"It's said it was caused by eating flies."

"Who believes it? There was once a man here whose back oozed pig fat all the time. Some people said he ate too much pork. But nobody believed it! I've got to raise the issue at the Committee."

"Early this morning, the rats in my storage room bit a cat to death."

"I'll prepare a file for this case, and put it before the Committee."

Lightning shook the sky as well as the earth. In the electric light the two faces turned green and ferocious. In the darkness, the barber's shoulder pole was heard clanging by. The whole of Yellow Mud Street was melting into a pool of ooze. The tiny light at the corner of the street looked like a cloud of will-o'-the-wisp waving in the wind.

3

Since discovering in the morning that the rats had chewed through the wardrobe, Old Yue had felt agitated. He had hardly sat down to his meal when someone came to report that Old Hu San was out of his mind. He had climbed to the top of the blockhouse and refused to come down. People tried to knock him down with a bamboo pole, but in vain. He had broken several big holes in the roof tiles.

At night a rustling sound came from the corner of the wall. This sound made Yue dream of centipedes. He also dreamed that the wall had collapsed in the rain. His wife became so frightened that she squeezed under the bed to sleep. She crawled out after a while, complaining that there was a spider underneath that kept creeping onto her face. She simply couldn't whisk it off. She touched the leg of the spider when she stretched her hand toward the wall. As she chattered she turned on the light, saying she could at least see if anything crept onto her face. With the light on, Old Yue had less hope of sleeping. A bunch of thorns stabbed his temples. He felt so pained that he wanted to curse. After much struggle, he was soaked with sweat as if the rain had poured down on his bed. His head had barely touched the pillow when the silhouette of a man's head appeared on the window shade. The man was knocking at the windowframe. Gathering his courage, Old Yue went to the window in the dark and asked, "Who is it?"

"It's me." It turned out to be Qi Er-gou. "I can't sleep. It's so annoying. I was just wandering around before coming here. I want to clear up something of vital importance to me."

"Oh?"

"Did you have any misunderstanding about our last talk? I've decided to come and vindicate myself to you."

"Talk?"

"Yes, *talk*, exactly! It's become a burden on my heart. I keep thinking about it and can't go to sleep." His tone became hurried. The window rattled from his voice.

"I'm trying to remember if I said anything bad or suspicious in our last talk. The trouble with me is that my memory is so bad I can't recall anything. I've suffered from this so much lately that I've gotten neurasthenia. I'm feeling terrible. The premonition of a big disaster is always with me. I believe the talk has completely destroyed me."

"Wait a minute," Old Yue interrupted him impatiently. He was now so drenched with sweat that he couldn't stand such agitation.

"You've mentioned some kind of talk? I can't remember a thing about it. How can that be?"

Qi was so excited that he didn't pay any attention to Old Yue's question. He continued, "Last night I was taking off my socks to go to bed, when the brilliant idea came to me that I should make a vindication, a thorough vindication! It came to me the instant I was taking off my socks. I can never count on having such clever ideas. If I did, I'd feel relaxed no matter whether I'd said anything bad or not. As soon as the idea came to me, I felt saved. I was so happy I couldn't go to sleep, so I put on my clothes and took a walk. That's how I've come to your place. What's your opinion about me? Eh?" His long figure reflecting on the window shade resembled a ghost.

"Prevent the transformation of contradictions,"* Old Yue said, staying calm and collected on the other side of the window.

"I consider this my only chance." Qi's teeth clattered as if he were having an attack of malaria. Then he started to pace outside the window. His footsteps were so light that he made hardly any sound.

"*Everyone has a blemish,*" Old Yue pronounced one syllable at a time. He stared at the thin shadow and bared his teeth.

"So you've forgiven me fully? Right? Good. Now I feel relieved." Qi rattled on. "Do you know what I thought? At first I thought forgiveness was impossible! I've never thought about vindication before. My thought ran like this: I found a man to exonerate myself to, but couldn't get any reaction. No one would admit to having heard me say anything. Thus I would have to be on tenterhooks all my life, without any chance of vindication. Then my situation . . . "

"Of course, you haven't said anything. Why should you criticize

---

*Maoist concept.—TRANS.

yourself?" Old Yue interrupted him coldly. Sweat was streaming down his body. He couldn't stand this heated talk any longer.

"What? Do you really think so? You mean you didn't hear anything? That means there's no hope for me? I'm done! Save me!" He drummed on the windowframe till dawn, driving Old Yue really mad.

All that rainy day, Old Yue waited for someone from the Committee.

Yang San asked Old Yue, "What kind of organization is the Committee?"

"The Committee?" Old Yue put on an enigmatic look and repeated, "The Committee? I should tell you that your question is a deep one. It covers an unimaginable range. Let me draw an analogy so you will have an idea of the whole thing. Long ago lived a man named Zhang. Once a mad dog bit to death a pig and several chickens. When the mad dog was running loose in the streets, Zhang opened his door and leaped into the street. He died a sudden death. That day the sky was pure white. The crows blotted out the sky and the earth . . . In fact, Yellow Mud Street has a whole series of unsolved cases. What's your personal reaction to self-reform? Mm?"

By the time Old Yue went out with his umbrella, the rain had flooded the steps. "Where is Old Hu San?" he asked Liang Xiao-san, sneezing all the time.

"Nowhere. When you use a hook to grab him, he jumps away. The roof tiles are all ruined."

"Where is this smell from?"

"It may be the overflow of excrement from the latrine. It's everywhere in the water. It may cause an epidemic of 'excrement disease.'"

Old Yue walked through the rain to a shelter at the corner of the street. Two vague figures appeared in the mist. He cried out, "Hello, are you from the Committee?"

The figures dashed away and disappeared. The rain banged his umbrella louder and louder and sounded more and more frightening.

In the street turmoil arose. Liang Xiao-san reported to him that some chicken thieves had arrived. They'd run into more than a dozen houses. Now everyone had hidden in their attics because they'd heard that the chicken thieves were desperadoes.

"The Committee still hasn't sent any people?"

"Hush!" Liang Xiao-san made a sign. "Don't talk so loudly. Haven't you heard that the big Committee in the city is no longer in existence? A telegram was sent from above saying it was a false Committee. There was nobody inside except an old man selling ashes as toothpowder. The so-called Committee was really a scheme of his to extort money. When someone from above was sent to catch him, he put on a disguise and made up his face with the ashes. Thus he escaped among the people." He clucked his tongue. "Such a man is indeed formidable!"

"Don't you see there's much complication inside? Eh? What a wretched rain. The water ruins everything! Once there was a man named Zhang who indulged in such wild fantasies that he ended up falling to the ground and meeting his doom. Have Yellow Mud Street people drawn enough lessons and formed a clear understanding ideologically?" He gave a snort of contempt.

While making his general remarks, Old Yue heard a vague, suspicious laugh somewhere at his back. At once he felt uncomfortable, as if prickly heat covered his body. Turning around, he tried to locate the sound. He searched further and further until he found himself entering old lady Song's house. He scowled. "Did you have a good sleep last night?"

"As sound as the dead." The old lady was eating rice porridge. She didn't even raise her head but continued, "So the centipedes are keeping you from sleeping again? How can there be so many centipedes in your house? At dawn I heard a gurgling sound as if someone were drinking tea. When day came, the earth had already drunk enough. So there are floods everywhere."

"Didn't you hear anything stir during the night?" He moved closer to the old woman, puffing his foul breath in her face.

"What sound are you talking about? I lay down and slept like the dead . . . This rain, can dead fish fall? Are you leaving already?"

"Your house smells too bad."

"Sure. The excrement is overflowing, stinking up everything. This morning when I was frying sausages, I found a lump of it inside one casing. I heard there's a Committee in the city. Why does nobody intervene in such ridiculous matters?"

"What's your opinion about the Committee?"

"What Committee? I've just heard about such a Committee." She gave a contemptuous snort. "Who can explain such things clearly! I don't want to bother about such a stupid thing and make trouble for myself. I think there might not be any such Committee. It's only a rumor perpetrated by the bad guys. I've never seen any Committee in my fifty-three years. It might indicate another flood. In the last flood, the Committee was said to have held a meeting at the bottom of the river. What farting around! Are you leaving now?"

4

The rain was strange. Its drops were as black as Chinese ink. The water smelled like sewage water from a shifting sand well. It wasn't the first time they'd had strange rains. There'd been the dead fish rain and the rat rain. But never before had people seen such a dark, stinking, and endless rain. It rained on and on. "We're living in a huge shifting sand well." Old people were reminded of the analogy by looking at the sky. Immediately, they began to worry and sigh as if they were dying that very moment.

One morning, old lady Song was getting ready to stir-fry the flies. She'd peeled the heads and wings off the flies she'd caught in the flytrap. When she opened the kitchen door, black water poured out carrying large clots of blood. In the knee-deep water in the kitchen lay a dead body. It was her father. The smell of blood was stifling. The crickets screamed viciously. The mouth of the corpse hung open in a queer way, baring yellowish-black teeth. Bending low, old lady Song pinched the ice-cold arm of the dead man and shouted hoarsely, "Hey-hey!" Her husband and sons came hesitatingly and stood there like logs. None of them had the courage to so much as glance at the corpse in the water.

"Last night a moth dropped on top of my net," her husband said irrelevantly. He felt uneasy as soon as he finished. He leaned hesitantly against the damp wall and kicked at the water awkwardly. At the same time, the two sons had already sneaked out the door without anyone's noticing.

"He might have been bitten to death by the rats." Old lady Song was staring at the body. "At old lady Qi's house, rats are biting everyone. Who knows? Maybe he was too impatient with life."

"In such weather boils grow in my ears all the time," her husband said. Meanwhile, he was sidling toward the door, ready to escape.

"Don't go. Let's talk about it." Old lady Song detected her husband's intention even without looking at him. She dashed over and blocked the door with her back.

After that, they squatted on top of the kitchen range and started a long discussion. They decided to make a pair of tongs. They clamped the throat of the corpse and pushed it out to the street. The torrential rain washed the coagulated blood away at once.

About three months before, the old man, in his seventies, had suddenly asked to be moved to the kitchen. He tumbled into the kitchen like a dung beetle, clutching his worn luggage. At one corner was a pile of hay. He settled in by spreading his ragged bedding on top of the hay. He had never been out the door since that day, not even for a meal. When the family finished their meal and put the rice pot back in the kitchen, he jumped up and scraped the leftovers from the pot with his black fingers. He never used any dishes and drank only the dishwater.

Since the old man had moved there, the kitchen had become extremely dirty. The stench of urine irritated everyone. Every night, he shat in the water basin, explaining that he couldn't move his bowels on the night stool. The excrement would stay in the basin until the next morning, when old lady Song got up and cleaned it. After a while, a species of delicate black mosquito grew in the kitchen. They flew in swarms. Cooking a meal in the kitchen would mean getting a whole bodyful of mosquito bites. When the cooking smoke filled the kitchen, the old man would cough with force on the hay and spit yellow phlegm on the ground.

He had very sharp ears. Whenever he heard people in the room, he called sadly in his hoarse voice, "Please come—" But upon inquiry, he couldn't tell anything particular. Usually he complained that the hay was too hard, that there were centipedes on the floor, that his throat was choked with sputum, that his teeth were falling out, and so on. At first, people ran to him when he called, but after being taken in several times, nobody paid any attention to him any more.

He had a spade hidden in his quilt. Every night he held it to his bosom in sleep. He thought he had hidden it well, and during the day, he sat on his ragged quilt, pretending nothing was out of the ordinary. In fact, the whole family knew about it, though no one wanted to bother exposing him.

Soon after that, old lady Song discovered more strange behavior in the old man. After the others had gone to bed, he would dig here and there in the room with the spade. He could also be found lying on the floor like an old dog, his ear to the crack under the door leading to her room.

"Father, what are you listening to?" old lady Song once asked, suddenly opening the door wide, her little face wrinkled up in an ugly way.

"The crickets are crying so fiercely. Something is swimming above my head . . . " he mumbled, crawling back into the kitchen like a dung beetle.

Since the discovery of the old man's strange behavior, the leftovers in the pot had been decreasing. The old man became so hungry that he picked every grain of rice out of the basin he shat in. He became more and more feeble daily. Finally, he shrank on the hay pile, dried up, got smaller. Without close attention, people could mistake him for a pile of rags. Old lady Song became more irascible each day. Once, in the middle of a conversation, she dashed into the kitchen and jabbed the rag pile madly with a stick. After this rage, there were no longer any leftovers in the pot. The strange thing was that the old man did not die. Whenever people were sure he was dead and went over to look, the rag would make a movement or two.

"With such a god of plague at home, there's no way to get rich," old lady Song said firmly.

"What's the nature of the question? Eh?" the husband agreed, half asleep. "I can see it's no longer an ordinary question of right or wrong. There's something wrong inside, which has far surpassed the usual range of dispute. Can it have something to do with the case of Wang Zi-guang? They say the barber is wandering around our house again. Yesterday when I was in the latrine, someone threw two stones in from above. I've been paying close attention to the situation. I feel so tense that I might have a heart attack . . . "

That particular night, the old man suddenly started neighing like a horse. He whinnied on and on, driving the whole family mad. Getting out of bed and opening the door, they asked what the matter was. He replied that his leg had sunk into the hay and several snakes were biting it. He begged the family to pull his leg out. Of course, no one really helped him. Instead, they returned to their rooms to continue their sleep. As soon as they lay down, the old man started begging for an orange. He complained that the family had hidden a whole basket of oranges from him.

"I have a scorpion here. Would you like to try it?" old lady Song offered hypocritically. She squeezed out a horrifying smile.

"Something is swirling above my head . . . " the old man said hesitantly. He retreated in horror.

"Stink dog!"

"Something . . . Maybe nothing . . . Certainly, I didn't really see clearly. I must have made a mistake."

Old lady Song could see the trembling hands holding the spade. They were as thin and gray as chicken claws.

The husband got up without attracting anyone's attention. He was still complaining about the swelling boils in his ear. He shuffled over and jabbed his fingers up and down in the air while talking: "Haven't I commented on the problem? It's not an ordinary problem of right and wrong. Now about the two stones yesterday, I've had many weird dreams just now. My heart is aching again. I suspect that throwing stones is a plot. I've made up my mind to investigate it thoroughly. Is there any possibility that someone is plotting against us?"

Old lady Song leaped forward, grabbed the spade, and shoved it down violently into that yellowish black bundle. It felt as if the spade had broken an eggshell.

The husband had already sneaked back to his room. Lying in bed, he covered his head with the quilt and started his dreams again.

"Are there really snakes in the sky? He must be lying," old lady Song thought. She stirred the straw and observed carefully. Clouds of mosquitoes swarmed from the straw, dancing in the dim light. At that minute, the clock on the wall struck two. Old lady Song could remember very well that the rain outside was pouring down. The room was steaming hot. A hole in the roof was dripping water. She left the room and bolted the door. She then returned quietly to her bed. She slept until dawn without even a dream.

In the morning, old lady Song scolded her husband. Then the two dumped the corpse into a big carton. They tied it up and carried it to the river. The box splashed into the water. The rain was still pouring down. On their way home, they met Factory Director Wang climbing out the window of Yan Si's wife. He was stark naked except for his underpants. He stood under the eaves gasping for breath.

"Would you two write a list of suggestions," he said in a dignified tone, his big belly protruding. "It's about the garbage on this street. Do you have any reasonable proposals? Eh? I'm collecting suggestions from the root units. I'll report up to the district . . . Hey, don't run! Stop!"

The two were frightened out of their wits. They scurried like rats into an air-raid shelter and stayed there till midnight before sneaking back to their own small hut.

"He died from swallowing nails," old lady Song told her neighbors on Yellow Mud Street. "When people are old, they often develop unexpected eccentricities. I didn't know it until he complained of trouble moving his bowels. He felt such pain that he couldn't use the night stool, so he used the water basin. Then I saw him put a rusty nail in his mouth. I grabbed it and threw it away. At that time I also discovered sharp nails in his excrement. It was disgusting." She started coughing. Bending down, she groaned, "Chest pains."

"When people become dissatisfied with their lives, many odd occurrences come out of nowhere." Qi Er-gou was telling others, "I have a relative who lost his will to live. So he sat on top of his hut and spat on passersby. Later on he became a famous Taoist priest!"

But people were still not satisfied. They went to consult old lady

Song's husband. He was squatting in a wardrobe, shivering, his head covered with rags. (Ever since the death of the old man, he had been suffering from light phobia. During an attack, he cried and yelled and hid in the wardrobe, refusing to come out.) When he heard the people coming, he called out angrily from the wardrobe, "Comrades, what is your reaction to such persecution? Isn't it a murderous trick? I have to report to the authorities about the two stones." He banged the wardrobe door threateningly.

Later on, people came to a unanimous conclusion about the death of old man Song: "He wanted to become an immortal, so he climbed to the roof to be raised to heaven. But he fell off and died. This poor old man was wishing in vain."

Some people believed he drowned in the rainwater.

5

That noon the rain stopped for a while. The sky was as dark as before and hung down to the rooftops. Old lady Qi lay in bed thinking hard. "The rain has stopped, and I still can't go to sleep. Will the thunder come?" Thunder came immediately. Roaches were shaken down from the crack in the ceiling and dropped onto the mosquito net. That reminded her of one of her dreams. Thunder rolled over the "Pure Water Pond," and hundreds of dead cats floated to the surface. The sky shone with red light. The dead trees beside the pond reflected a blue color as if they were puffing out smoke . . . Turning over, she heard rats chewing at the wall.

The day before, her husband fussed all day, swearing the rain would continue nonstop till December. He sneered viciously while talking. Old lady Qi could see he was hoping the rain would last forever so the wall of the back room would collapse. Whenever there was a big rain, he kicked the wall with his big leather boots, yelling, "Why don't you collapse!" If people objected, he cursed, and vowed that the wall would collapse that night and crush them.

He told others he had dug the foundation of the wall loose. One roll of thunder would do the job. Now her husband was sharpening a knife. He had been doing this for a long time. In the mirror on the wardrobe she could see him waving the knife and making gestures of chopping and cutting.

"Hey!" she called as she rose up.

"Cut off the ear." He made a face and again raised the shining knife.

"The rumor is unbelievable." She was hesitating.

"At night a chicken sneaked under the bed." He waved the sharpened blade of the knife before her eyes. "Without turning on the light, I chopped off its head."

"Rumor . . . ," she said again. She glanced at the knife now hanging at the man's waist. Her hair stood up like thorns. "Murder!" She dashed out, crying along the way, "Comrades, be on guard against the vicious slander of rumor!"

Yellow Mud Street people crept like rats from their dark little huts. They smiled meaningfully at each other. Nodding and sticking out their tongues, they whispered to each other, "Hey, did you see? Chopping off ears!"

"Good chop! Good man!"

"Old Yue says he's going to report this to the Committee."

"There's no more Committee. The old man selling ashes for toothpowder has already been killed and thrown into the river. So it's been thoroughly chopped!"

"It goes without saying, completely and thoroughly."

"Bah, what 'completely and thoroughly.' There's half left to be chopped next time."

"Black mushrooms grow at the corner of my wall. Too much rain has steamed them."

"Can the ear grow back again after being chopped off? One year when Cao Zi-jing had his thumb chopped off while cutting vegetables, a new one grew out the next morning."

Some people suggested they go see Yang San. In jubilant spirits, the whole mob surged toward his house.

The door was fastened with a big lock. An old lady in her eighties hobbled over. Rubbing her rotten red eyes and waving her hand, she said, "How can he have the face to live on in this world? He melted long ago. When he came back this morning, he mentioned that people would come to look, and it would be better to melt by himself. This would at least be a clean way. I pulled back the quilt, but not even a ghost could be found inside. Only a pool of blood and some bloody fingerprints on the quilt. It must be very painful to melt away." She stretched out her hand and rubbed her eyes affectedly. As she squinted her eyes, a yellow secretion oozed out as if she'd squeezed a tube of eye ointment.

"So he's melted? Leaving nothing? What a pity." People postured. They were still reluctant to leave, hoping to see something special.

One day Liu Mi-zi put on his cotton-padded cap with the earflaps pulled snugly down. Thereafter, every man on Yellow Mud Street wore his cotton-padded cap.

Rumors flew up and down Yellow Mud Street.

An old blind man came to the street. He walked here and there looking for something. Someone found a broken jar he had hidden. It was full of ears, and blood ran down the side.

"The case of Wang Zi-guang is keeping everyone stirred up." Wearing his cotton-padded cap, Old Yue lectured in the street, "I believe the key lies in the attitude toward the Committee. A recent rumor says the Committee is a false organization. I'm going to provide a large quantity of evidence to refute this shameless slander. I'm here under orders to tell the public that the Committee in the city is working normally. No one should have any doubt about the functioning of the Committee or lose heart and give himself up as hopeless . . . " He was sweating all over from the talk, and his ears swelled badly inside his cap.

One day, word circulated that the district head was coming to Yellow Mud Street to solve the problems raised by the rumors. So people crowded in front of Secretary Zhu's house, banging loudly on the door.

"What do you want?" Secretary Zhu stuck his head out.

"Is the district head inside?"

"We want to see him. We're dying from missing him."

"Hush!" Secretary Zhu raised a finger. "The district head has a bad cold. He's wrapped up inside the wardrobe. You may have a look at him, but very quietly. You can only come in one at a time." At this, he dragged one person in and bolted the door behind them. The people outside waited for such a long time that they grew impatient. They banged and pushed, almost breaking the door.

"Look through this crack." Secretary Zhu pointed out a thin crack in the wardrobe. "He might fall asleep very soon. I can never tell if he's really asleep. He works hard like this all the time. All right, be satisfied. Don't stare too long. Go out and let one more in."

"The district head has been here for a week now," Secretary Zhu told the second one. "For some reason, he's had a cold the whole time. He's been sick for a week now. I've had to wrap him up in a thick quilt and lock him in the wardrobe. I heard the rumors are running wild outside. Hey, don't go too close, OK? You'll wake him up. That's enough. You ought to be satisfied . . . "

Thus the district head greeted everyone from the wardrobe.

After that day, old lady Qi's husband stopped making rattraps. Instead, he sharpened his knife every morning.

"Someone will come to chop off your ear. Haven't you heard the rumor?" Old lady Qi was feeling happy at others' misfortunes. She dug a piece of dried-up mud from her foot, rolled it into a ball, and tossed it into her mouth. She chewed the wad, making a squeaking sound. "Yesterday, someone saw two small ears growing on Yang

San's head. Now people are gossiping that it's nothing to have the ears chopped off. Just soak your head in rainwater, and your ears will grow back again."

Her husband was still sharpening the knife, his head bent low. Every now and then he felt the edge with his hand.

"You always spit in the corner. The mosquitoes in this room are all from your sputum." She spat the wad at his broad back.

Her husband moved his body, and old lady Qi started, jumping toward the door.

"You sweat so much lately. You smell terrible." She swallowed a mouthful of water. "Who knows, you may die a sudden death some day. Didn't Zhang Mie-zi die suddenly? Old Song died a sudden death also, all because of too much sweating, and too much rain soaking . . . "

"A lump of something green is growing on my intestines." The husband pointed at his belly. "Look, here it is. One intestine has a hole rotted in it. You can see some green spots around the hole. Priest Liu Bao told me last month that I won't die, but will live forever. I tremble with joy when I think of this. Last night a chicken sneaked in. By instinct I chopped at it with my knife. Its neck was cut, and it flapped its wings several times."

He dropped his knife and went to the back of the house.

The rotten vegetables could be smelled.

The men on Yellow Mud Street still wore their cotton-padded caps because the old ear collector was still wandering the street. People felt so nervous that they complained about life. The cotton-padded caps were so hot they made people feel dizzy. Everyone's ears were badly swollen.

According to Old Yue, an investigative group would be sent from the city. The men felt a bit easier at the news. They hoped the group would make everything clear by finding the evil one who had spread the rumor. Days passed in expectation.

Every now and then people would chat with each other.

"The investigative group is coming pretty soon."

"The authorities have the situation of Yellow Mud Street in mind."

"We will feel immensely satisfied soon."

However, the investigators must have run into some kind of obstacle. They never showed up.

It was not until a long time later that Qi Er-gou, who lived next to the latrine, admitted that all the rumors had been made up by him. But he had been acting on special orders from above. The Yang mentioned in the rumors was not Yang San-dianzi, but Old Yang the garbage collector, who had died of a stroke several years before. As for the ears, old lady Qi's husband had chopped off only two dog's ears rather than human ears. He too was following instructions from above. He had even received twenty yuan in reward money.

Thus talk about the chopping off of ears ceased. Why hadn't the wretched Qi Er-gou let out his secret before!

RELOCATION

1

It was a windy season.

When the wind blew, people's vision was blurred. Everything seemed indistinct and enlarged.

People out walking looked like tatters of rags dancing with the wind.

Shading their eyes from the dust, Yellow Mud Street residents sat under the eaves and squinted at the sky. The wind grabbed here and snatched there, stirring people's hearts into confusion.

Old lady Song leaned against a wall and spoke loudly: "The wind is fierce. Something bad might happen."

She was right. One day a passerby, blinded by the dust, was blown into the sewer. He yelled day and night and frightened the residents so badly that no one dared pass by the spot. After several days, the yelling stopped, and people began to wonder why.

"A man was seen falling down the sewer."

"Who can be sure it was a man? It might have been a cat or something else."

"Yelling was heard from below. But it's hard to tell. It might be an illusion. Illusions occur all the time."

Soon after, they started using evasive language to talk vaguely about some impending event connected with their feeling of approaching disaster, the kind of event that can only happen covertly, undetectable through appearances. Once, talking in a dream, Old Hu San cried out a word which seemed close to reality and yet at the same time remote from fact. At the moment, he was moving his night stool, making a screaking sound. Then he mumbled the word: "Relocate?" Everybody was stunned by the sound; they sank into their own private thoughts.

Then they went into a panic.

The wind blew all that night. When the roof beams cracked, old lady Qi's nightmares started. She dreamed repeatedly of a faceless man bending down to dig out her intestines, one bloodstained strip after another. She couldn't go on sleeping, so she got up and squatted outside the house.

A black figure jumped out from behind the house.

"Old sister, are you waiting for someone at midnight? And he never shows up? Ha-ha!"

It was Qi Er-gou. Old lady Qi could dimly see a swarm of mosquitoes fly out of his mouth. He squatted down beside her, his brows furrowed, and they listened to the howling wind for some time.

Then he lowered his voice: "The wind is blowing far away. I have planted a pot of cactus under my bed. It blossomed in the past. Last night I was sleepless, so I turned on the light and took out the plant. Oh, the flower had turned black! At that moment, the big clock in the city struck three. I became suspicious and searched very carefully around the house. When I went into the kitchen, I found the cat dead on the floor! Let me tell you, never walk near the wall. I can hear the sound from underground."

Old lady Qi grabbed a handful of dirt and put it into her mouth to chew. She then lit a cigarette and sucked it into a flashing red glow. She said in deep thought, "The wind is upsetting me so much. I feel I'm living on a rocky mountain. Lately I dream constantly of dead cats floating on the pond and of trees puffing with smoke as if they were burnt . . . They say the people sent by the city have already been here. But what did they do? Someone saw them bury a boot somewhere. Maybe he didn't see clearly. Could they have buried a secret document?"

"Hmmph. Do you know why I've come out at night? Someone saw with his own eyes a trap in Yellow Mud Street. It was huge. When conditions are right, the whole street will sink in. But where is it? I've been looking around but can't locate it. There must be a plot here. Have you heard any sounds at night?"

"I'm tired out by the dead cats these days. Chicken claws have grown out of Jiang Shui-ying's toes. Have you seen them?"

"In the trap lies a skeleton. Don't tell others, will you?"

"Sure. The claws even have fingernails. They're so dirty. Don't you want to go and see?"

"There's also a pair of children's eyeballs. Please don't tell others."

"She's so proud of them that she often shows her claws to others as if she's showing some rare treasure. Not long ago, she sent word inviting me to visit her and her claws. Bah! It will ruin my eyes! Oh, what a pity you didn't see them. They're sickening."

"Have you heard the talk lately? I mean when you're half asleep—for example, when you're just waking up in the morning—can you make anything out of it? Take me, for instance. This morning I saw a red cat. Isn't that strange? I started to hide from it, but the animal dashed away and disappeared immediately. You really haven't heard about it, eh?"

"What?"

"The talk."

"Jiang Shui-ying is a whore. I have enough evidence to expose her."

"The talk includes the word 'relocate.' But I'm not sure of the exact word."

"Oh! Relocate! Vampire! Thief! Ah—!" Forgetting her fear, old lady Qi jumped up and shouted into the wind, "Comrades, we're falling prey to a plot!"

The wind blew all night and continued to blow in the morning.

People got out of bed enveloped in nightmares. With baggy eyes, they shuffled out under the eaves of their houses.

Everywhere was a rustling sound. The wind blew the Chinese fir bark from someone's roof and a ragged mat from beside the sidewalk. It blew the garbage on the street into a whirl, and it broke a windowshade and tossed it into the sky. The strange wind frightened the residents of Yellow Mud Street.

The mob under the eaves whispered to each other.

"I dreamed of dead cats covering the pond and also of the tip of a tree . . . "

"Last night a clump of poisonous mushrooms sprouted under my bed. I intended to hoe them, but my wife stopped me. She was so scared her face turned blue. Toward dawn, the roof was banging as stones fell on it. My wife told me it was a star shower."

"Comrades, a single armed marshal has entered the revolutionary committee building. His steps are as light as a spirit's. Yesterday noon, I noticed that the clock in the city struck wrong once. Also, crows appeared in the sky. What does all this mean?"

"Lightning struck the little hut of Zhang Mie-zi. Red light flashed . . . "

During the day, old Hu San stood beside the well in front of his house fetching water with an iron pail full of holes. Every time, just as he raised the pail to the lip of the well, the water leaked out. So he let the pail down again and fetched more water. He stopped every now and then to blow his nose into the well.

Qi Er-gou offered comments while jumping about like a grass-hopper: "Comrades, now the whole truth is out." In the evening he went to old Hu San's house and said, "I have to ask you to sacrifice yourself, granddad."

"New information?" Old Hu San rose from his night stool. He stared at the spiderweb in the corner of the wall and grabbed frantically at the air in front of his face. He caught an insect and inspected it carefully. "Is the situation most gratifying to the people? Is there much hope for the rebels?"

"Please, granddad, take the whole situation about the trap into account." Qi Er-gou's ear started to ring, and for a long time he hopped about on one foot in the middle of the room. Then he continued, "Of course, I'm not talking about the trap. I mean at the hazy moment of waking up in the morning, do you feel a kind of omen? In other words, don't you feel startled at realizing something? To put it in a more direct way, for example, if a skeleton rolled out of your room, what would you think? Of course, I don't mean a skeleton will roll out of your room. I mean have you seen the severe nature of the problem?"

"Let the God of Thunder strike you, you pestilent pig!" His daughter dashed out of the room with her braid flying. Her eyes looked like two black holes. "Go and sacrifice, you pig!"

"Why should I sacrifice?" Old Hu San blinked his eyes as if he understood something. "I'm in good health, and I'm not in a hurry to die. I plan to do some work in the future. Yesterday I caught a spider and swallowed it in one gulp. Just look, my stomach is full of leeches. You go. The room stinks. It's been a week since the shit was taken out."

"It's a long time since cars ran on this street. This place is vicious," Qi Er-gou said. Walking to the table, he opened a drawer and found a nail. Baring his teeth, he dug in his ear with it.

While tightening his pants, Old Hu San commented, "A ball of light keeps stopping at the windowframe, making me so hot that the blood throbs in my temples. This is a great place to live. The crack in the ceiling sprouts mushrooms. Flies fall like rain on the mosquito net." He climbed into bed and let down the mosquito net, sneering from inside.

"This should be reported to the higher-ups." Old lady Song's voice could be heard from outside the window. She had been eavesdropping all along.

When those people came in, Factory Director Wang was fighting with a lizard. He got up several times during the night to check the dead dog in the yard with his flashlight. He suspected the dog was pretending to be dead. Putting on his clothes, he sneaked toward it. The dog didn't move when he jabbed an iron bar into its belly. Then he used the iron bar to push the dog into the sewage pool. He worked so hard that he was sweating. Raising his head, he saw a bloodred star shower fall on somebody's roof. "The problem of Yellow Mud Street is a puzzle," he said to himself. Then he closed the door and lay down on the bed, but his ears were full of the barking dogs. The noisy barking lasted all night, and he tossed in bed the whole time. Opening his eyes in the morning, he saw a lizard at the center of the ceiling. He jumped up and jabbed it with a bamboo pole.

"Director Wang—" the mob called out timidly.

"What? Damn it, it's run away! The wind is really something! I dare not go out the door for fear something will crash down from overhead. My wife suggests that I put on my straw hat when going out. Last night the pop-eyed barber was here. Did you see him? I have a suspicion he's the old toothpowder seller in disguise."

"Haven't you heard the talk? I mean have you noticed a tendency? For example, at the instant when you wake up in the morning . . . ," Qi Er-gou said hesitantly.

"True. I'm sure of one thing. In the past, I never had such a thing as a lizard in my room. It's been a headache for me. I wonder where these things come from?"

"Relocate! Bah!!" Old lady Qi could hold back no more. She started scolding them.

People made a hubbub. Then Qi Er-gou elbowed to the front timidly and lowered his head shyly. Blushing, he said, "What's your opinion about it, granddad? I mean about the meaning of the word. Isn't it something unheard-of before? Why should the authorities do such a thing? Can it be a mistake? Of course, you understand what word I'm talking about. You must have had some deep thoughts about it."

"What word?"

"To be exact, it's the word Comrade Qi mentioned. I find it so difficult to repeat. I'll get a cramp if I open my mouth. The word's so powerful, it's like—" After some thought, he decided to exaggerate. "The word makes us all feel electrocuted."

"Absolutely," everyone agreed.

"Right!" Director Wang furrowed his brow. Suddenly he lit up. "The fundamental reason is, comrades, I remember something." The thing he remembered was that he had only his underwear on. Consequently, he opened the wardrobe and dug inside. He found a worn shirt and placed it over his shoulders. Then he paced about the room. "The fundamental reason is that the garbage problem on Yellow Mud Street should be put on the agenda. After working around the clock, I have made a table that lists the people who've died of garbage pollution, more than a dozen in all. Shocking! I've already recommended that the authorities abandon one latrine and change it into a garbage station. These days, I've been preparing a file about the garbage problem with Secretary Zhu. I find that some people are frightened by this, and they sabotage our work in any way they can. The lizard case involves a lot of problems. I intend to get to the bottom of all these matters."

"We can't abandon the latrine! What would we do with the excrement? We don't have enough latrines even now. Every time we have to wait impatiently for a toilet. If the latrine is abandoned, people will shit on the street corner."

"Oh? This is a very constructive suggestion. This suggestion is very valuable. I have to consider it." He paced back and forth with his hands folded at his back, his head bent low. Finally, he stopped, rolled his eyes, raised his chubby fist, and hammered downward through the air. He said, "All kinds of problems concerning Yellow Mud Street must be solved."

"Absolutely! Absolutely!" Qi Er-gou jumped up with joy and clapped his hands. "The day when we feel proud and elated is coming. I'm now feeling what being proud and elated is like. Comrades, what is your understanding of the director's talk?"

The people looked stupefied and then put on an air of thinking hard. They stared blankly at the ceiling, when suddenly old lady Qi took the lead in applauding.

"Immense satisfaction, immense satisfaction." Their palms grew red from clapping, and they pushed each other with joy. Someone said he was "beside himself with happiness" and stood on his hands. Others drummed their heads against the wall. The clamor lasted for some time.

"Lizard!" the director screamed oddly, his body trembling. Raising the iron bar with his shivering hand, he jabbed at the wall. A big piece of lime fell down. "Is that dog barking?" He was gasping for breath, and his face turned white.

"It's nothing but the wind," Qi Er-gou said, puzzled by the terrified face of the director.

The wind blew down something in the yard and broke it with a cracking sound. "Ah—" Director Wang said. "What a wretched wind! Yesterday afternoon I was killing a lizard in my room when a mad dog dashed into the yard. Its hair had fallen out. It hung around the sewage pool and refused to leave. I kicked it, beat it, and stabbed it with a knife, but no use. It was determined. The whole thing was outrageous. Then my wife came with a basin of boiling water and poured it on the dog. It still didn't move and just died right there. I can't eat well when I think about this. The rice sticks in my throat. What does this mean? Someone wants to resist stubbornly to the end? Hey, what do you think of this problem? The district will hold a meeting. The meeting will spend five months talking about planting trees in the whole district, then three months talking about the garbage problem on Yellow Mud Street. Though time is short, the district is full of determination. I'll certainly bring all your suggestions to the meeting."

A loud noise was heard from the yard. It was even sharper and more irritating than before. It sounded like a big glass tank being broken. Director Wang's tongue suddenly got stuck. His face turned purple at the sound. Digging out a large blanket, he wrapped his body up tightly. His eyes stared blackly, and his forehead dampened with cold sweat.

"This house is haunted," his wife exaggerated. Her voice sounded happy at his fear. "Ten years ago, this house used to be troubled by ghosts."

"Have you discovered any suspicious traces?" Director Wang was shivering all over. His tongue felt twice as big in his mouth.

"Someone wants to resist to the end," old lady Qi remembered.

"Good!" He stopped trembling. "Be on guard against sabotage by our enemies. The pestilent dog in my yard yesterday was a sign. I'm determined to investigate thoroughly. Very good!" He threw away the blanket and stabbed the iron bar at the lizard with all his strength. He then smashed the lizard on the ground until it turned into a mess.

"It turns out to be the district head." Qi Er-gou returned from the yard and let out a relaxed breath. "The district head was crying just now. The dog had been with him for five years. I saw him climb out of the well after he blew his nose."

"Ah—" People lowered their heads and pretended to be indifferent. But they were planning how to escape.

"Can it be a mistake?" Liu Tie-chui asked. But he was scared into retreat by the glance of old lady Qi.

After they left, Director Wang lay down again to read his "Strange Cases of Present and Past." Several minutes later, he shouted toward the inner room, "Has the dead dog been taken away?"

"Not yet. It's still lying in the yard."

"Why not remove it? What do you want to do? Eh? It's murder! What a wretched world. Everywhere there's a plot . . . Stinking pigs! I'm going to hang you one by one!" He flew into a rage. After his explosion, he felt relaxed and aloof.

A face appeared at the window. It was Old Yue. He worked his whole face into a wrinkled smile. "I've practiced handstands the whole night. I kicked a lot of holes in the wall, but I'm making great progress. Would you like me to give a performance?"

"I'm coming. Damn the wind! It blurs my thoughts. This wind is going to blow till the end of the world."

"I heard the investigation will start again?"

"Certainly. We have to investigate the dogs one by one, or we can never know if there're any mad dogs. Shoot! It's rotten already. Come out!"

His wife came out lazily.

2

Old Hu San sat under the eaves with Wang Jiu-po peeling taros. He was feeling drowsy. His eyes drooped, and his head nodded until it finally bumped against the wall.

"The taros this year are only so-so," he mumbled.

"No good, as usual. It's said there will be a big flood this year. The air smells moldy. When I combed my hair this morning, I found it had gone moldy after a night's sleep!"

"I plan to steam a spider for the taro dish," Old Hu San said.

"The night stool in the room is full again. I don't intend to clean it. So what?"

"They say the relocation will start in a few days. I plan to die in my bed tomorrow morning. I've tried, and it's not too difficult."

"Lightning struck this morning, but it's cloudless again now. I can't keep my eyes open on a fine day."

One day the district head came in disguise to Yellow Mud Street for a secret visit. He had decided on the spur of the moment to conduct these secret visits.

Wang Jiu-po died in her bed. People went to see her with their handkerchiefs over their noses.

The district head went to the "S" factory office to check the "Registration of Cause of Death":

—Zhang Mie-zi, 36 years old, male; cause of death: overeating (sickness from a diseased chicken).
—Song Jin-cia, 70 years old, male; cause of death: rhapsodic symptoms (brought on by the rain).
—Yu Zi-lian, 18 years old, female; cause of death: voluntary (swallowed glass).

The list included the names of more than fifty people who had died in the past few years.

The district head stuck his nose to the paper, trying to find some problem between the lines and the words. After a while, his eyes felt swollen.

The room was suffocating. Cicadas bumped against the window pane and fell to the ground. He spat on the floor, raising a cloud of dust. "Isn't there any case of persecution?" he wondered anxiously. Opening the dirty window, he saw a woman digging something out of the garbage heap outside. She had her hips stuck high in the air, and she was chewing on something. She looked familiar. After some thought, he remembered that her name was Qi, and he had seen her on the street just now. She used to be his classmate more than twenty years ago. She loved folding paper figures. Her drawer in the school desk was full of waste paper. When had she settled on Yellow Mud Street?

After pacing back and forth several times, he decided to go for a shit. The floor in the latrine was slippery and smelled terrible. He had hardly entered when mosquitoes swarmed up. He supported himself by pressing against the walls firmly with his hands and squatting down carefully to avoid a pile of feces. "Damned place," he muttered, at the same time feeling a sharp pain on his right eyelid. "Hope I'm not having rotten red-eye."

Since morning, the district head had been worrying about having rotten red-eye. Back in the office, he took several salves from his briefcase and put some of each on his eye. Then he shut his eyes and rubbed them for a long time. He still didn't feel at ease. While his eyes were closed, he heard a strange bird cry. When he ran over to open the window, he saw only the woman still digging in the garbage.

"Hello—" He shouted at the top of his voice.

The woman ignored him completely and continued to keep her rear end toward him.

Before he left home, his wife had sprayed spittle in his face when she shouted, "How dare you go to places like that? There are several epidemics going on in that street. Every family there is pickling dead men's flesh. Last year one of my relatives stayed there for just a few days, and got some disease when he came back. His intestines rotted into pieces. They say there's a haunted house, too, in which a nonexistent person called Wang Si-ma lives . . . "

Walking on the street, he saw many dead-fish eyes, as well as many big snoring mouths. "Isn't there any case of persecution?" He tightened his eyebrows and stared at a cactus that looked like a sore on top of Zhang Mie-zi's hut.

Someone was hanging a thief. The district head joined the spectators. A skinny man with protruding teeth was throwing one end of the rope that bound the thief over the branch of a tree and pulling it down gradually. And the thief, accordingly, was rising gradually. After one minute, he started groaning.

"Good!" the Yellow Mud Street residents sang out, their tiny eyes shining with joyful light.

Two more minutes later, the thief started yelling. His face had turned pale, and his sweat was beating small holes into the dirt.

"Very good!" The Yellow Mud Street residents began to applaud. Some of them were keeping time with their pocket watches.

After half an hour, the thief passed out. The toothy man tied the rope to the tree and put a slipknot at the end. Then he took out a sling chair and lay down, waving his big palm-leaf fan. "Seventy-five pounds worth of grain coupons and more than six yuan in cash," he told the audience and pointed at the thief swinging against the sky.

The sun was hot. The people were sweating. Yet they were reluctant to leave, hoping to discover more details.

"Is there a case of persecution in Yellow Mud Street?" the district head whispered into the ear of an old man.

"Oh?" The old man's face changed color. Retreating two steps, he examined the district head, then said, "There have been two dead-fish rains in the past, and dust rains all year round."

"Forty-five minutes," someone called out the time.

People dilated their nostrils to smell the sweat of the thief and waited patiently.

A band played beside the coffin.

The stench of a rotting corpse could be smelled in the air.

The mob whispered to one another.

"Last night, Wang Jiu-po's three pigs jumped out of the sty and ran to the outskirts of town."

"So gold bars can be dug out of the 'S' garbage pile?"

"Yesterday a headless man arrived at Yellow Mud Street. They say he was beheaded in the city. At midnight the barber passed by the street, holding human heads in his hands. They were all tied up with wire."

"Is Wang Jiu-po's death true or false?"

The district head could see Old Hu San dozing on the roof. His back was bent, and his face was buried in his hands. A sparrow perched next to his feet.

"Hey, get down!"

"Oh, district head! I heard the district head was making a secret visit in disguise."

The old man climbed down a ladder like a spider.

"Is Wang Si-ma a real person?" he asked abruptly.

"Wang Si-ma?" Old Hu San was startled. "Is Wang Si-ma a real person?" He repeated the words mechanically, his chin trembling. Then he brought a bench from his room as if he had suddenly remembered something. He invited the district head to sit down with him. He murmured into the district head's ear, "Ssh! Don't speak so loudly. My heart is pounding. Let me tell you something." His old brownish yellow eyes dimmed, leading his memory into the distant past. "Long ago, the ceiling of my room grew a black mushroom. Flies dropped on top of the net like rain. At night the ghost driver passed by, 'crack, crack.' I used to count his steps until dawn. At the corner of the street hung a yellow lantern. I used to mistake it for a big moon. The latrines were so clean. Creeping oxalis blossomed on the roof of every house . . . Now people try to lock me in the air-raid shelter! Is the relocation project making any progress? These days, I have been hiding on the roof to observe the situation on Yellow Mud Street."

"Is Wang Si-ma a real . . . "

"Hush! Don't be so loud. Something might happen these days. Look, can't you see that the sun is melting away? Last night a mad dog was making noise in a yard. The barber came again. I saw everything as clear as day from the roof."

"How long has the old lady been dead?"

"She died only this morning. Who knows? She smells putrid. I've just now smelled it."

"I've smelled it, too. Can there be some factor of persecution involved?"

"It's only the smell of the wind. When the wind blows, the whole Yellow Mud Street is full of this putrid corpse smell. It might be the dog that died a few days ago. The dog has been dead in the yard of Factory Head Wang for a week now. Nobody dares to touch it. They're too frightened."

Old lady Qi passed through, chewing something. Her cheeks looked full.

"Is everything well with this woman?" the district head asked.

"There's a sewage pool in my yard which spawns mosquitoes like crazy. What did you ask? How can she be well? She's pretending. She has a malignant tumor in her ear. She applies medicine every day. She's feeling miserable inside. Even though everybody knows her secret, she keeps on pretending. And she chews all the time. My cheeks feel sore whenever she chews. See how swollen my cheeks are."

"What are they digging for in the middle of the street?"

"Planting shaddock trees. They did that in the past also. That time they planted orange trees. Then they dug up the orange trees for cotton roses. Now they're digging up the cotton roses for shaddocks. Yesterday when they were digging up the cotton roses, they found a woman's hand which was said to have been chopped off and buried there by the barber. Since the municipal document ordering tree planting was issued, people are thinking of experimenting with planting trees in their kitchens. Even now they are digging the holes."

The narrow street had been completely destroyed. No one could pass through. The district head sheltered himself from the dust with his straw hat and rubbed his eyes vigorously. Thus he advanced by feeling his way, leaning against the little huts along the street. He felt something as big as rice grains in his eyes. His eyes were so painful by now that he dared not open them. Suddenly he raised his head and saw a long black memorial banner hanging to the ground. He tried to read the words on the banner, but they were all surrounded by circles of dazzling light.

The band played madly beside the coffin.

"Is there any case of persecution?" He made a great effort to resume his original line of thought. His eyes were giving him severe pain. He entered Eternal Spring Drugstore to buy a bottle of eyedrops. He put at least ten drops into his left eye. The result was that his left eye refused to open at all. He had to hold a handkerchief on it.

"The man Wang Si-ma . . . Is he a real person?" The district head asked Qi Er-gou.

Qi Er-gou's face flushed, and he started explaining, waving his hands. "There used to be a barber here. He shaved off a whole jar of ears and hid it in the blockhouse over there. Strange rains fell in Yellow Mud Street, three times already: one dead-fish rain, one leech rain, and the other was a black rain. The raindrops were as black as Chinese ink. Hey, in your opinion, are one-fourth of the residents on Yellow Mud Street idiots? Old Hu San's ceiling keeps growing black mushrooms, acutely poisonous. I've seen him poison two dogs with my own eyes. He mixed the mushrooms with meat. That old beast."

The district head's left eye was as swollen as a walnut. The tip of his nose was oozing grease.

"Can you prove that Wang Si-ma *is not* a real person?"

"Sure. No place can be compared with Yellow Mud Street in complexity. This is a strange and unique place. For example, certain people are living on roaches even today. Have you heard about it? Such a decadent life should not be allowed to continue, should it?"

"Who lives by eating roaches? I have to register it."

"Come along, I can show you. In Old Hu San's kitchen there's an entrance to an underground tunnel. A skeleton rolls out of it every night."

"Impossible! Where's this digging sound from?"

"That's from Old Qing's house. They're thinking of planting a shaddock tree in their kitchen. Showy! Ha, what's wrong with your eye? Is it fire eye? It'll be OK if you wash it with water from the eaves when it rains. Be sure not to use eyedrops! I have a relative who was suffering from fire eye, and he went blind because he used eyedrops. Eyedrops are simply disastrous!" While talking, he tried to touch the district head's eye. Quickly the district head jumped back.

"Don't touch it! It's contagious."

A bat dropped from the eaves, hitting the brow of the district head. His teeth clattered with pain.

"Ouch! It's killing me! The hell with this place!"

"You should never use eye medication. When the rain comes tonight, I'll get some eave water for you."

The band played on beside the coffin.

Fireworks were set off. The funeral procession started.

Factory Directory Wang came over, sticking out his big belly. The district head cast a scornful sidelong glance at him. The district head was a thin man.

"What movie is on tonight?" the district head asked.

"*Sparkling Red Star.*"

"Good movie." The district head thought for a moment, then said, "Suggest that the masses go watch it."

"I've seen it six times, but it's still not enough. I want to see it again. When they open fire in the movie, my blood runs faster, as if I'm experiencing something new."

"We should make the cultural life in Yellow Mud Street rich and colorful."

"Of course, we've already produced a wall poster. Oh, I forgot something. Will you follow me? Please notice above. Do you see now? It's true that somebody has already covered it with mud, but there used to be a hole there! Haven't you heard any talk about it? Everything is going from bad to worse! In this house Secretary Zhu was doing the file work for the Wang Zi-guang case. This hole means that for three months, someone has been spying so as to grasp the situation. Now we have to declare the documents invalid and restart the entire work from scratch."

"Are there any clues?" The district head asked anxiously.

"What are you talking about? It's impossible! The whole thing was planned so well that we have no place to get started. I would list everyone as suspects. There's never any decent arrangement on this street. I have the feeling I've entered a deadend lane. My experience tells me never to overdo anything. In this way, problems will be solved unexpectedly in dreams."

"This experience is a great enlightenment for me."

"I've gotten a disease recently. I don't know what kind of disease it is yet. It might be a severe potential danger. I have a premonition. Haven't you noticed that I eat like a horse lately? I can't sleep well, and I have to get up and eat at midnight. What's the matter with your eye? You can't expect to recover once you get the sickness! You should go see Old Granny Li. She's the only one who can cure such eye diseases."

The district head returned to the "S" office building, covering his eye with his hand. He lay down. Toward afternoon, he could no longer stand the pain. It was no use even to put on a cold towel. His eye burned so much that he felt his eyeball was going to drop out. He jumped up and down in the room for a long time before he finally went to the corridor and knocked at the next door.

"It's the district head."

Secretary Zhu came out with mussed hair.

"Please fetch Old Granny Li for me."

"To treat your eye?" Secretary Zhu said gravely. "She's a witch, and she's blind with superstition. Sometimes she destroys people's eyes completely. How can you trust your health to such a person? Your disease isn't serious. Stick with it till fall, and you'll recover. I've had the same disease before. Every time it heals in the fall."

"It's going to fall out." The district head pointed at his bloodshot burning eyeball.

"Doesn't matter. You should have confidence. Wait for the fall . . . I have a nephew who had a sore on his leg . . . " He went on and on.

The district head sighed deeply. He returned to his room and lay down again. He was lying there half asleep when a dream started in which his eyeball dropped out.

3

Factory Director Wang sat before his house watching the sparrows on the roof across the street. There were three of them. Their tiny feet scratched at the grass. "One more sparrow and mushrooms will grow out of the roof," he said to himself.

The day before, he finally had had the dead dog taken away. At the time, Wang hid himself in his room with doors and windows bolted tightly. However, the fleas from the dog remained. No matter where he stood, they jumped on him and bit him crazily. His body was covered with bites which he scratched insanely. The dog's smell also remained. He had spread lime, then sprayed perfume, but to no avail. The stubborn smell could penetrate anything.

Last night, the district head knocked at his door and called him out. Wang was forced to take a clearcut stand as to whether the Wang Si-ma case was an instance of persecution. He remembered that he had talked a lot about nothing in hopes of stalling the district head with vague answers. But why should he stall the district head? He himself didn't know. One possibility was that he didn't know the answer.

"Is Wang Si-ma a real person?" the district head had asked abruptly.

Wang's backbone felt chilled, and he was startled. He hadn't answered, but mumbled something about the mysterious relationship of Wang Zi-guang to Yellow Mud Street, the omen in the dream, the exit of the secret trap. Finally he'd raised the issue, "We must beware of ideological confusion." The district head was not satisfied at all. He peeled off his socks and scratched his toes impatiently. Then the director took out a rolling pin and carefully ground a kind of powder, saying it was used for eye treatment.

Why couldn't he answer the district head's question? He had no explanation, even now. At the time, he took it for granted that the district head was not asking him for an answer, but only asking because of his eye pain. The district head might have been testing him? He had cast several glances at the district head and found the district head glancing back without a smile. Therefore, he'd concluded that the district head was not really asking him.

He recalled a cadre in the past who intended to investigate the cause of death of a person. He spent a long time on that with no results. As a consequence his gums swelled, and he had trouble opening his mouth. The next day the cadre rolled up his luggage and fled.

They talked and talked until two in the morning. They talked repeatedly about the meaningless Wang Si-ma case. He couldn't go to sleep for a long time after he returned home. That's why, even now, he felt confused.

"Hey, what's the result of your consideration?" The district head was approaching. He looked dry and mannerless. His clothes hung on him like a gunnysack.

"How's your eye? Let me see. Oh, it's full of pus and badly infected. There's no cure for such a disease!"

"I feel a mood of resistance among the masses."

"Have you heard about the chicken claws growing on a woman's feet? It's been drizzling for two days. Even my quilt is damp. My wife has been complaining. She wants to light a fire to dry the quilt lest something grow inside."

The rain got heavier.

A man with a knife chased a frizzy-haired woman down the street. The woman was covered with mud. She screamed as she ran. Many people looked on. Beneath their oilcloth umbrellas, they jostled each other and stretched out their necks to watch.

"What's that about?" the district head inquired.

"Eating flies again, of course." Director Wang kept a straight face. "Her husband has forbidden her to do so, yet she still gets up at midnight to eat flies. This is not the first of their arguments. Such a woman."

"It's outrageous, outrageous." The district head was still deep in his own thoughts. "Why don't these people organize a literacy training class?"

"Lately everyone is gossiping about the relocation. This woman's been eating more and more flies," Factory Director Wang said while glancing toward the street. "Sometimes even in broad daylight. She claims it's a waste not to eat the flies because she won't have anything to eat at the new place. Not only does she eat them herself, but she even invited a good-for-nothing man home to have a fly feast with her. This started the fight. They say her husband is determined to chop off the man's feet. That good-for-nothing has been hiding in the air-raid shelter for more than ten days now."

"Outrageous." The district head continued his thinking. "Why don't they organize a literacy training class? By the way, how is the investigation going concerning the hole in the wall? Have you found any clues? I can't open my eye. It's flopping like a frog. I'm beginning to think I have cancer."

"Beyond doubt your eye disease is incurable. I have a nephew . . . "

"How can it be that there's no case of persecution?" The district head started his grumbling again. A strong body odor poured from his loose clothes, a mixture of sweat and something else strange. "A few days ago, we explored a case of severe persecution in the district . . . Do you want to maintain the tradition of the old revolutionary base area or not? Please notice that I have only ten days left here. I intend to start with the case of Wang Si-ma, then go on to the real identification of Wang Zi-guang. The only effective approach is that put forward by Secretary Zhu's plan, in which he focuses on the way Wang Zi-guang dressed. It goes without saying that the resistance to relocation is unimaginably strong. I can't even decide if Wang Si-ma is a real person. The problem involved is impossible to clarify. The scope of the investigation has to be unbelievably wide. Nearly everyone on Yellow Mud Street seems to be a Wang Si-ma. We have to rely on the practical and realistic spirit, as well as the tradition of the old revolutionary base area . . . Please excuse me, my eye can't go any longer without treatment. I'm in constant fear that it's cancer. I won't come again for a few days." He was holding his eye, from which tears were running continuously.

The fight over eating flies had ended. The street was empty. Director Wang's murky gaze was fixed on the eyesore of a cactus on the roof of Zhang Mie-zi's hut.

"Is there a case of persecution? Is Wang Si-ma a real person?" Director Wang spoke his monologue aloud. His voice sounded dry and hollow. It startled even him. So the district head was using a stratagem! Was it a threatening hint? Could this talk about cancer be an innuendo? There may not be any cancer! Was he only bluffing and blustering? After sitting there for some time, Wang started to spit. The sputum tasted sour, and the coating on his tongue felt thick and heavy.

"Only ten days left." Secretary Zhu flew from nowhere like a crow and stopped at Wang's foot. "Do you have any idea about the persecution case? I feel uncertain at this time. I have a feeling we've made a mistake. I'm in the process of collecting detailed information. No one can guess the intention of the district head. His every move is mysterious . . . "

"Puh!" Director Wang expelled a last mouthful of sputum. "Maybe we should hold a mass meeting and let people speak out?" Secretary Zhu lowered his uncombed head and dropped his big hands in a modest way.

Director Wang glared at him sarcastically. "Hope to catch criminals on the spot? What a good idea! Nobody will expect that! Bah! the fleas are like hungry wolves!"

"I see the uniqueness of the recent wind. It doesn't appear to be stopping." Secretary Zhu remained cool. "It keeps on blowing. I often dream of myself standing on a steep cliff. Yesterday, a strange-looking bird dropped into my kitchen. It called all night, leaving my wife sleepless the whole time. Even now the bird is calling. Today we had to cook our meal in my bedroom! Some people from the lower orders complain that certain individuals refused to dump their trash in the garbage station, but instead dumped it on the street. When they were caught, they defended themselves by explaining that the garbage station was overflowing. The so-called garbage station is nothing but a formality. I feel listless these days. You know I'm having trouble maintaining the confidentiality of my work. Someone is after me! I've turned this thing over and over for several nights. Sometimes I can see some clues, but then I'm disturbed by trifles such as the noise of the rats, a gust of cold wind, the firecrackers. In short, I no longer have any hope. Dejection and disappointment overwhelm me."

"Have you heard about the secret investigation in disguise? I see something tricky in it. Just think, all of a sudden—a secret investigation in disguise."

"I've lost heart in everything. I feel enveloped by depression." Secretary Zhu shrank into a knot and squatted down at the foot of the wall.

"It might be the queer temperament of the District Head, or a bad suggestion by some conspiratorial villain. I believe the truth will come out soon. There's a change going on in my body. It could be a malignant disease. I've already consulted the medical book. It fits. Every night, I dream of death. I've asked Li Da-popo to tell my fortune. But she says the opposite. She could be lying. Such a woman is not worth believing after all. Since the death of Wang Jiu-po, I can't deal with dead people any more. Passing a dead body causes rashes on my body. Who dumped garbage on the street?"

"Who knows. He was caught by some lower-class person. They're confused themselves. It seems there are two of them. But they've denied the whole thing. Maybe they caught two cats?"

"Tie the saboteurs up!"

The district head departed for three days for treatment of his eye.

During that time, Director Wang started to arrest people.

Rumors arose on the third night of arrests.

Many people had received anonymous letters in plain envelopes. The letters said that ten people on Yellow Mud Street had grown chicken claws on their feet. These people went about in clever disguise. They wore hightop leather boots so no trace showed.

One day a Taoist priest arrived. He sat down on the stone steps of the post office and put down his long, full bag. Then he took off his shoes and drummed them on the ground while shouting to the passersby, "This street is so boring!" Then he asked the telegraph clerk, who was leaning in the doorway. "Hey, are there white rats around here?" The clerk's face turned white, and he spoke haltingly, "Are you a medical doctor? At the time of the plague, a doctor came. So many people died. Like mosquitoes, they fell down dead at one slight tap . . . "

The priest sat in the bar till dusk. He drank so much that he staggered when he left. He forgot his bag under the table. When the waiters opened it, they found it was full of sand from the river. It was so heavy that nobody could lift it.

The pop-eyed barber appeared again. He circled around the

street at midnight, knocking on every windowframe with his razor. People were frightened half to death. The first thing they did when they got up in the morning was dash to the doors and windows to check the security of the bolts.

"A broad conspiracy of restoration* is brewing on Yellow Mud Street," Director Wang announced.

Altogether, there were twenty-one suspects. They were shut up in the meeting room of the "S" office building. The door was locked to prevent their escape. As a result, they had to pass their excrement and urine in one corner of the room. While moving their bowels, they cursed, "Even the right to shit is denied." One suspect had two bats in his pocket, which he released to crawl on the ground. The rest watched them, yelling and spitting.

"What's all that noise?" The district head blinked his swollen eyes and furrowed his eyebrows.

"They want out, but I've locked the door," the director replied with respect.

"Unlock the door."

"No, you can't do it. They might kill someone. I have evidence." Director Wang dug in his pocket for a long time before pulling out several crumpled letters full of black fingerprints. "Anonymous letters. A big movement of restoration is brewing. The mad dog in my yard was a sign. Yesterday, the manure collector dug up a gun in the latrine. My sickness gets worse when they start to make trouble. I have to eat meat all the time. Yesterday I was napping under the Chinese scholar tree. I dreamed I changed into a wolf chasing a gray rabbit. Isn't it ridiculous? A priest passing by asked about white rats. As soon as he left, the telegraph clerk fell into a fit of spasms. He was injected with two bottles of analgesics, but he is still twitching upstairs in the post office. These days there is chaos. Be sure to put on your straw hat when you go out."

"Bring one of them here. I'll interrogate him."

---

*A common phrase during the Cultural Revolution, 1966–76.—TRANS.

"It's very dangerous. Be careful." Sticking out his rear end, the director went over to open the door. The district head saw that one of the director's shoes had its back folded in. As a result, he made a loud noise when he walked.

The person brought in was a woman with no hair. Her hands were cuffed. According to Director Wang, she was "utterly evil." Her scalp was light pink and covered with leprosy scars. She didn't even have eyebrows. As she approached, she yelled, "Upright magistrate as bright as the blue sky!"* She knelt down and kowtowed noisily. Then she yelled again, "I'm an innocent person being wronged!" Jumping up, she scolded, "Spy! Manslayer!" The spittle flew from her mouth like strings of white worms.

"Go out and investigate." She stopped abruptly, then whispered to the district head mysteriously, "My neighbor gets up every midnight to listen to the radio. In his quilt there's something lumpy. It's a transmitter. He throws bricks at anyone coming near his house. He broke my husband's head. . . . Don't disturb him when you go in. You can climb over the back wall into his kitchen. Just don't make any noise. I can't be wrong. I've been watching him for several months. Almost every family in Yellow Mud Street grows a kind of ghostly pen mushroom. It looks ghastly and covers the straw mattress. . . . There's a cat. It's been mad for three days. It hides in the haystack in the yard. You've got to be very careful when you sleep. Don't turn off the light, don't open the window, and search everything in the room repeatedly."

"Release this dirty chicken." The district head waved his hand impatiently.

"She's lying. They've made this whole thing up. Please don't be taken in!" Director Wang protested.

"Scram!"

"Scram!" Director Wang shouted at the woman's back.

---

*A feudal mode of flattery for addressing legal officials.—TRANS.

The door banged shut. Even at a distance, he could smell the district head's body odor. He didn't understand why the district head hadn't changed his clothes.

"Wasn't it your idea?" Director Wang smiled cautiously. "The talk you gave that night . . . I've been thinking about it for a long time! It involved so much deep philosophical theory. It took me a whole evening to condense your speech into one word: Eat! Isn't that right? I think my understanding has improved greatly this time. Since you left, I've been studying political documents every day. Thus my thinking is improving. Of course I still make mistakes, such as in the problem of cats or human beings . . . Ah?"

"Unlock the door for me, you porcupine! You fat meat!" The district heat smashed his fist onto the table. He continued angrily, "I once had a cerebral hemorrhage! My eye is killing me! Oh? Early this morning a cat dashed in front of me . . . You pig!"

Director Wang unlocked the door with trembling hands. The prisoners dashed out like a pack of mad dogs. He said to himself, "Is the district head pretending to be crazy? That old trickster!"

4

Director Wang was brushing his teeth. His whole face was covered with foam. He meant to turn back to reach his towel, but he stopped short and remained motionless. He opened every drawer with a bang and dug around inside. The room was full of dust. Finally he came up with a dirty bottle of balm for treating minor ailments. He applied more than half to his neck, then tried to turn his head, but the slightest effort caused such severe pain that tears ran down his cheeks.

"Damn the wind," he said to the back of his wife's head. "All night I dreamed the wind was breaking my neck. My head rolled off my shoulders. The weather forecast says the wind won't stop till October. What's the reason for it?"

"Oh, the wind, they say, is going to blow till the end of the world." His wife didn't move. She was eating melon seeds while planning how to catch the tailless rooster at her foot.

"Can it be cancer?" he said suspiciously. He felt the pain getting worse. He pressed his neck till purple marks appeared. "I have an omen about having an attack of the disease. Lately, no matter where I go, I see a black cock. A voice warns me in my ear, 'Face the north.' Yesterday the voice came again when I was in the latrine. I thought it was somebody's joke. So I turned my face south instead. The pain came immediately. I thought it was a cold. But who knew it would be as bad as this?"

"Yang San's mother died of tongue cancer. She stank so." She suddenly caught the rooster, then threw it high into the air. The rooster crowed and flew into the shadows on top of the wardrobe. It hid itself up there. She peeped out the door. "More strange diseases are occurring since that wretched garbage station was built. Never before have I heard of cancer of the tongue. Yesterday afternoon, a dead baby boy was dug up in the garbage heap. Now people pour everything onto the pile. Nobody cares if it's already full. The whole street is covered with garbage. Last week somebody opened the door of Zhang Mie-zi's little hut and shat inside. At least, they say, it's better than shitting in the street."

"It's all caused by the dead dog." While saying this, Wang was about to lie down on his bed. But he suddenly jumped back when he saw two lizards crawling side by side on the ceiling.

"Bloodsuckers!" He rasped out a curse. Raising a spear, he jabbed at the ceiling. Lime dropped in chunks, and honeycomb cracks spread overhead.

"The ghost-pen mushroom is flourishing in Yellow Mud Street." His wife left for the market after making this remark. From a distance, he could still hear her heel plates scraping the ground.

"The slick district head . . . " He barely started thinking when yawns came upon him. What's the reason for this? Every time he starts thinking, he grows drowsy. His mind goes blank. He spat out a big glob of sputum and hopped vigorously three times on one foot, counting at the same time, "One, two, three!"

"The ghost-pen mushroom has appeared on every roof." Old Yue's gloomy face appeared at the window. At first glance, the director mistook him for the old man who bathed the dead. "They even appear under the water vats."

"Tell me what's growing here." Director Wang stretched his neck toward Old Yue.

Yue hesitated. "Maybe, it's a little bit red." This started his long speech. "In the city there's a dentist. Whoever sits down in his dental chair, he rubs their neck with a dry towel. He rubs and rubs until he scratches the skin and causes a lot of pain . . . "

"That's crap! Touch this side, and this hollow place. Eh? It's killing me! I am more and more sure it's cancer! Now that I think about it carefully, the pain started here several months ago."

"How did you get such an ailment?"

"It's caused by the damned wind. A voice keeps telling me not to face the south. I thought it was only a joke. Who can foresee such disaster? Oh, Comrade Yue . . . " He suddenly felt emotional and called him "Comrade Yue" in a clumsy way. "According to the weather forecast, the wind won't stop before October. Is that true?"

"They say the wind doesn't appear to be stopping," Old Yue said, discouraged. "For days running, the wind has borne a rotten corpse smell. It turned out to be a baby buried in the garbage! He was dug out yesterday. He was rotten all over. The district head has called in Yuan Si's wife. It looks like she committed the offense."

"She soaks her head up to the neck in the night stool every morning. You can always smell urine when you get close to her hair."

"Can you go and buy me ten tubes of sulfa eyedrops?"

"You're having eye trouble?"

"Well, I'm constantly gripped by fear. My long pondering tells me my neck needs sulfa eyedrops. Who knows? It may help."

"The district head is tracing the rumor about relocation to its source."

"He can trace it to the end of the world." He suddenly blew up. "Where on earth did he sneak from? This man, this man may not be the so-called district head, but only someone who has assumed his title. Is the whole thing a trick? The day he came there were no traces at all. He sneaked into the audience watching the thief and said something crazy. Consequently, rumor has swallowed up the whole Yellow Mud Street. People are frightened out of their wits by the idea that a district head has come. . . . But who can prove it's him? Why doesn't he change his clothes for years running? I've suspected for a long time that he has some scandalous purpose for coming to Yellow Mud Street. Is he playing a trick on us? I think we've become stupid pigs ourselves." His eyes stared blankly as he spoke.

"Factory Director?" Old Yue was scared.

"Good!" He kicked the wall violently and knocked down a lizard. He stomped on it with his other foot. "I hate such things the most," he said. His face was as red as if he were drunk.

After the dead baby was buried and the street was deserted, old lady Qi sneaked into Zhang Mie-zi's little hut in a hurry.

In the darkness appeared a pair of eyes. It was Yuan Si's wife squatting in one corner. Old lady Qi squatted down in another one.

"How many times have you moved your bowels?"

"I've been shitting all morning," Yuan Si's wife replied. "I'm feeling pretty joyful here. In fact, I was talking to myself when you came in."

"I've just buried the little devil. Bah! It smelled so bad."

Yuan Si's wife was chuckling.

"Why did the district head talk to you?"

"Why did the district head talk to me?" She stared at old lady Qi indifferently. Then a flash passed over her eyes. She grasped old lady Qi's hand warmly. "This is something good that no one can guess. This is a secret of the treasured bottle gourd. Ha! Yesterday morning I inspected the weather and said, 'Brightness overhead indicates a fine day.' Then I went to fetch water in the kitchen. I couldn't find my gourd ladle. I was at a loss! But everything good was gathering up at the same time. Just think, if there had not been a power failure, if I had slept soundly, if there had not been a rope in the drawer, how could the good luck have rotated to me? Yet the good luck, instead of going to anyone else, came right to me. Just now I was hiding here alone, laughing and laughing. I was laughing so hard! I'll never understand the whole thing."

"What good luck did you have?" Old lady Qi wasn't even looking at her. She was humming to herself comfortably while shitting.

"Exactly, you couldn't even dream it! Oh, Lord! I can't hold it back any more. I'm going to tell you. *The district head came to my room.* Hey, do you hear? You know my room is so dark that you can't see anything without turning on the light. He felt his way in. Possibly he mistook me for somebody else. I was overjoyed with this unexpected accident. With one grab, I held him tight! I wasn't sure at all. He felt like a wisp of empty smoke that might drift through my hands at any moment. You'd never guess what an excellent idea I thought up, within just a second, too. I held him with one hand, and with the other I opened the drawer and found a rope. So I tied him to my body. I wound the rope around him several times before I felt secure. Just as I expected, he quieted down and stuck to my body. He's still sleeping on my bed. You can go and peep in with me, but not for long. He's snoring, too. He's so lovely! There are so many things in this world that can't be predicted. Though he found the wrong person, once he was in my hands, hmm! Now my whole fortune has changed! I would rather die than let out the secret and cause trouble for his work. At present, I'm still thinking about the matter. I'm really happy."

"Obscene guy! It's nauseating! There's no one good in this world!" old lady Qi shouted.

"Hush, don't shout like that. It may ruin my good luck."

"You're so dirty, and yet he goes for you. Who will buy this? Bah! The pig, he can start without opening his eyes! Mean and filthy vile character! Hypocrite! Poisonous snake! I once gave him a pair of shoes as a present! I am so annoyed!"

"Please don't shout. I don't understand, either. I am so dirty, how can he come? Of course, he mistook me for someone else. Not everyone can have such a chance. That's my luck."

One day old lady Song was at the well fetching water when she saw Yuan Si's wife in the distance. She clapped her hands in excitement and said in a loud voice, "Ha! Yuan Si's wife is really good-looking!"

All the males on Yellow Mud Street felt shy in front of Yuan Si's wife. When they met her face to face, they blushed and sidled nervously past her in as wide a circle as possible. Then they would stop in a daze and stare at her back till she disappeared in the distance.

The females said, "Yuan Si's wife is growing more and more delicate and charming."

"Yuan Si's wife doesn't look like a woman in her forties. Sometimes she looks only eighteen."

"The district head is a man with foresight. He never makes mistakes in his choices. Even without a light, his eyes see as clearly as a cat's."

"Yuan Si's wife should grab the chance and indulge him as deeply as possible."

Thus Yuan Si's wife passed some days in contentment.

All of a sudden, another rumor started.

It began with old lady Qi. She went to every household to

spread her news. "Don't be taken in, fellows! Just think what kind of thing she is. Nothing but a whore. Who witnessed the district head entering her house? Such a claim should be based on real evidence. Once everyone accepts such nonsense, where will the reputations of our leaders be? In fact, the district head has also been to my house once. It also happened at midnight. The room was without light, too. Then what? I can tell everybody that the district head and I sat well-behaved the whole night through, that nothing happened. Of course, there was every possibility for something to happen. Something might *really* have happened, but I would *never* go and gossip to everybody. We can't get lost in our fond dreams. I hate people with wishful thinking the most! For example, the district head came to my house, and, in fact, he meant to show a certain intention. But I have never boasted for myself, because I don't allow my fancy to run wild. All I want to do is be honest and know my place. Daydreamers are disgusting!"

Later on, she told others with excitement, "Comrades, the truth of the case of Yuan Si's wife is coming out now. It's kidnapping! In this incident, the district head became the victim of the most vicious villain! From this incident people have seen the real nature of a certain person! An appalling self-exposure! A trick of perpetrating a gigantic fraud!"

That night, the district head was so disturbed by the mosquitoes that he couldn't sleep. When he opened the window to let in some fresh air, he looked out by chance and saw something white moving in the garbage pile.

"Who is it?" The district head lit his flashlight.

"It's me," a hoarse woman's voice replied. It was old lady Qi.

"Still looking for the gold bar? You might find a human skull instead!"

"I'm determined to find the truth. Be careful of the manure pit under your feet," she sneered. Her mouth was moving as if she were chewing something. "I was so deep in thought about the problem of persecution cases that I couldn't go to sleep. So I decided to come out and search around, thinking maybe I could find something."

"That's good, you have high vigilance," the district head praised her. His spirit dropped suddenly. "This Yellow Mud Street is horrifying. Fortunately I have only a few days left here," he said aloud to himself, staring at the yellowish light. A moth bumped into the lamp stupidly and fell to the floor.

"The latrine smells terrible." Secretary Zhu drifted in like a shadow. The scales of sleep, big as mung beans, hung at the corners of his eyes. "The smell is keeping me sleepless. Who're you talking to? That woman is a thief. You have to take precautions against her."

"She used to be my classmate."

"That doesn't mean anything. She'd respect nobody once she started stealing. Besides stealing things, she steals men. (That is to say, she's good at seducing men.) Not long ago, her husband cut off the ear of one immoral man. A yellow weasel dashed in downstairs. Didn't you smell the stink? Is the investigation on Yellow Mud Street coming to an end? The weather forecast reports that the wind will continue to blow until October. What miraculous weather! I feel myself living on the edge of a steep cliff every night."

The district head folded his hands behind him and paced the room for a long time. Finally he spoke. "So there's no case of persecution in Yellow Mud Street? The signs here don't fit my expectations at all. Can it be that a strange antibody is borne in the organism?"

"Excellent!" Secretary Zhu became excited. "Your judgment is exactly the same as mine. Whenever I suffer from insomnia, I ponder the same question. If you are living in the attic facing the street, you can hear many sleepless people at night."

"We have to do something about the urgent problem at hand; for example, run a literacy training class."

"Right, in order to heighten the understanding, which is the key to solving the problem. I'll start the preparation tomorrow. I already have a list of participants in mind, including old lady Qi and Yuan Si's wife. They are among the first batch to be cultivated. The latrine is too stinky. It gives me a headache. Tomorrow I'll get two workers from the team building the air-raid shelter and make them responsible for the hygiene of this latrine. When can 'S' factory resume production? The situation is pressing."

"I still haven't received any document from above. I heard that in the past a man called He Hu-zi choked to death on chicken bones. I also heard that he melted in a pool of blood. What was the matter? How can the cause of death be so complicated?"

"Who knows? You can never set such things straight, not even after three days and three nights of thinking, not even when you break your skull in thinking. I believe it belongs to the realm of psychology?" Secretary Zhu put on an air of meaningful and profound learning. His tiny triangular face blurred behind the cigarette smoke he puffed out. He was pleased to have used the intellectual term "realm."

"You might be right," the district head agreed. He was still staring at the greasy yellow light. "It's a pity I can't stay here for long."

"A new problem has arisen. The ghost-pen mushroom is growing crazily in Yellow Mud Street."

"Mm," the district head said vaguely.

After that, the two went to the latrine together. The district head slipped and fell beside the urinal. One hand landed in a pool of urine. A swarm of mosquitoes attacked him.

All night he felt too nauseated to sleep.

5

It turned out that the district head was Wang Si-ma! When the Yellow Mud Street residents woke up from their nightmares that morning and started thinking about it, the district head had already disappeared. The news was brought to the people by a monk with one eye. The monk sat under the eaves of old Hu San's house. He wore a black robe, and his bony shoulders towered so high that from a distance he seemed to have three heads. As soon as the monk left, old lady Qi discovered two dead cats in the middle of the street. They were already rotten. A bloodred silk quilt cover hung right in the street, shining with red light. "Bad omen," she thought. "Someone is trying to exploit the masses."

"The ghost-pen . . . " somebody whispered.

The pop-eyed barber was approaching. When she discovered this, old lady Qi scurried into Zhang Mie-zi's hut and bolted the door. The barber shouted in a thrilling voice and put down his shoulder pole right in front of the door. He was gasping for breath. The room was very damp. Among tiny dots of phosphorescent light, two big balls of light floated deep in the darkness.

"I've been shitting the whole morning." The two big balls of light turned out to be the eyes of Yuan Si's wife.

"Hush!"

The sound of the barber receded.

"There's a snake," Yuan Si's wife jabbered on, "that's been crawling on the roof beam right above my head the whole morning. I'd been staring at it until you came in just now. It's crawled away. It's a pity you can't see it. What're you doing?"

"I'm looking for the snake. It may be coiling somewhere."

"No, you can't do it! It will cause an accident. Do you think I'm really shitting? I'm hiding here. They plan to capture me. Early in the morning, I jumped out of my quilt and hid myself here. Please look at this pair of binoculars. The district head gave them to me. The whole morning, I have been using them to observe the situation on the street."

"I was sleepless all night, but I listened carefully with my ears to the wall. Just now I saw dead cats on the street. My legs almost fail to carry me around. Oh-oh . . . something is going to happen. There's red color everywhere on the street. That night he was sleeping against the wall of 'S,' I was looking for something on the garbage pile. He called me 'old classmate.' Isn't that strange?"

"The Song woman is arguing with the reprobate." Yuan Si's wife suddenly remembered the news. "They were fighting over a flytrap. The flies were swarming everywhere. The woman is an out-and-out whore. What're you doing now?"

"I have something to say. Have you heard anything about the new treatment for people who have made contributions?"

"No. I dare not even step out the door. Why should they capture me? They pester me endlessly. They don't have any sense of the general situation."

"The one-eyed monk has brought the news. I'm going to the district to inquire. Yesterday, someone revealed to me that they use dice to decide the recipients of the awards. How can that happen? Why haven't the authorities dealt severely with such deeds? I think there must be a good bit of sabotage by tricky, vile characters. I'm going to turn the sky upside down if they don't select me this time."

She arrived at the district and dashed into the room of the agency. She banged the desk with her fist.

Despite the hot weather, the agent wore a black cotton-padded cap with the ear flaps pulled down snugly. He held a big cup of hot tea at his chest as if to warm himself. From behind dusty glasses, his eyes stared at a piece of yellowed newspaper. The paper had lost all four corners and had several big holes in the middle, showing the red paint of the desk underneath. He was so intent on studying a picture of a rooster in the paper that he did not notice the newcomer.

"Hey!" old lady Qi shouted at him and knocked on the desk again.

"Please have a clear recognition of the seriousness of the question," he mumbled to himself without raising his head. "All power should be passed down to the root units."*

"I'm here inquiring about the new regulation concerning people who have made contributions," old lady Qi raised her voice.

"Is it the canvas factory? Your questions concerning housing should be discussed with the housing department." He waved his hand with force and peered over his glasses. He cast a wicked glance at old lady Qi as if he could penetrate her deepest thoughts. "The fourth door on the right."

"I have proof here . . . " Old lady Qi stepped back. Sweat dripped down her back after the long walk.

"The fourth door on the right, eh?" He blew his nose with a dignified gesture.

"People can prove my contribution . . . "

"So what? Please don't claim credit for yourself and become arrogant! The fourth door on the right." He circled around the desk and approached two steps toward old lady Qi. He made a gesture with his hand and said in a low voice, "Whatever your problem, it will be readily solved!"

"I'm here to inquire . . . " Old lady Qi intended to explain further, but her feet had involuntarily carried her toward the door. Several black figures rushed past in the corridor. Old lady Qi's head hummed like a kettle on the stove.

"Make a mountain out of a molehill!" The agent bolted the door and sat himself down. He put his cup of hot tea to his chest in a hurry. Immediately he emitted a string of sneezes.

The same day, Director Wang locked himself in his room. According to him, his cancer started in his neck. From that day on, he refused to put on any clothes. "It will cause deterioration," he said. He moved about in the room without a stitch on, his gigantic bottom sticking out. He panted like a pig and gave out stinking

---

*Revolutionary saying.—TRANS.

belches. One day his wife brought him some clothes, which he promptly hurled back through the door. He yelled at her in a rage, "I've brought shame on you, eh? I want to let people see me, so what? Eh?" Later on, he blocked up his door, and even his meals had to be passed in through the window. While eating, he would complain that people had poisoned his rice. Then he would break the bowl. He made an uproar claiming that the members of the family had united to murder him. They had stolen his clothes so he had to go naked all day.

"It's a plot planned long ago!" he screamed while punching the ceiling with a spear.

With a sneer, his wife told everybody who came to visit, "It's the mosquito bite that has caused all this. The Yellow Mud Street mosquitoes reproduce like crazy. His disease started only with a neck pain. But now he is rotten up to his eyeballs. What kind of question is this? Who can prove the identity of that nonexistent person?"

Every night when people were asleep, he let loose a torrent of abuse and shouted that someone had buried a dead dog under his bed, that the stink in the room was driving him mad. "Don't laugh too soon, you! Am I really sick? Bah! I've bulged forth with this tumor on my neck on purpose, because I can't stand vicious reality! I'm feeling much relieved thanks to this tumor." He kicked his door so loudly that the whole family was awakened. So the doctor was called, but when he arrived and knocked at the door, nobody answered it. The snoring inside was as loud as thunder.

"He's seriously sick." His wife turned her back to the doctor.

"He's seriously sick," his wife's sneering voice resounded in the empty room.

In the morning he could see the back of his wife's head, which looked like a big broad brush. "He's seriously sick," she was telling somebody excitedly. This was followed by the clang of her iron soles on the street. Suddenly he felt blue. He remembered how he couldn't go to sleep last night and had gotten up to catch bugs. He caught three in succession and squeezed them to death one by one. Blood splattered on the bedsheet. When he unfolded the sheet he saw the blood stains. "Who can prove the identity of the nonexistent person?" he argued loudly. He remembered the sweat-stained worn jacket. The hairy arms stretching out of the clothes looked moldy and rotten. "He's nothing! Nothing but a rumor, a fantasy. He's only a kind of fantasy! Dead fish fell on Yellow Mud Street. Dust falls all year round. Now ghost-pen mushrooms grow everywhere. Moths are as big as bats. Who can explain all this? Self-indulged, daydreaming!" He made all kinds of powerful gestures. "Once upon a time there was a conceited fellow who allowed his fancy to go wild. Consequently, he came to Yellow Mud Street to do an investigation. He popped his eyeballs wide and spat everywhere. But what was the result? His intestines rotted through, and he died in two years! Nobody needs to pop his eyes. We Yellow Mud Street people have tiny eyes. Yet we are good at smelling out what is right and what is wrong! Hey, are there any suggestions about the garbage station? Isn't it epoch-making? Eh? Now about the experiment of planting shaddock in the kitchen, what is your impression of it? A big plot is cooking!"

"Isn't his sickness serious?" His wife was heard talking to somebody again outside the window. Her voice was as meaningful as she herself was dry and dull, full of edges and corners. She went on, "When I got up to go to the toilet last night, I saw a fireball stop at Yellow Mud Street. One more pig died at Wang Jiu-po's house. It was killed by somebody and was thrown into the sewer. Don't you smell the stink? They say the wind is going to change direction in September. The wind is blowing people out of their wits these months as if the doomsday of the world were coming . . . Listen, it sounds like my old Wang is killing lizards again. He punctures the ceiling with a spear and makes a honeycomb of it!"

"How can the district head become Wang Si-ma, and how can

Wang Si-ma change into the district head? I have turned the whole thing over and over in my mind all day, but simply can't solve the puzzle. I wondered upon his arrival, 'Secret investigation in disguise? What does that mean? Maybe he is neither Wang Si-ma nor the district head, but some important figure from above coming to inspect the people's life?'" This was a woman's voice.

"I may need a 'pain-killing plaster.'" So thinking, Director Wang opened the drawer and took out a whole pile of plasters. He applied five or six on his neck and patted them firmly. He felt much more relaxed. "I might really need to cut the lymph nodes." He recalled the doctor's diagnosis and felt nervous again.

Old lady Song's tiny wrinkled head poked in through the window. Her glance circled the room before she whispered, "Hey, your ailment is nothing." After a pause, her voice became sharp and anxious. "Just try, it's not a big deal! Apply fly blood wherever the pain is, eh? I once suffered from cancer also, and it was cured by applying fly blood. Don't be afraid of the pain. Why should you wear only a pair of shorts? This wind, it's getting cold . . . " Her gums were a purple similar to fly blood.

"Now I'll shit. It makes a great stink," he said smilingly and made the gesture of peeling off his shorts.

The old lady shrank back and left without a word.

"The ceiling has become a honeycomb," his wife continued, her voice sounding dry and sharp. "He always gets up at midnight to do his punching and make a roomful of dust. His sickness has no cure."

The broad brush appeared at the window, waving threateningly. The voice quieted to a whisper. A gust of wind wandered through the room, stirring up a stink.

"The whole house smells of death. The wind comes from the graveyard, doesn't it?" Director Wang asked loudly. He picked up the chamber pot and poured the urine out.

The whispers stopped at once.

"No cure for it! Such sickness!" A dry, sharp voice was heard from the street. Iron soles seemed to be crushing the broken tiles.

His neck started aching again. "I should have bought the sulfa eyedrops long ago. Old lady Song is a reincarnated pig. There's excrement everywhere in the street."

Two bony dogs rolled in the dunghill.

"I want to buy ten bottles of sulfa eyedrops," he said in the Eternal Spring Drug Store.

"Do you have piles?" The young clerk grew excited. His face was as pale as a winding sheet. Putting his soft, long palm over his mouth, he said quietly, "Why don't you buy the Zebra Brand Eyedrops? Recently there's a lot of cases of piles. Everyone is washing with Zebra Brand Eyedrops, and it's said to be very effective. The cactus on Zhang Mie-zi's roof is fumigated to death by the stink. Have you seen it? Now the whole house is full of excrement. Those people are boorish." His mouth smelled of moldy beans.

"Ten bottles of sulfa eyedrops."

"As soon as the priest arrived, he sat on the steps of the post office. I was passing by and saw with my own eyes five centipedes creeping out of the stone crevice. When the priest drummed his shoes on the ground, the telegraph clerk's stomach bubbled." The young guy scratched his head with force, and a large quantity of dandruff drifted down onto the counter. He sighed deeply and continued, "This street is very strange. I've been working this counter for ten years, and I always hear a clattering sound from underground. It never stops. Sometimes I think people are digging in the latrine, and sometimes I feel the digging is right under the drug counter. At night I've been awakened by the clattering and can't get back to sleep. When I have to sleep in the drugstore, I always rig two wine bottles behind the door. If someone broke in, the bottles would make a noise. I've done this for ten years, but nothing has ever happened. Anyway, I keep doing it for safety's sake. Who knows? Anything can happen because of one moment of carelessness . . . My hometown is in the countryside. We have a grape vine there. The sun looks like a golden cherry . . . " His talk was followed by his snore.

6

It was moonless that night; not even a star could be seen. Standing on the garbage heap, old lady Qi could see the curtain on the window of the office building blown by the wind and flapping up and down like a strange black bird. The big clock in the city was striking two. A groan came from the garbage heat. With a spade, old lady Qi dug violently toward the sound. "Ouch," a man moaned. Not the man in the heap, but high in the office building, leaning against the wall.

"Former classmate, what are you digging for?" the voice grumbled. It turned out to be the district head. So the district head hadn't left? How could the district head be Wang Si-ma? And how did Wang Si-ma change himself into the district head? Long ago, there had been a butcher who visited Yellow Mud Street in the disguise of a rich man. When he sat down with a family, pork fat started to ooze out of his back. Within half an hour, his back was wet and greasy. It smelled miserable. What a shame it was! Old lady Qi kept thinking about the Wang Si-ma problem before she went to sleep, tossing and turning. Her back was covered with sweat. Then she went to the kitchen to fight with the roaches for a while before she lay down again. As soon as her head touched the pillow, she heard the rats chewing her scalp.

"The night is very dark," she answered unaccountably. In her heart, she wondered why he called her "former classmate." That was strange. That monster, that lizard crawling on the wall, why should he come to Yellow Mud Street? She had even given him a pair of shoes for nothing. She was planning to go home, but her feet seemed to be tied up by many twisting vines. She struggled hard to free herself. Every effort was accompanied by a fit of groaning from something.

"The former doorkeeper in the Number Twenty Municipal High School has committed suicide by drinking chemical fertilizer," the man on the wall said coolly. On the approaching wind, old lady Qi could vaguely smell his body odor.

She stood firmly in the darkness and replied while chewing on tile splinters, "People die of plague in Yellow Mud Street. A perfect man can die a sudden death. He can appear lively and fresh and still have all his vital organs rotted away. Someone was sent to do a lab test. They concluded there was a virus, in the water, in the earth, even in the air. In this garbage heap, ten skeletons are buried. I come here every night, stamping on top of it, listening to their moaning. Now Yellow Mud Street is overrun with ghost-pen mushrooms. They can even be found on the ceiling beams. At the dinner table, mushrooms drop into your bowl unexpectedly. Sooner or later, we will all be poisoned to death . . . Relocation won't stop the growth of ghost-pen mushrooms."

"What's that smell in the wind?"

"The wind is blowing from the graveyard, so you've smelled the greasy smoke from the incinerator. Bah, it's disgusting! I once raised a cat. It was bitten to death by a bunch of rats. The rats here are terribly big!"

Later on, Wang Si-ma indeed left. Why did he leave? He was frightened away by old lady Qi. He was climbing the wall of "S" factory at midnight when he was discovered by old lady Qi, who pressed him with several questions he was hard put to answer. In response, he showed her a clean pair of heels.

THE SUN SHINES ON
YELLOW MUD STREET

1

A shabby garbage truck crawled onto Yellow Mud Street. The body of the vehicle was plastered with such a thick layer of yellow mud that people had difficulty telling where the window was. Several strange-looking people jumped down from the truck. They were all in rat-colored uniforms and their heads were wrapped tightly in canvas hats.

"This street is so small," a voice was heard to mumble from one of the hats.

"What street, it doesn't look like a street at all," another chimed in.

"Pah!" a glob of spit flew from under the hat of the third one.

"The cleanup is starting at the other end," Qi Er-gou was telling old lady Qi. "Have you heard the cawing of the crows? It's a real scene. Mosquitoes swarm into your nostrils like dust."

"Nothing exciting!" Old lady Qi gave a snort of contempt. "Fussy. There's nothing to be surprised about. Ignorant!" She cracked a bamboo chair with a kick and frightened Qi Er-gou away.

"Damned ghost-pen mushroom, it knows how to use every bit of space. It's even growing in my shoes." She picked up her greasy towel and dipped it in the basin. She gave her face a fast wipe and hurried to old lady Song's house. "Why so much stink? Is there another dead infant?"

"The wind last night blew the soul out of my body," she began. "The cleanup is starting at the other end. I can hear the spade digging at the cement. It feels like they're digging at my scalp. Where are they from, those people? They're disturbing our lives. Who gives them the right and power? What's our situation in the mind of the authorities? Is there a cure for Yellow Mud Street?"

"Hmm, I've heard this long ago. Early this morning, I saw three black figures . . . Whose idea is this? Can something serious happen? Are we leaving immediately? Those mosquitoes, they're robbing and killing us!"

"A snake has been dug up." Yuan Si's wife walked over with a big bowl of porridge. She was sucking loudly as a pig. "I wonder if it's the snake in Zhang Mie-zi's hut? Those people have vicious intentions. Anyone can see that. But have we overestimated those weird people? Who knows, there might not be anything tangible inside those rat-colored rags. Maybe that's all they are—mad rags. No one has ever seen anything inside them."

Those strangers were digging here and there frantically. People felt they were digging not garbage but the residents' own intestines, green, yellow, black, sticky and messy. Their spades ground irritatingly on the cement. They stretched their necks and belched. Their mouths gave off the smell of spoiled rice. To hell with the cleanup! Undisturbed, nothing was at all dirty! But once it was turned upside down, the whole street became suffocating with the stink. This unreasonable cleanup has stirred up a large quantity of mosquitoes. Would this start an epidemic of malaria? What was the opinion of the authorities toward Yellow Mud Street? It was so abstruse that not a soul could see the truth.

"Wretched garbage station. Everything grows in it: mosquitoes, flies, rats, moths. I entered it just once the day before yesterday, and a huge sore developed on my leg."

"We used to pour everything into the river. It was never that smelly. I've been against the garbage station from the very beginning. Just see now what a big problem it's caused."

"This cleanup will make the street stink all month. It will be like living in the latrines everyday."

"Is the whole thing a plot? The crows are cawing so vigorously."

"I told you long ago it's not a good thing to have this wind."

"In the past there was no wind. There was peace everywhere."

Dung beetles were crawling out. The three strange men stuck their heads out the window and spat loudly.

"Yellow Mud Street's days are numbered," Old Hu San prophesied. Then he sighed sadly and closed his eyes in misery. He rubbed his wrinkled chest with his greenish fingers, saying there was too much dust in his chest and he had to spit it out. He rubbed and rubbed till he appeared to be ready to spit. People made room for him and waited to see. But he didn't spit. Instead, he said, "These are not good days we live in."

After the garbage cleanup, all the roofs on Yellow Mud Street leaked.

Although there was no rain and no one poured water from the roof, water dripped endlessly for no reason. The water from the roofs was as black as Chinese ink and as stinking as fluid from a corpse. People believed the water came from the rotten straw on the roofs.

Old lady Song's roof was the first to break down.

That night she was eating flies in bed, wrapped in her quilt, when a big warm messy glob landed beside her feet. She turned on the light, and discovered it was straw from the roof. It was wet and appeared to be alive, shining in the light. "The straw on the roof must have been dead for years and years. Yet it now looks alive. It feels so warm in the hand." Then she looked up and saw a hole as big as a bowl right in the center of the roof. She was about to call her husband when the second lump fell down. Now the hole was the size of a basin. Through it, she could see the green stars looking like will-o'-the-wisp. A gust of cold wind poured in through the hole.

"The roof has rotted through." Old lady Song's voice was muffled by the splitting sound coming from all directions. The roof straw fell like rotten meat all around her. In half an hour, every single straw was down, and the three rooms had become bright and light. Old lady Song and her husband sat on the biggest pile of rotten straw. She said loudly, "It's like dead human flesh falling down." They started to struggle, trying to push each other off the pile. This game was followed by their drooping heads and snoring.

The big clock in the city struck three times. The sound was quivering and prolonged.

As soon as she heard the clock, old lady Song pushed her husband's back with force. Her hands felt sore from the pushing. She told him, "I knew the cleanup this morning would lead to some accident. You see, it turns out to be true. I've analyzed the situation carefully. Everything leads to one question. All the clues are linked. Have you noticed this?"

"Jiang Shui-ying turns out to be a whore." The man was rubbing his eyes.

"I've heard some kind of sound." Her bony neck shrank back. Blinking her rotten red eyes, she sank into deep thought. "Can it be the nonexistent man? I heard he sleeps on the wall like a lizard. Whenever he sees a woman, he calls her 'former classmate.' The whole thing makes no sense at all."

"Yuan Si's wife has set up a door plank on the street and lies down with the so-called district head to sunbathe their bottoms."

"It's nothing serious that the roof has rotted through. Flies fall through all the time anyway. I've caught several containers of them.

They all grew in the straw. Unconsciously, I link these clues with the case of Wang Zi-guang. I feel very uneasy about it."

"Wang Cui-xia is also a whore. I can see through her with one glance."

"When the roof fell down, I was dreaming of a big sunflower. Many flies were smelling it. What did this dream show? I can't make sense out of it."

"I've counted as many as seven or eight whores on Yellow Mud Street! How can there be so many?"

"The flowerpot was as big as a washbasin. I was about to pick it up when the flies swarmed over it. They were numberless!"

"What literacy training class? They should run a whore training class."

"Hey, can you explain the omen in my dream?"

"Nowadays, I dare not go to the street. Every time I leave the house, I meet whores. What bad luck!"

"I think it's better to sleep. Is there a smell in the room?"

"The problem of whores is disturbing me so much."

Old lady Song snored for a long time, leaving the man troubled by the problem of whores. He was too upset to go to sleep.

That night, more than a dozen roofs rotted through.

At dawn, some people pushed their way out of the rotten straw piles. They stood trembling against the wall and sneezed loudly.

A half-doglike creature dashed straight up the street.

"Head shaving . . . " The sound came from a great distance. It sounded half real, half fantastic.

Beside the latrine, Qi Er-gou was sharpening a pair of scissors. The sound of his grinding spread afar in the faint rays of dawn.

Old lady Qi appeared at the road side with disheveled hair. Her eyes were glazed—she had dug in the garbage heap half the night, looking for the corpse of a baby boy.

"Ah—Ah—" Old Hu San expelled a big yawn. He entered the latrine half asleep.

"It's very cold without the roof. It's like living in a cave."

"The wind whistles all the time. I feel I'm living on a cliff."

"I woke up to a glow overhead. The stars seemed irritatingly bright. I thought I was sleeping in the graveyard."

"A roofless house isn't livable. Without protection, some disaster will come in. I couldn't close my eyes all night for fear something might crash down from above."

"When the roof was falling down, it blotted out the sky and the land! I thought doomsday was coming, and I was ready to hide under the bed. It took my wife and me a long time to wriggle through the rotten straw. The whole room smelled like a pigsty!"

"The problem of whores on Yellow Mud Street has no solution," old lady Song's husband shuffled out the door and shouted to the people by the wall. He made faces and farted at the same time.

Zhang Mie-zi's little hut had collapsed. It became soaked with water and fell gradually. Yellowish green night stool liquid oozed from the mud wall and flooded the street. Director Wang passed by with a walking stick. Rubbing his neck, he uttered "Tragic!" a dozen times before entering the restaurant to buy eight steamed buns with pork stuffing. He swallowed them almost with one breath and then sat down at the table for a nap. In his drowsy mind, he saw a long funeral procession. He stepped toward it and shouted, "Comrades! Today is a day of great significance! You should recall seriously . . . " Someone pushed him hard. Jumping up in anger, he demanded, "Who is against the idea of the garbage station? Isn't the question of the mad dog a signal?"

"Wang Si-ma is clinging to the wall of 'S' office building," the shop assistant responded listlessly. He yawned after he spoke. Right in front of Director Wang, he dug his finger into his nostrils and mixed whatever he dug out into the flour. "Black wings grow out of the wall at night. I don't know if you've noticed. Every night the street twists and turns like a snake. I often wake up with my whole body ice-cold. I sit on a stool at the window and peep out through the crack to watch how the street zigzags . . . "

"Dirty pig!" Director Wang suddenly blew up. He belched and left the restaurant. The whole day his stomach churned as if he had a rag inside. A greasy stink came to his mouth whenever he belched. "I've already used up a whole drawer of sulfa eyedrops," he complained to Old Yue.

"This disease has no cure. You know that!" His wife sneered.

After all the roofs had rotted through, Old Hu San dreamed some outrageous dreams on top of the rotten straw for most of the night. This time his dreams contained bacon and cured fish, all with a sweet, rotten smell. Waking up, he saw several centipedes, thick as a man's finger, crawling on the moldy wall. He had breathed in too much dirt during the garbage cleanup the day before, so now his nose and throat felt dry and itchy. He wanted to cough, but couldn't. Now, seeing the centipedes, he meant to shout, but all of a sudden he coughed something up. It made a pool of something pink. He moved closer only to find numerous small worms wriggling inside his sputum. "The roof is like human beings. It rots from inside gradually. When it has rotted through, it turns into worms. In this world, everything rots, be it iron or bronze. It turns into worms eventually. Is there any hope for the rebels?"

His daughter stood under the roof with her arms akimbo. She looked very happy.

"With the roof gone, you can move to the old people's home," she said jubilantly. Her huge black lips stuck out to suck porridge, and at the same time her greasy hair fell into the bowl. She always did that. When she raised her head again, her hair stuck to her clothes. Hence, her jacket was always wet with porridge stains. "How many on Yellow Mud Street can live more than eighty years? There's no reason to do so. Why should one insist on living for more than eighty years? To put it bluntly, it's only a thought to go against the wind." She twitched her mouth in contempt. A belch exploded from her lips.

"How can the ceiling fail to support the falling roof?" Old Hu San was wondering vaguely. "Maybe the ceiling is also rotten? No wonder mushrooms and flies grow out of it. It's rotten from inside."

He moved slowly to the street and forced his eyes open. He could see the sun and the dusty yellow sky. The air was murky as if there was a fog. The bloodred fireball hung in the branches. It was much brighter than the sun in the sky. He dared not glance at it lest his temples swell and ache.

"Is there any case of persecution on Yellow Mud Street?" The voice sounded far, far away.

Ah?

The bowl of memory was suddenly stirred. Old Hu San closed his aged brown eyes halfway and said rapidly, "A woman's arm was buried under the wall over there. I saw it with my own eyes. Blood drips from the eaves. The fireball always stops at the windowframe. Who's planning a murder? Just look, the fireball is on the branch! Be careful about your eyeballs! I find centipedes and spiders in my food. I have an antibody for poison. You can test me on the spot! Dust is falling these days. Many good things fell in the past . . . " While rattling on, he opened his eyes and was startled that nobody was listening. It was all a dream. But how can dreams come during the day? He remembered several such experiences lately. Sometimes in the sun, sometimes on the night stool. Dreams came whenever they felt like it. Then he always talked, always talked . . .

"There are so many maggots in your sputum. No wonder there are so many flies in the room." His daughter stuck her head out the window. With a contorted face, she chuckled and said, "Now we no longer have a roof. I'll go to the old people's home to apply for you tomorrow."

Before the roof collapsed, many tiny things fell from the crack in the ceiling and rattled onto the top of the net. There was a thick layer of them. He often observed those small things struggling on top of the net, making the net swing.

"Maggots are growing in your lungs. It's contagious." She glared at him, half smiling.

"The rotting of the ceiling started with a hole," he replied in confusion. He could see innumerable mayflies swarm in through the window.

2

More than a dozen big bats perched on the wall of the "S" office building. Their bellies were full of human blood. When old lady Qi dumped rubbish at midnight, she noticed the bats hanging on the wall like a dozen black flags. Something shrieked in the wind. The whole scene was gloomy and gruesome.

"A sound is calling me 'old classmate,'" she said. "It's a weird sound. It resembles a human voice but also something else. When I listen carefully, the sound disappears. I believe it's the crying of a bat. Does this mean that Wang Si-ma is a bat? I've wondered for a long time how Wang Si-ma could stick to the wall. I've never thought that only a bat can hang on the wall!"

"But how can Wang Si-ma be the district head at the same time?" Yuan Si's wife asked anxiously. "And how can the district head turn into a bat? Isn't the district head a human being? You're making fun of me, right? But wait, I'm really puzzled. I definitely did tie him to my body. It was pitch-black. He mumbled something that I've never figured out. It must have been something profound. I think the idea was very upsetting for him. His body was boiling hot and wet through. He was pitiful. Yesterday, I heard people say that Wang Si-ma is, in fact, Zhang Mie-zi. Please don't tell others about it."

"Once a butcher came to Yellow Mud Street. Pork fat oozed

from his back. One opinion says that Zhang Mie-zi's little hut was ruined by the night soil. Why do I get up every midnight? It's the problem of the spy that disturbs my sleep. I'm dying to find some clue."

A mob gathered in front of the "S" office building. They glared at the gray wall with their straw hats on. Because people used to pour water out the windows, under every window there was a slippery spot.

The direction of the wind had changed. It was now a west wind blowing thick black dirt like a storm. The wind smelled of fish.

Nobody could really tell if there were bats on the wall. The crying, a choking and sobbing, was carried by the wind from the cemetery. A bird screeched strangely from a crevice in the eaves.

"A black wing is sticking out of the second window," old lady Song told a woman in the crowd nicknamed Excellent Situation. The woman had only half a face, the other half having been cut off by something.

"The whole truth has come out concerning the case of Wang Si-ma." Qi Er-gou was suddenly startled. "The crows on the iron gate are making suspicious movements."

"Eh?"

"It's said that more than ten rats are buried under every wall."

"The shouting of the barber last night was particularly horrifying. It seemed he was hiding in some corner right in the house. I had to cover my head with the bedsheet, but the sound still penetrated. What a mad year!"

"According to Director Wang, the bats have something to do with the remaining problems."

"The problem of bats is a signal!"

Old lady Qi shouted through cupped hands, "Beware of spies! Beware of spies!" When she approached Excellent Situation, she was suddenly struck dumb. The woman was squatting on the ground, her butt naked, fishing clothes out of a wooden basin to wash.

That night, Old Yue was awakened by a clatter as if many things were bumping against the windows and the door. "The bats," he remembered. He felt uneasy. But as he stretched out his legs, he was distracted by the cold quilt.

"Shall we sleep under the bed . . . " his wife said, half asleep. Her heavy body made the bed squeak. After tossing and turning for a long while, she belched several times and went back to sleep.

"Puh!" Something dropped in the darkness. Turning on the light, he found a bat struggling on the ground, its tiny ugly head turning back and forth. He got up and stamped on it with his leather boots. "Squeak—" The little thing screamed and stopped moving. He smashed it with his heel.

"Throw it into the night stool to drown it," his wife advised him.

"There are so many bats outside." After the exertion, he stretched his body. "I'm afraid they might break the window."

"Have the authorities declared their position about the Committee? You've been waiting for so long without any results! Someone has spread the news that there's no case of persecution on Yellow Mud Street . . . Why? Snails are crawling on the wall of the 'S' latrine. Why is that? Had you not taken the lead to wipe out the moths, there would not have been many more things growing. It seems that nothing is right now. A scorpion is hiding in the cupboard. Have you cleaned it out?" She was both belching and sighing, too upset to go back to sleep.

"There must be a bat's nest under the roof. I've climbed up on a ladder and searched for a long time. They say that such bats suck blood from human beings. I felt some kind of bite on my neck as soon as I went to sleep. My head felt numb. Can there be any bats hiding inside the house?" While talking, he was turning everything over with a stick, stirring up a whole roomful of dust.

"I see that it's all a waste of time. Has the bat died yet? These days nothing is to be understood. Yesterday, somebody saw two will-o'-the-wisps. Don't even think of catching them with a hook!

Why should I dream about snails all the time? My stomach feels upset whenever snails occur in my dream. Please give me a cold steamed bun with stuffing."

"Bats are hanging from the eaves. They swing like a curtain in the wind. I've thought about it for a long time, but didn't see until recently the truth that the district head is an escaped prisoner! Just think: a secret investigation in disguise. Once he came to me for eyedrops. His bad eye glared at me gloomily through the slit in the guaze. Long hair grew from his nostrils like the whiskers of a cat. My teeth chattered when I saw his appearance. When he asked me what was wrong, I told him I was suffering from piles . . . Qi Ergou's kitchen has fallen down. He's dug out a whole nest of carpenter ants. I'm so nervous whenever the wind blows. Who's that?"

"Did you say I couldn't swallow centipedes?" Old Hu San was banging on the window frame with a big stick. He stared at him seriously.

"Your daughter is applying to send you to the old folks' home."

"Don't play tricks with me. I am asking you a question. Someone heard you say I couldn't swallow centipedes. May I ask what evidence you have? I discovered long ago that you are insanely jealous of me. You resent every success I have. Whenever I'm in the limelight as a result of my own skill, you spread rumors and slander, attempting to put me to death . . . Test me on the spot!" He poked at the window with force, and a piece of glass crashed out. One more jab, and another piece dropped.

"You're not allowed to run about once you enter the old folks' home," Old Yue said, climbing quickly to the attic. "Please use five centipedes for the experiment! Let's start at once! Even with ten! I can swallow as many as you can supply!" He jabbed the attic ceiling with his stick and shouted, "I'm going to show you strong evidence! Only a cur will desert on the eve of battle!"

The attic was full of bats hanging in neat order along the ceiling. Old Yue believed the bats had grown out of the several piles of ashes that could be found in the attic. After looking around, he picked up an old broom and started knocking the bats down. They dodged everywhere. Several dropped to the floor and were stomped to death under Old Yue's foot. One was seriously wounded. It flopped under a broken wheelbarrow. Old Yue picked up a shoemaker's awl and stabbed the little creature in its furry back. The awl drove through and pinned the bat to the floor, its tiny eyes popped out of its sockets. Old Yue looked out the window and saw flocks of bats completetly covering the setting sun. The sky darkened immediately. "A bat's eyeball is just like a human's," he thought. The dirt in the attic crept into his nostrils and made him sneeze.

Qi Er-gou was grinding away at his knife again.

"The sulfa eyedrops have cured him." Iron soles clattered along the street. Twisting, bony bottoms flashed through the window.

"Two bats are falling!" the wife was yelling downstairs. "I've dropped them into the night stool, but they're still flopping in there! The sky is full of bats. The room is so dark I have to turn on the light! Please check the window and see if they can sneak in!"

Before bedtime, he strolled around outside for a long time. Through old lady Song's open window, he could see a fog inside and hear the sound of splashing water. A dim oil lamp swung in the wind. People inside were chuckling. The old lady was doing something under the light with her head bent low and her hands waving up and down. Old Yue moved over quietly and hid himself in the shadow beneath the window.

"Anything can grow in Yellow Mud Street." The old lady was talking to someone. "Once I put a wool sweater in the chest and forgot to wash it. The next year when I opened the chest, the sweater had disappeared! It had turned into a fishnet. Worms as thick as a person's finger were crawling over it. So I threw it into the fire, where it crackled for a long time! Even today it gives me goosebumps to talk about it."

It turned out that the old woman held a wet dead bat in her hand. She was patiently plucking its fine fur.

"A rat has bitten off half my toe," an invisible man said.

"The whores in Yellow Mud Street must be rounded up at one fell swoop. They should be thrown into the incinerator." It was the voice of the husband, who rasped as though a glob of sputum blocked his throat.

After this, the people inside made a joyful melee, accompanied by a lot of kissing sounds. It seemed they were fighting over the bat. They dashed here and there, making faces at each other and playing hide-and-seek, until a thermos bottle was broken with a big bang.

"The bats this year are fat and tender," Old Yue popped his head in the window and said smilingly. "Some of you might remember the case of Wang Zi-guang. Since the investigation and analyses of Secretary Zhu have become widely known, many vicious people have taken advantage of the situation. I think if we had dealt with Secretary Zhu's report in accordance with the principle of dividing everything into two and controlling the key terms,* the situation would have developed in more hopeful directions. In short, the case of Wang Zi-guang was a severe lesson for us. The idiots on Yellow Mud Street have messed up the whole thing, putting us into a hopeless deadlock."

"The Committee problem must be investigated thoroughly." The old lady was staring at him with one eye. She had obviously thrown away the thing in her hand.

"I have discovered someone is fooling around with people. This is a serious problem," the invisible man said glibly.

"I've sent a report to the district about the problems of whores in Yellow Mud Street," the husband said with a triumphant air,

---

*A key Maoist concept and practice.—TRANS.

while still hiding in the darkness. His teeth squeaked with chewing as if he were eating the bat.

"There are so many bats. Can we try to cook them and eat them?" Old Yue narrowed his aged eyes, trying hard to detect the situation in the room.

"We've put cement tiles on the roof." The old lady's voice was heard over the splashing of water. "Nobody dares to come in for fear a tile will drop on him. It's far less safe than the straw roof before. Don't come in here. I have the feeling the tiles will fall at any moment."

Bats flew overhead. Dust arose. Everything looked dim and vague.

Under the bluish light of the bar, the shoulder pole of the barber appeared again, the razors sparkling.

"Several bats have died since you left. They're all in the night stool now. It can't hold any more," the wife came over and complained. "Where are they from? Our window's been closed tightly. Not even a mosquito can squeeze in . . . "

"Don't sleep too deeply at night. The bats will suck your blood."

The pop-eyed barber was asking someone in a fierce tone, "Close-cropped or bald? Shave, or a shave-and-a-wash?"

The next night, Old Yue's wife woke up in pain. She discovered her hand had been nailed to the bedside. Blood dripped alongside the bed.

"Save me!" she screamed, half awake.

"I've thought of trying for a long time," Old Yue's cynical voice was heard from the shadow in the corner of the room. "Blood is streaming down from the nail hole like a fine string."

The next day, Old Yue disappeared. People said his disappearance was the continuation of a certain case.

While Qi Er-gou was sharpening his knife in his doorway, old lady Song came. Her back was bent low and her face all black.

"More than ten big bats have been crucified. The wall of the 'S' office building is dyed bloody red! What does the disappearance of the man mean?" She blinked her eyes, looking worn out from sleeplessness. "I feel so agitated that I want to bite somebody."

Qi Er-gou put down his whetstone and yawned several times before saying, "I feel so drowsy." The mosquitoes from the latrine swarmed around him and left numerous little welts on his neck. He pulled off his shoes and climbed into his bed, letting the black net down. So many problems were bothering him. He had just decided to think them over when he dozed off. He had several dreams about his body's becoming swollen from mosquito bites.

"Old Yue is hiding in a crevice on the roof of the office building. He comes out every night to kill bats," somebody was saying. Yellow Mud Street residents looked toward the sky and pulled in their necks. They put their hands into their sleeves and said, "It's a bit chilly." Shivering, they sneaked back into their small huts.

Not long after that, dead bats were discovered in the latrine in "S" factory. There were several dozen of them, and each had a nail driven through its neck.

At midnight old lady Qi noticed a black figure on the garbage heap. The figure was floating, not walking like a human being. She intended to catch up and find out more when a pool of blood splashed down from the sky. Her shoes were bloodstained. "The shoes are still in my basin for washing. I can see it's the same problem of thousands of human heads." She peeped around nervously. "Such a threat is simply endless, driving people nuts. Have you heard about Jiang Shui-ying's clandestine love affair?"

Yellow Mud Street residents had bolted their doors tight and made snoring sounds even when they were awake. Their windowpanes shook with the noise.

Old lady Song was cooking bats at home openly. The tempting smell wafted out her window from morning till night.

"Catch that fireball! There's a fireball!" Old Hu San was so afraid of going to the old folks' home that he pretended to be crazy every day and shout at people from his window. He mistook every passerby for the district head. He would grab the man with all his strength and start jabbering, "That was such a good time! The grass on the roof was as tall as a man. On the street the blind fortunetellers sang at midnight. Good fat meat flew out of the sewage! When can the rebels regain power? I've lived for eighty-three years, but I still don't want to die. Hey, what do you think of it? Eh?"

Qi Er-gou squatted beside the latrine catching mosquitoes and flies to feed the bats. He was raising more than a hundred in his attic. They were all big and fat. Old lady Song came every dusk for bats.

"The weather is so bad," she would sigh loudly, putting on an air of anxiety. "The general mood of society in Yellow Mud Street is a big problem." Qi Er-gou agreed.

Her leather shoes clattered as she climbed to the attic with perfect assurance.

"The old lady is fat and tender from eating bats," Qi Er-gou's wife said in envy. "They say she only sucks the blood without eating the meat. Otherwise she wouldn't need so many every day."

Qi Er-gou popped his eyes toward his wife and said. "There's a thick layer of dirt accumulating behind your neck. Why don't you wash it when you clean your face? An ant has built a nest there. I hear the chewing sound at night."

3

By the time Qi Er-gou returned from killing the flies beside the latrine, the water had overflowed the threshold of the kitchen. Through the window lattice he could see his wife, her rear end high in the air, struggling to plug the crack in the wall.

When the rain came during the evening, it seeped in through a small crack in the wall. But it was a slow leak, since the crack was only the width of half a finger.

"We have to find some way to plug it, or the house might collapse. This damned weather." His wife searched endlessly in the chest for rags as she spoke. The harder she tried to stop up the hole, the bigger the crack got. Trickles of dirty water seeped into the kitchen. During the night, she got up every half hour to plug the crack with a fresh handful of rags. This went on all night. By morning, the crack had widened to nearly a foot.

"Stop! Forget about plugging the damned crack. The wall is beyond saving. It was already about to collapse when last year's rains came." In disgust Qi Er-gou pulled his quilt over his head to block out the annoying light and cursed at his wife. "The more you plug it, the faster it collapses!"

The water spilled over the threshold, but his wife would not give up her efforts. Her mind was as small as a soup spoon. Once she formed a notion, she would follow it persistently, like an earthworm digging deeper and deeper into the mud.

Qi Er-gou had barely sat down when old lady Song came in with a big basket. "I'd like to go upstairs and look for something." She waded toward the stairs. Soon a banging could be heard from the attic. She must be catching bats.

"That wall is going to fall on your ass," Qi Er-gou said to his wife. He kicked a clump of rags into the air.

The woman rubbed her dirty hands with a piece of rag. Her fingers had turned pale from being soaked in the water. She entered the bedroom with her head hanging low. The noises emanating from the bedroom sounded as if she were fighting with someone. This lasted until noon.

"Tomorrow I'll knock the wall down," Qi Er-gou said while eating lunch. "It's too bothersome. The kitchen is merely an extra, a breeding ground for roaches and rats. It's much better to cook in the bedroom. Hey, what's wrong with the taste of the rice?" Throwing down his chopsticks, he glared at the bowl.

His wife, continuing to eat indifferently, replied, "Nothing. I used the sewer water for cooking. It wasn't very dirty. You've already eaten two bowls of rice. Why did you just now notice the taste?"

"Ha—you intend to poison me, eh? You don't mean to poison me at all, right? Woman are queer! A woman is a little spotted dog!" He stuck out his tongue and laughed loudly. "One bat upstairs has grown as big as a child's stool. You should go have a look!"

"The moon these days is so big, big and yellow," she said absentmindedly. She twisted her neck and continued in a worried tone, "When the moon is up, a beam of light appears vaguely on the window frame, as if something were walking outside. There's always something wandering on our street at night."

When the legal medical expert came to inspect the corpse, Director Wang was in the room feeding his black hen. The hen was purple-black with a fat body and only one eye. Every day it pecked rice from his palm. His hand felt the pain of the pecking. Once he had a sore on his foot that ran with pus for three months. The one-eyed hen circled his leg several times before it pecked right on the sore. It picked out a worm. Afterward, a bean sprout grew in the sore. After feeding the hen rice, he continued the meal with a pile of roaches he had caught that morning.

Old Yue poked his tiny head through the window. "There's a long nail in his nostrils. His face is as purple as an eggplant. The fact is he's raising more than a hundred huge bats in the upstairs of his house. At night they fly out to suck human blood. Everybody knows that his catching flies in the latrine is only meant to fool people. To whom does the series of problems on Yellow Mud Street lead? Where do you think I've been all these days? To tell the truth, I've been hiding in the air-raid shelter. I've discovered how mysterious the problems of Yellow Mud Street are. For example, several families keep their lights on from midnight till dawn. Besides this, there's the problem of the bats—the water in the air-raid shelter is very deep and there are so many bats, simply terrible! Every midnight, I stroll along Yellow Mud Street."

Director Wang said nothing while giving Old Yue a good look up and down and wondering what he was talking about. Finally he said, "Do you think this hen can solve the problem? She can almost understand human talk. Of course, she once had an infected eye, which finally went blind when the pus dried up. Still, she's an unusual chicken. Yesterday I devoured eight steamed buns. Something's wrong here. The worse the pain gets, the hungrier I become. Why? Am I going through a critical change?"

"He was killed by a nail driven through his nostril. Isn't that odd? Odder still, there was no motive for the crime. Who drove the nail? Did he do it himself?"

"That's very possible. This is certainly a highly representative case. I will prepare a file on it so as to report to the district." Director Wang suddenly felt agitated. Kicking away the hen, he said in a loud voice, "It's a bitch!"

"He had been very gloomy lately," Old Yue recalled. "At the time, a blue light was shining on him. I saw him tearing the leg off a bat. He looked crazy. On the night of his death, his wife had a dream that three beans were buried in a jar. What omen did the dream carry? The rumor is going around that a huge python is hiding in the sewer. Shall we dig up the ground to have a look? I feel distraught. The weather is no good these days, either. The wind is simply not right. To tell you the truth, I'm fed up with the present general moral mood. There's a crack in the wall of Qi Ergou's kitchen. Have you been there to inspect?"

"*A crack?*"

"A crack as wide as your foot."

"The chicken is shitting in the cupboard!" Director Wang jumped up and shouted in disgust, "Come on, people! Is everyone dead?"

The crack looked ordinary from the outside. A big clump of rags, dripping dirty water, was stuck in it.

When the district head rode his bicycle toward Yellow Mud Street, the people on the street suddenly realized *he was a real person, though not Wang Si-ma*. They felt relieved, as if a boulder had been lifted from their hearts. As a result, they returned to their old habits of teasing and making obscene jokes with each other, playing the fool, making all kinds of faces, shouting at each other, making empty shows of strength and so on. They became extremely ugly and frivolous.

"Are there rats in this room?" the district head asked. Frowning, he pulled the stinking rags from the crack one by one. After long observation and scrutiny, he finally made up his mind. Bending down, he stuck his shriveled head near the edge of the crack to study every inch of it. His face was now covered with mud. After he straightened up and looked at the people around him, he said sharply, "So that's the case!" Then he put on the air of having urgent business and hurried away to the district with his black briefcase under his harm.

"So that's the case!" people echoed. They stopped their fighting and joking to stare with admiration at the back of the district head. "The district head has on a pair of 'Labor' brand overshoes."

"I have the feeling he's found something." Qi Er-gou's wife hunched her shoulders as if she felt cold. She sniffed two dribbles of mucus back into her nostrils.

Old lady Song squatted at the wall and stuck her head near the crack as the district head had just done. Then she got up and spat dirty blood from between her teeth. She said with a sigh, "There are bats in the house."

"Isn't it very strange?" Old Yue's voice sounded as if it came from the crack.

While the rumor of murder was spreading, Jiang Shui-ying was cutting her toenails. They were long and sharp, very much like chicken claws. After she finished one foot, she lit a cigarette. She was about to pick the dirt from her fingernails when Yang San came in.

"So that's the case!" he said.

"Mmhmm," Jiang Shui-ying agreed vaguely. Lowering her head, she continued picking at her nails.

"It is known to all that the moon that night was big and yellow, as if a plot were brewing. When the district head came to Yellow Mud Street, he was wearing 'Labor' overshoes . . . So that's the case!"

"Someone wants to . . . "

"I've been to court once. The judge never used 'murder' when he was talking about murder. Can you guess what terms he used? It was absolutely weird! He said, 'A horn grows on the head.' Those clever devils. You can never understand their meaning. I believe the key lies with the crack in the wall."

"True, the crack in the wall. Someone wants to . . . "

"Doesn't the shape of the crack resemble a foot? Why did the district head bend his head so close to the crack? Attention should be paid to walls. As soon as I arrived home, I inspected my walls carefully."

"He caught another cat the day before yesterday. The cat seemed mad. It meowed every night. Can you fix it for me?"

"Hand me a knife."

When they approached the cage, the wildcat was twitching and huddling up in a ball. Green foam dripped from its mouth.

"No, it can't be done." Distracted he walked back toward the house. "Such a cat has a soul. I can see that. You'll never sleep again if you kill it. One of my relatives killed a cat with a soul, and he heard a cat meow every night for three years running. When I saw him, he was all skin and bones."

"What should I do with it? Someone . . . "

"Just keep it. It might recover."

Jiang Shui-ying was still thinking about the mad cat long after Yang San left. At night, the cat scratched at the door attempting to enter the room. It scratched and meowed the whole night. The wretched sound was terrifying. Toward dawn her husband caught it and threw it into the cage again. Her husband caught everything: a bird, a snake, a small pig, a dog, anything he could lay his hands on. He shut them in the cage till they were starved to death. She couldn't figure out the cage, which was tall and spacious, made of strong wooden bars. Its four legs resembled those of a buffalo. It stood in the back yard like a fiend. At midnight, when the cat was meowing, Jiang Shui-ying saw her husband staring at her insidiously, as if looking at some monster. When she woke up, he told her in an unctuous tone, "Somebody's hut has collapsed again." Pretending that he wanted to watch it, he went to the window.

She replied in confusion, "The wind is blowing through the cage. It's cold inside."

The man turned his back to her and said, "Women are as stupid as pigs." Turning off the light, he got back into bed.

In the darkness, she was quite happy she had exposed his trick. Yang San's words came back to her, and she got up and felt the wall all over. Still she felt insecure. Finally, she decided to give up trying to sleep and shuffled out to the street instead. Early in the morning, she saw Yuan Si's wife and a bald man dash into Yuan Si's house like a pair of wild cats. The back door banged shut.

About twenty stealthy-looking men squatted in front of Qi Er-gou's kitchen wall. The district head was bent over measuring the crack. He moved a vernier caliper up and down clumsily. "It doesn't look like human digging." He blinked his grayish white eyes. His forehead was dripping with sweat. "Are there any wild animals around here?"

"It doesn't look like human digging!" Yang San rubbed his fingers with excitement. He lowered his voice and whispered into the long, bony ear of the district head, "*That thing? Some people here say you are Wang Si-ma!*"

"What?" The district head's face changed color.

"Some one is spreading the rumor," Yang San raised his voice, "saying you are Wang Si-ma, and Wang Si-ma is you. You're mixed together, and there's no way to distinguish the two."

"No way to distinguish!" The district head thumped his chest in regret. He shouted, "Please pay attention to the implications of such a ridiculous fallacy: No way to distinguish! These villains are misleading the pubic! Vicious, mean characters! Comrades, let me remind you again that the obstacle to the solution of the Yellow Mud Street problem is unimaginably big. We have to retreat in order to progress. The struggle is just starting . . ."

"The corpse is rotting. Do you smell it?"

"'That thing' has been here four times," old lady Song said. For some reason, her eyes were full of yellow secretion which accumulated faster every time she cleaned them. "Now my house is covered with cement tiles. They clatter whenever the wind blows. What's the matter now? It seems everything is going wrong."

"The problem of Yellow Mud Street has to be solved before December." The district head was determined. He went over to push his bicycle.

Jiang Shui-ying was watching the mud-stained "Labor" overshoes. She said in a frightened voice. "There's a cage in my house. Someone wants to . . . What kind of problem is this?"

"Everything will be solved eventually." The district head raised a hand and chopped it downward with determination. While talking, he got on his bicycle.

When Jiang Shui-ying shuffled back home and lay down, the sun was peeping in brightly through the tiles. For a long time, she wondered if there were any leeches on the district head's shoes. Then she fell asleep. In her dream, a roach chewed a hole in the wallpaper and poked its little black head out. It chewed slowly until, gradually, its body emerged. It crawled down along a water stain toward her pillow. One of its legs brushed her neck. She swatted at it and woke up to see her husband stretching out his hands to throttle her. "Oh—oh—," she moaned. The man withdrew his hands and gave a dry laugh.

Looking outside, he said, "I think the cat is not going to die. At night a cat's meowing can improve sleep. Yesterday I saw it chewing wood in hunger, so I fed it a fish. This morning, it ate another fish. Tonight it's going to meow harder. I'm going to feed it a fish every day."

"So he's fully recovered. Isn't it a miracle?" The mocking remark of Director Wang's wife was heard outside the window. "I see that people like him can never die!"

After a while, Director Wang was heard saying as he walked, "Now I can eat nine steamed buns with stuffing. I don't feel well. Is there any medicine? Am I done for? Eh?"

"Tomorrow morning I'm going to whip this cat to death with the branch of a tree. It's lived long enough. Why should I feed it?" The man was talking. He was still looking outside toward the yard, deep in thought. Wrinkles piled up on his forehead.

A billow of smoke floated into the room from somewhere. The air became blue with the smell of mosquito-repellent incense.

"That's the smell of burning corpses in the incinerator," the man said, showing his long front teeth.

That night the cat yowled again. This time the sound was even more horrifying. It sounded as if the cat was chewing the bars of the cage. Jiang Shui-ying dashed to the street clutching her head with both hands. Her mind was full of red eyeballs and green eyeballs.

"Tomorrow morning I'm going to whip it to death," the man said in front of the window.

4

Old Hu San staggered down the street. After every few steps, he stopped to ask loudly, "This year is . . . which year?"

The Yellow Mud Street residents were startled. Poking their tiny wrinkled faces from the dust-covered windows, they replied as if in echo. "This year is . . . "

The sun cooled down. The crows and sparrows shivered. The oxalis and wormwood withered and yellowed.

"What's the matter with the sun? Something is wrong!" Yang San-dianzi smashed a wineglass on the street and continued talking as he walked. "The sun used to be so fierce. It burned the maggots out of everything! Now all the cactuses are dead. Where's the grass on the roofs? My joints are as swollen as steamed buns! Once we had a grievance committee. Everyone went there to appeal. Spittle flew in all directions . . . "

Yuan Si's wife and the bald man squeezed the upper parts of their bodies through the window of the hut. Rubbing their baggy eyes, they yawned in a singsong tune. Then they started weeping. "Wu . . Wu . . . "

"Everything on Yellow Mud Street is deteriorating gradually," old lady Song mumbled. She glanced at the cement tiles on her roof. "What are those tiles made of?" The tiles looked bare, but a layer of mud and sand was collecting on top of them. They made a strange sound in the wind as if they were about to break loose and crash down. A few days before, she measured the house and found it had already sunk about ten inches into the ground. As a result the doorframe touched her head, and her husband had to stoop over to get into the house. Yesterday, when he had gone out to clean the night stool, he forgot to bend down. He banged his head on the door frame, and spilled the night soil on his body. In a rage, he smashed the night stool with his feet and let the contents flood the doorway. All morning he sat on the threshold and cursed. He claimed somebody was plotting against him and said the whores on Yellow Mud Street were maneaters. He also complained that he'd broken his forehead and might die from this, and so on.

Old lady Qi came out of the house after killing the last roach. She found Liu Tie-chui standing in front of the window. He said, "There's a living corpse on Yellow Mud Street." Clicking his tongue, he continued, "Hey! Its legs are moldy. Its eyeballs can still roll around in their sockets. It's wrapped in a bedsheet. Have you heard about the sinking of the houses? They say the ground is going to open like a big mouth and swallow the whole street before closing up again. Yesterday, my wall cracked. I watched it widen all night . . . crack, crack . . . "

"The cold wind this morning again smells of blood. What's your opinion about the problem of chicken claws growing on human feet? Should it be put forward at the meeting for public debate? Someone . . . " She stopped short as her hand touched something hard protruding from her hair. "What's growing on my head?" she mumbled to herself, thinking of looking in a mirror.

"The living corpse turned out to be Yang San's old mother," her husband told her. He stuck out his tongue like a snake. "Hasn't she been dead for half a month? But it seems she's not really dead. Isn't the whole thing mystifying? I must carry out an investigation."

"My head . . . " She suddenly blew up. She banged on the table and screamed in discomfort, "I'll buy a medicine to apply to it! I'm going to die! Thief! Pestilent pig! Everything is hopeless!"

"Which year is this?" Old Hu San's voice was heard outside like the voice of a ghost in the graveyard. "That's a bloodball!" he yelled severely.

"Humph! How could such disease disappear without any after-effects." Director Wang's wife sneered and clacked her metal heel plates unnervingly. "What has the guy who's going under some-body else's name done on Yellow Mud Street? I can see that some people are following him blindly. Pay attention to this problem, everybody."

At midnight, old lady Qi's husband turned on the light and began digging at the corner of the wall with a pick.

Old lady Qi was just returning, puffing cold air as she spoke. "It's pitch-black outside. I saw a snake creep in the window of Yuan Si's wife. I'm not sure if she's raising it in secret. The street is extremely quiet. Every wall is cracking. I'm so worried . . . What are you digging for?"

"A skeleton."

"How can there be any?" she asked. "I've been wondering about the snake. It's certainly not an ordinary snake. Hey, you ought to look around instead of digging aimlessly like this. All the walls are cracking. I heard the sound with my own ears."

Old lady Qi did not wake up until the cock crowed. She found her husband still digging, his broad back in the burlap shaking with the movement. A deep pit had appeared in the corner. Broken bricks and mud were piled in a small hill in the middle of the room. The damp smell of rotted things was choking and suffocating.

"How can there be any?" old lady Qi commented again. She tossed a handful of mud into her mouth. "Who can tell if this is anything more than bluster? I want to go and see the whore Jiang Shui-ying."

When she returned at noon, the man was still digging.

"The sulfa seems to have softened the lump on my scalp a little." A sham smile played across her face. "Now people on the whole street are applying sulfa, believing it can cure every disease. Why don't you try? I have the feeling you've had some trouble recently. When do you plan to finish the digging?"

"There are twenty-four skeletons buried underground," the man whispered to her. He ground his teeth with force.

"What do you think of the situation at present?" Old lady Qi stepped back in fear, rubbing her scalp hard.

"Within this month, more than thirteen major problems are to be solved on Yellow Mud Street," Director Wang was heard saying to somebody outside. "Yesterday I received a report that one family is raising a whole nest of snakes. Hey, what does that mean?"

"The house has sunk about ten inches. The kitchen is useless now. I don't see any hope of things changing for the better." Old lady Song sighed endlessly. "The moon last night was again big and yellow. But it looked dim. I squatted in my yard for a long time with my coat over my shoulders. Yellow Mud Street turns into a dead snake at night, icy cold. In the past, something always grew at night. Eerie yelling and fighting could be heard clearly. At that time, I had a boil on the back of my head, and I couldn't sleep. So I would listen till dawn. As soon as the sun was out, my face turned rosy. Why did that bastard Qi Er-gou commit suicide? In fact, I've worked out an excellent plan to save the whole street. I'm going to carry it out in due time."

"There's no hope in anything." Old lady Qi stuck her head out the window. A moth smashed against her forehead, leaving a pool of yellow fluid.

"What year is this?" Old Hu San asked harshly and jabbed her nose with his stick.

Old lady Qi was numbed by the blow, and her whole body felt weak.

"Someone catching white rats was once here . . . "

"Why should the fireball hang on the windowframe the whole night?" he was asking again. His resounding voice sounded like the hammering of galvanized iron.

"Nothing. Humph! Who is his 'old classmate.' I think there's a spy involved in the Yellow Mud Street problem! Comrades, beware of spies!"

"Ah—ah!" Old Hu San stretched his arms and shouted to the sky, his snow-white hair swinging like a horse's mane.

The frizzy hair of Yuan Si's wife and the bald man's head were seen outside the window. Rubbing their baggy eyes, they chuckled and snickered.

After eating some peppers, old lady Qi felt an itching on her scalp. With one scratch, she peeled off a small wrinkled piece of skin dripping with blood. She peered at it and gave out a shrill cry. Hurriedly she looked into the mirror. Her scalp was wet and had started swelling. Before long it had swollen into a soft bun. It dimpled at a slight touch.

"Do you think it's cancer?" she asked Yuan Si's wife, filled with apprehension.

"The snake has already dropped down. It turns out to be dead! It smells rotten. What cancer are you talking about? I believe it's poison. I've had similar things on my body, also poison. There's such poison everywhere on Yellow Mud Street. Even dogs have it in the same way. They intend to imprison me just because I once almost had good luck. I have to thank the rope. Indeed, how is it that the rope happened to be in the drawer? Just think of it, nothing would have happened without the rope. Yet, the rope did happen to be there! Eiya! It was so funny!"

"Can you cut it open for me with a brick shard? It's so swollen."

"Bah! You can't do that. That's dangerous. You have to wait till it breaks open. Then you can press it clean. You can let out some blood on your palm though."

"The pain is like someone sticking me with a needle from inside." She was hopping on one foot in the middle of the room, her face all purple. After a while, she said, "Now it's better. The whore is shut up in a cage by her husband. Is it because of the clandestine love affair? I said long ago there's no way to change the general moral decadence of Yellow Mud Street."

"My back wall makes a cracking sound. All night I was floating in the black water, and a saw was cutting back and forth through my skull. Old Hu San's shouting in the street is scary. Some people believe he's been dead five days now and it's his living corpse walking the street. But according to old lady Song, the living corpse is not him, but Yang San's old mother. I'm totally confused. Living corpse, bats—I simply can't think about them lest the pinkeye disease start."

"The kitchen has sunk seven more inches," old lady Song's voice came from next door.

"The living corpse is steeped in sulfa water?"

The district head was choked by the dust as soon as he approached the corner of Yellow Mud Street. He coughed loudly and rubbed his infected eyes. He felt as though the dust had condensed into strings of little lumps in his lungs. The passersby huddled together across the street and hid their faces as if they were thieves. The tree from which they once hanged the thief was now dead. The black rope was still wound about it like a dead snake. Crows gave dubious cries. Several people with jars dashed past him and vanished. He scratched his back and remembered the story Old Hu San once told him about pig fat oozing out of the back. Slowly, he closed his square palms into fists and raised them to his nose. He said with determination, "The obstacle of Yellow Mud Street has to be wiped out!"

Old Hu San jumped into the street like a monkey. Grabbing the district head's sleeve, he jabbered, "What's your opinion about the present situation? We have unlicensed prostitutes here. Please count thirteen doors from the corner . . . What do you think of the weather? It's cold. All the ghost-pen mushrooms are frozen to death. Someone is planning to poison me. Hey, have you changed your idea about the incident of my swallowing spiders? In the jars they're carrying, there's sulfa water! Now people are gossiping that I have been dead for five days. Why? Please count clearly: the thirteenth door, on the righthand side . . . "

"Good!" Director Wang appeared in the street with a jar in his hand. He pushed Old Hu San away from the district head and made a face. He whispered to the district head, "Do you want some sulfa water? I've got fifty bottles. They're unopened . . . Now about the effect of sulfa on piles, I've already prepared a report, which will be sent to the district. It is epoch-making . . . Please pay attention. Old Hu San is a living corpse. He died five days ago . . . "

The district head concentrated on picking his nose. He said, "How are you carrying out the thirteen major problems? I believe that looseness and indifference will only lead to doom. Aren't there incidents of bats eating human beings? Do you still keep the tradition of the old revolutionary base area? I'm here to hold an emergency meeting on Yellow Mud Street about the solutions to the thirteen major problems. Have you dealt with the aftermath of Qi Er-gou's death? Shoot! I haven't had any sleep for three days and nights. Party Secretary Liu suggests I prepare not to sleep for five days and nights. Now I'll fall down if anyone gives me a push. I could sleep for seven days and nights!"

"Which year is this?" Old Hu San asked unexpectedly, his voice gloomy and miserable, interrupting the dialogue.

"Ah?" The district head felt his legs give away and his forehead break into sweat. His back felt acutely itchy. "Pah! Can it be fleas?" He took off his cotton-padded coat and turned it inside out at the roadside.

The street was full of people carrying jars. They were all acting stealthy and sneaky.

That night an emergency meeting was held in the blockhouse. The district head droned on till two in the morning, by which time everybody's head hummed. He suddenly opened his eyes in his muddleheaded condition and saw a whole roomful of bees. For some reason, he finally let loose a torrent of abuse. The meeting did not end until he became exhausted from his scolding.

The next morning, one side of the district head's face swelled up. While brushing his teeth, he remembered that one sentence of his abuse—"Liu Ma-zi, skunk, son of a bitch"—should have been "Wang Ma-zi, skunk, son of a bitch."

Old lady Song's kitchen wall collapsed. Inside, bats' bones were found everywhere.

5

The little sun paled. The firmament was as shabby as a ragged tent.

A will-o'-the-wisp burned above the withered grass.

A will-o'-the-wisp shone on the nameless little purple flower.

The walls cracked, about to break.

The sinking huts were shorter than ever.

Carpenter ants bred madly.

Strange, muffled groans arose. Someone asked in a humming voice from underground, "Which year is this?"

The last man with a jar passed down the street. Blood dripped from the edge of the jar.

A cat rolled in the dust, pus streaming from its rotted belly. The shadow of a man whipped the cat ferociously with a branch.

Old lady Qi shuffled to the window and stuck out her head. She complained, "No hope to leave the room in such weather! I wish something would fall from the sky and pile up as high as a man, to block the doorway so we could have a good sleep." She went back to bed and let down the black mosquito net.

Snow never fell in Yellow Mud Street.

Dust fell all year round. The dust tasted salty. It came from the greasy smoke of the crematorium. One morning, the street was coated with white. Some people mistook it for snow, but stepping into it, they found it to be ashes, just dead ashes.

A group of people with their faces hidden sneaked along the wall, leaving a trail of footprints.

"Sulfa can cure cancer," Director Wang said smilingly.

The district head frowned. He asked with a heavy heart, "When can 'S' Factory restore production? How many different opinions are there concerning this question? Please organize a special discussion on this issue. I haven't had any sleep for half a month." He scratched his head. Dandruff fluttered onto his collar. In the afternoon when he went to the latrine, he found dead flies scattered in the corner. A decayed footboard was breaking. Yellow urine was pooling on the ground.

"Despite the fact that four people have been assigned to take charge of the hygiene of this latrine, similar problems occur every now and then," Secretary Zhu said quietly, as if telling a secret that weighed on his mind. Lately he appeared restless. Every night, he jumped up and down next door, making all kinds of noise.

The dead Hu San wandered the street every day, yelling, "Spider, so what? Eh? I can swallow it down in one mouthful! Try me right now! Why am I thought to be dead? I used to have a ceiling that grew mushrooms. It was destroyed by the carpenter ants. Though such unfortunate things have happened, who dares to say I can't swallow a spider? I welcome repeated tests!"

Jiang Shui-ying roared in the cage, her blue-veined hands clutching the bars of the cage, her eyes hollowed into two deep blue holes.

Yan Lao-wu spat a mouthful of thick sputum on the street and mumbled to himself, "What time is it? It seems the sky is darkening without even lighting up in the first place. Nothing is clear nowadays."

Director Wang, his cotton-padded coat removed, sat under the chinaberry tree sunning the fat meat on his back. After a while, he began to snore. Old Hu San, bending low, whispered in his ear, "When did it happen? Do you still remember? Two crows were flying in the bloodred light. All at once they smashed dead against this windowpane. You were not around at the moment. . . . Someone locked the door. The room was so damp that ghost-pen mushrooms flourished on the floor. I'm determined not to die! I've had enough misfortune in the past. The ceiling fell down. I fled like a wolf. They were overjoyed by this, believing I was done for. Hmmph! I'll give a public show of swallowing spiders today in order to shatter certain people's willful fantasies. I already have the psychological weaknesses of certain people in mind."

The district head slept in the "S" office building. Swarms of flying creatures bumped here and there at midnight. He covered his head with his quilt. Then the ceiling cracked. A bunch of dead flies fell down, piling up on the floor like a small grave mound.

Secretary Zhu stuck his head in, complaining while sniffing back cold mucus, "A thief outside my room fooled with my door bolt all night. I had several spells of cold sweat. Just now I tossed a shoe at the door to scare him away. Did you hear the thump? How many flies are there in this building? Look at this pile. How strange."

Yellow Mud Street simply couldn't escape its endless dreams.

They dreamed of spiders and flies; they dreamed of green grass at the foot of the wall, of long-horned beetles with spotted backs, of little purple flowers; they dreamed of everything having to do with summer. Bats and wasps flew over their heads. Their snores reverberated in the little pitch-black huts, shaking and cracking the black, dirt-covered windows. The little sun was pale, and several rust-colored clouds hung motionlessly over the ragged umbrella-like roofs.

They woke from their dreams with waxen faces and baggy eyes. They mumbled in confusion. "What did I dream this time? Now I'm really done for. My head bleeds night after night. It must have bled more than a barrel of blood."

"This dream is lifelong once it starts."

"Sometimes I try to wake up, but in vain."

"With such high blood pressure, I hope I won't die in my dream."

"The quilt is moldy. The smell of mildew sends me into dreams."

"Every caw of the crows causes me to dream. How can there be so many crows in Yellow Mud Street?"

The cat with the rotten belly rolled about all the more violently. Big puffs of dirt and dust swirled up in a mushroom-shaped cloud.

"It seems to pull down the wall."

"It's extremely fiendish."

"It rained last night. Leeches are crawling all over the place. They make me shiver. At first I thought they were roundworms from the night stool. It's almost winter. How can there still be leeches?"

The brandy nose of an old man appeared in an open door. Flipping a gob of snot into the middle of the street, he complained, "What weather, deadly weather!" He shut the door again.

Old Sun came back from jail in September and hanged himself on the iron gate of "S" factory. No one saw the corpse, but his voice was heard in the dark of night, "There's an imperial robe. It's true, comrades. What do you think about this? How's the situation at present?" The moon cast its ghastly, bloodcurdling light on the sharp barbs of the gate. Flocks of bats cast huge shadows on the ground.

Jiang Shui-ying's husband put one foot on the cage and stared at the sky, saying, "It's been like this for a long time. Whatever I catch, I shut up in this cage. What do you think about that? I've calculated that a cat can live for fifteen days, and a rat for thirteen days, but mad dogs never die . . . Bah! She squeezed in herself. Everybody knows she makes trouble all night, jabbering on and on about guessing my plot in her dream. Snoring like thunder, she pretends to be dreaming. Yesterday she jumped into the cage and refused to come out. She said it was a good place to be, much safer than our room. Just now when I was brushing my teeth, I swallowed my toothbrush."

"Can I get sick from eating? Eh? What do you think? How can I eat so much? Eh? Just think, nine stuffed buns in one meal! It's like filling a hole. Like cooping up chickens! Like a spider laying eggs!" Director Wang sighed with surprise, observing his swelling belly with worry and anxiety.

After waking up one morning, every resident on Yellow Mud Street remembered dreaming of an old man with eight legs. His whole body was covered with a hard shell. His belly was green. He crept to the middle of the street like a crab. Stretching out his eight thin legs, he let loose a big splash of excrement. Everyone on the street had had the same dream. How could it be? Nobody could explain it.

"Such weather. I'm so sleepy!" Sitting down on their thresholds, they fell into a bad mood. They stared gloomily at the street. "Five crows have floated up from the bottom of Pure Water Pond."

"Recently, I've lost confidence in the problem of the garbage station," old lady Qi said softly. "It seems so meaningless. I can't stand the social mood here. Someone is raising poisonous snakes at home. Have you noticed that? My biggest weakness is my too-strong sense of righteousness. There was a time yesterday when I felt so blue I wanted to give up."

"You're stirring up a whole roomful of dust. You want to choke me to death, don't you?" Qi Er-gou was heard talking in the darkness. "Such disturbance day after day is a way of killing a person, isn't it?"

The woman was banging around under the bed. "A rat has given birth to a whole nest of babies. I'm going to stamp out the source of the problem," was her muffled reply. It was cold and damp under the bed. She was feeling around with her hands, pursuing the squeaking sounds. She was nervously poking her hands under the bed when suddenly her fingers felt numb and hot.

"I feel I'm sleeping in a grave," the man was saying again. "In fact, I'm dead. I never thought of that before."

"Comrades," Old Yue was pointing at the dim, shadowy circle

outside the window, "how can the sun become like this? Shouldn't it be big and red? It's really supposed to be both big and red, big and . . . Which year was it that we planted trees in the city?" His voice dropped gradually into a whisper. "This world is making giant strides . . . " The roofbeam cracked loudly. Old Yue's face changed color. "Damned cement tiles. Is it necessary to hide?"

The district head walked down the street. Two sulfa-poisoned patients lay along the curb. They were having a contest to see who could spit the highest. When the sputum fell back into their own faces, they made a fuss, yelling and rolling around, smearing their faces with dirt.

"We've been taken in once." They quieted down when they saw the district head. "Sulfa is taking our lives away."

"Who are you?" The district head sniffed their poisoned bodies. He was struck by the sweet smell of mixed pickled vegetables.

"Sulfa eyedrops is a kind of bacterial weapon." They were astonished by the district head's ignorance of such an important point.

The pale little circle was about to disappear behind the roof of Wang Si-ma's house.

At that time, spiders stopped spinning webs and fell into dreams also.

Winking his red, rotten, lashless eyes, Liu Tie-chui asked in a low, muffled voice, "What month and day is this? How long have I been sleeping?"

"I smell something. I'm afraid something is floating down the river again," his wife said. She picked her teeth with a match, spitting after every picking.

The pop-eyed barber cut off the head of a rooster, holding the flapping body at arm's length, the blood pooling on the ground.

The blue clouds looked like the coagulated faces of ghosts.

As soon as Director Wang lay down, he discovered a nose popping through the crack in the ceiling. When he jumped up and jabbed at the ceiling with an iron rod, the nose disappeared. Panting and puffing, he lay down again, but the nose reappeared. It had sores on its tip, and it wrinkled up and down, making all kinds of odd contortions.

"What are you jabbing at?" his wife asked with a bitterly sarcastic tone. "Every jabbing sound startles me. I don't think you've recovered from your sickness. Two cancer patients have died. People say cancer is incurable."

"The world is leaping forward . . . " Old Yue's raised voice passed in through the window.

"I've found out," Secretary Zhu said, "that the thief is, in fact, the wind. I paced my room all night. My head was splitting with pain. When will this murderous wind stop?"

The district head was holding his pajama bottoms while looking into a peeling mirror, inspecting first his left side and then his right side. Suddenly he yelped, "This ear has already turned black! Oh, look at the green spots on it. . . . How can things get so bad? Agh! It's the worst, like a head of rotten cabbage! They said this is the nameless poisonous swelling. Tch, tch, nameless. What a place, as dirty as . . . You have to take responsibility for cleaning the toilet. Say, have you worked out those major issues I mentioned to you yesterday? You should think about these things. Some comrades are overwhelmed by victory. Do you want to keep up the tradition of the old revolutionary base area? Eh? What's your opinion?"

"Hush!" Secretary Zhu jumped up and made a gesture. Frowning, he put his ear to a crack in the door. "Again, the wretched wind . . . " He shook his head with disappointment. "A blue corn is growing on my foot. I've broken two razors trying to cut it away. It's hard as a rock."

"How're you coming with the investigation of the woman shut in the cage?" the district head asked. He rubbed his ear and glanced outside cautiously.

"I'm organizing a massive investigation. Someone revealed that the person in the cage is none other than the dead Old Hu San—Lord knows what the truth is. In a word, it's impossible to clarify the problem of Yellow Mud Street completely. I'm considering whether it should be included in the category of moral education. Once upon a time . . . I've emphasized particularly that the good tradition of the old revolutionary base area should be widely propagandized."

In the dead grass, the tiny, nameless purple flower was shining with a dim cold light.

The will-o'-the-wisp floated about, resembling thousands of eyes drifting in the air.

Half frozen, the mosquitoes doddered up and down along the window frames.

A nightmare, like a big black overcoat, paraded in the dim starlight.

Someone was digging in the garbage heap with a rusty spade, making an irritating sound.

The salty dust from the crematorium drifted down.

A figure dashed into the lightless public latrine; then the splashing of urine in a wooden board could be heard.

"In my dreams, I always see scarabs, always scarabs . . . " old lady Song complained in her quilt. On top of the quilt, a baby rat crawled past. "My body aches all over! Why isn't the 'S' Machinery Factory roaring away? Ah? Which year was that?"

At the dim corner of the street Old Hu San narrowed his eyes and in a low voice told a story. "Once upon a time, the sun was as fierce as fire. There were rotten fish and spoiled shrimps everywhere. Maggots grew under the beds. Everything oozed oil and bubbled in the sun. We always slept in the sun and never took off our cotton-padded coats. We sunbathed until we warmed up and sweat dripped from our bodies. . . . Can you guess what year it was?"

Qi Er-gou's wife crept around the house like a crab, collecting every piece of rag and worn-out shoes to block the crack in the wall, which was big enough for a dog to get through. She kept bumping into things and falling heavily to the floor. She groaned with clenched teeth. By dawn her clothes were soaked with sweat. Then she fell into a nap, dreaming of a bat biting her neck. "There are bats everywhere," she yelled in her dream. "Where are they from?"

"Wang Si-ma is back." Yang San yawned and listened carefully to the footsteps in the street.

A nightmare circled in the starlight, a black, empty overcoat.

From the sky came the sound like someone gnawing at bones.

An owl gave a sudden cry, thrilling and soul stirring.

Dust fell from the incinerator like raindrops.

Dead rats and dead bats rotted on the ground.

The pale, shadowlike little ball was about to rise again—into the sky above the roofs of little huts resembling ragged umbrellas.

The little boy's face was scaly like snakeskin. As he stretched out his hand, I saw that it, too, was covered with scales. In the center of the back of his hand was a purple ulcer.

"So many cancer patients have died. They fall like poisoned rats," he told me. He blinked his swollen, rotted red eyes, and concentrated on spitting out the dust collected between his teeth. "There's no such street," he finally said in an empty, dull voice.

As I passed out through the iron gate, a dead rat fell at my feet. The gate was rusty and decayed. I could smell the greasy smoke from the incinerator. I walked on, leaving a damp narrow trail of footprints in the dust. My tracks looked both intentional and random at the same time.

Oil oozed from my back. The hot air jumped on me with swarms of mosquitoes. The water in the sewer blew out big bubbles. When I touched my hair, it crackled dryly as if it were going to burst into flame.

I once tried to look for Yellow Mud Street. I spent such a long time in my search—several centuries, it seemed. The shards of my dream have fallen at my feet. The dream has been dead for a long, long time.

The setting sun, bats, scarabs, creeping oxalis, the remote and strange old roofs. The setting sun glows. This world is both dear and tender. The pale tips of the trees give off a blue smoke. The smoke smells strange. In the distance, dust fills the air like clouds. It envelops the tiny flamelike blue flowers. The blue flowers dance vaguely.

OLD
FLOATING
CLOUD

ONE

1

The paper mulberry's large white flowers were so heavy with rain that they fluttered to the ground every few moments. Geng Shan-wu dreamed all night under the influence of their irritating fragrance, an odor inducing dizziness like the stench of sewer water that sends one into wild spirals of delirium. He saw red-faced women squeeze their heads in through the window. They had long, asthenic necks, and their heads hung down like poisonous toadstools.

During the day his wife, on the sly, made a hook and fixed it on the end of a bamboo pole to pull down the flowers one by one. After mashing them up, she cooked them in a vegetable soup. Bent over her work, with her rear end stuck out, she cooked busily, secretly, evasively, thinking to keep what she was doing under wraps. At night, having drunk this strange concoction, she would rip off a long chain of stinking farts.

"There's a thief crouching in the corner," Shan-wu shouted, puffing and blustering, and turned on the light.

Mu-lan started up, her hair disheveled. With her feet she felt under the bed for her shoes.

"It's only a dream," he breathed in relief. His face bore a mysterious smile.

"Something may happen today," he thought as he was about to leave home. "Besides, the rain has stopped and the sun will come out soon. Everything will be different when the sun is out. It's like a rebirth, a new beginning, a . . . " He searched his mind for grand expressions.

He was startled as soon as he opened the door. The yard was blanketed with gleaming white flowers. The petals beaten down by the rain appeared full of life and sensuality. They stood erect next to each other as though still sucking water from the ground. He tramped angrily on one of those arrogant little things and dug a shallow hole with his toe to bury it in the mud. While he was stealthily patting down the mud, the thin face of a woman in shock flashed past the window and disappeared into the darkness of the room.

"Xu Ru-hua . . . ," he thought in the blankness of his mind. Suddenly he became uneasy because he realized the woman had seen what he was doing. "The odor of the fallen petals is driving people crazy. I thought it was the smell of rotten cabbage," he said in a loud, defensive tone, his head tilted to one side as he scraped the mud from his shoe on the doorstep.

Mu-lan was tossing about in bed. Sighing, she mumbled, half asleep, "That's right. What are these flowers for? My appetite rouses every time I see these cursed things. It's just senseless. I eat and eat and soon become so confused I don't even know where I am. I always imagine I'm lying in a swamp, surrounded by muddy, bubbling water."

A soft sigh floated from the neighbor's dark window. Shan-wu's face felt hot. Lowering his head, he stumbled away, trampling a flower at every step. He dared not look around but fled like a thief. A rat scurried into the sewer ahead of him.

He rushed to the street out of breath, but a pair of eyes seemed to gaze on his narrow back. "Spy," he cursed indignantly. Making sure that there was no one around, he flung a gob of snot to the pavement and wiped his thumb on his coat.

"Who are you cursing?" A boy with a dirty black face stopped Shan-wu. He had a handful of dirt.

"Huh?" The dirt came right at him. Shan-wu felt a slashing pain in his eyeballs.

That morning Xu Ru-hua was also watching the fallen flowers. She had awakened at midnight, hearing her husband cracking something in his mouth.

"Old Kuang, what are you doing?" She was a little startled.

"Eating broad beans," he said, clicking his teeth. "That odor out there is agitating. The rain has rotted the flowers on the tree. Don't you ever dream? According to the doctor, dreaming before twelve o'clock is harmful to the nerves. So I keep a pack of roasted broad beans under my pillow. When I wake up from a dream, I eat some and fall asleep again. I've tried it for three days, and it works well."

Sure enough, in a few minutes he had turned the thick wall of his back toward her and started to snore loudly. In the intervals between snores, she heard her neighbor toss and turn, suffering from some neurosis, the bed creaking under his weight. On the roof, rats scuttled back and forth. The dust they raised settled on the mosquito net. Long, long ago, when she was a girl, she had dreamed of becoming a mother. But when the paper mulberry came into red berries, something in her body dried up. She often patted her belly and joked, "In here grows nothing but reed stalks."

"By dawn the fallen flowers will be everywhere," she nudged her husband awake and shouted in his ear.

"Flowers?" Old Kuang responded, dazed with sleep. "The broad beans are more effective than sleeping pills. You should try them, eh? They work miracles."

"Every petal is soaked with water," she went on, rattling the bed. "That's why they fall so heavily—'bang'—do you hear them?"

Her husband was snoring again.

Small insects wriggled on her chest. A black wind passed through the branches of the tree and separated into several skeins. The tree was a sieve for the wind.

At dawn she opened the window and saw the white flowers on the ground. She sat entranced at the window.

"The broad beans are wonderful. I suggest you try them," her husband's voice sounded behind her. "I had a sound sleep after midnight. I struggled awake just before dawn, when I worried in a dream that a thief had come to rob us."

At that point the neighbor's long thin back appeared. He was concentrating on digging a hole with his toe. Below his cap was a tumor on one of his ears. It quivered with his movements. Xu Ru-hua's mind turned blank.

"Shall we spray some insecticide? The flower odor may attract insects." Old Kuang tapped the edge of the bed with his finger and let out several overnight broad bean hiccups.

At dusk Xu Ru-hua was bending low, spraying insecticide in the kitchen, when someone threw a small wad of paper through the window. Opening it, she found a nearly illegible scrawl: "Don't spy on others' private lives. This is an arrogance more objectionable than direct interference."

Peeping out the window, she saw her mother-in-law walking toward the house with a rolling gait.

"Your place is like a pigsty." The mother-in-law planted herself sternly in the middle of the room, rolling her shifty eyes and snorting loudly.

"I found a cure for neurosis recently." Old Kuang forced out a horrifying smile. "Mother, I've discovered that azure has an ideal effect."

"How dare you play the radio in such stormy weather!" she roared, clapping her hands at the same time. "I once had a neighbor who turned on the radio when lightning was flashing. He was struck and cut in two instantly! You always do something odd to show off!" She stepped over and snapped off the radio. She spat violently as she rocked out the door.

As soon as his mother was gone, Old Kuang shouted in high spirits, "Ru-hua! Ru-hua!"

Xu Ru-hua was spraying insecticide under the stove.

"Why don't you answer me?" Old Kuang looked a bit annoyed.

"Oh!" Ru-hua roused with a start from her daydream and smiled, still in a trance. "I didn't hear you—were you calling me? I thought it was your mother shouting in the other room! Your voice resembles hers so much I can hardly distinguish them."

"Mother's always angry with me. She's gone already," he answered, scowling. His spirits dropped dramatically. "She's right. We simply don't have the ability to live independently."

Ru-hua was still speaking as if in her sleep. "Sometimes when you're talking in the yard, I think your mother has come. Maybe something's wrong with my ears. For example, today I didn't have any idea you were in the room. I thought your mother was talking to herself in a loud voice."

"The old shoemaker down the street grows osmanthus in his ears. It has such a sweet scent." Old Kuang tried to give his spirits a boost. "On my way back from work, I saw a big crowd push and shove until they broke down his door." Moving next to Ru-hua, he made as if to put his arm around her.

"This insecticide is really strong." She shivered, her teeth chattering. "I may be poisoned."

He jerked his arm back and moved a little away from her as though afraid of being infected.

"Your physique is too frail." He swallowed his spittle.

A large white flower floated to the windowsill, quivering vigorously in the dim light.

Shan-wu found the sparrow in a ditch. It seemed it was just learning to fly when it fell. He put the drenched little thing on the table. Its young, delicate heart was still beating. He turned it over and over, thumping it absentmindedly until it breathed its last.

"Big deal!" he heard Mu-lan say behind him. "Big deal!" his fifteen-year-old daughter echoed stiffly. He imagined her pointing her broken nails at his back.

"Some people are unreasonable." Mu-lan changed her tone. "Did you notice the neighbors have built a shed to grow flowers in? It's crazy! I've lived next door to them for eight years, but I can never guess their next thought. I think that woman's treacherous. Every time she passes our window, she's in a trance. You can't even hear her footsteps! How can a person go around without footsteps? A human being should have a certain weight. What else can she be? I'm scared she might break in and murder us. The odor of the paper mulberry leaves no peace of mind."

Geng Shan-wu found an envelope to put the dead bird in. He sealed it with two lumps of rice and patted the seal with his hand to fix it.

"I'm going out," he called, putting the envelope in his pocket.

He circled to the outside of his neighbor's kitchen. Squatting down, he hurled the envelope through the window. Then he returned home with his shoulders hunched.

The woman next door exclaimed, "Oh!" It seemed she was talking to her husband. The sound drifted, unreal, through the cracks in the wall. " . . . at that time. We often played Drop the Hand-kerchief on the lawn. The sun was going down, and the grass was still warm. You might even catch a praying mantis if you were lucky. I often surprised everybody by tossing down a dead rat! Last sum-mer a cricket sang under the bed for three days and nights. I'll bet it died of mental and physical exhaustion."

In his mind Geng Shan-wu saw a pair of woman's eyes, deep and gloomy like a pond of dead green water. He couldn't stand the idea that these eyes were fixed on his long thin back.

"The paper mulberry flowers are all gone. The heavy fragrance will disappear soon," she continued in an unsuitably high pitch. "Someone must have lost something and is looking for it among the fallen petals. I've seen countless footprints. . . . Are the flowers beaten down by the rain, or are they too impatient to blossom and simply fall? Late at night I pace my room. I see the moon hanging on a branch like a pale yellow ball of knitting yarn."

After a while heavy steps were heard at the door. It was her husband coming back. The woman's voice came to an abrupt stop. So she had been talking to the wooden wall? Or was she reading an endless letter?

For lunch Shan-wu chomped on a lump of cartilage.

"Great, great!" Mu-lan said in appreciation. Her Adam's apple bobbed. She gulped a mouthful of sour soup.

The daughter followed their example, chomping and gulping.

The meal was over. Shan-wu stood up, wiping the soup from his mouth. Picking his teeth with his fingernail, he addressed himself to no one in particular: "The spider on the windowframe has been trying to catch mosquitoes for more than an hour, but how can it?"

"During the workbreak exercise Old Lin emptied his bowels in his trousers," Mu-lan reported. A hiccup brought up a stream of sour soup. She swallowed it again.

"The ribs we had today were not thoroughly cooked."

"But you had tenderloin." She glanced at him in surprise.

"I had tenderloin," he said, still fixing his eyes on the spider. "I mean the ribs."

"Ah!" Mu-lan made a face. "You're tormenting me again."

During the night amid the remaining fragrance, Geng Shan-wu and the woman next door had the same dream. Both saw a turtle with bulging eyes crawl toward their house. The front yard had turned into a mudhole. The turtle crawled and crawled along the edge of the muck on its muddy feet but couldn't reach its destination. When the wind in the tree stirred their dream to pieces, they woke up in a sweat in their own rooms.

When Shan-wu graduated from college, he had his head shaved and carried a military knapsack on his back. Sweat oozed from his armpits. It had a sweet smell. At that time the sun was very bright and the sky was like a huge glass cover. He always squinted.

"I fell into a mudhole last night." The woman was talking in a shrill voice. "My body still feels sticky. At dawn the branch cracked, broken by the wind."

Shan-wu felt puzzled. Why could he alone hear the crazy remarks of the woman next door? Why couldn't Mu-lan hear them? Was she pretending?

Mu-lan kept her head down, trimming the nails on her short fingers. She didn't even raise her eyelids.

"Did you hear anything?" He tried to sound her out.

"Yes, of course," she answered casually without lifting her head. "It's the wind rustling the window shade. That family looks run-down and miserable. The man went so far as to put a glass tank out back with two black goldfish in it. It's childish! I've put up a big mirror on the back wall so I can watch everything they do. It's very handy. I'm disgusted by their raising goldfish."

The trampled flowers had turned black.

As he opened the door, the first thing to catch his attention was the woman's head at the window next door. She, too, was looking at the flowers on the ground. Her eyes sparkled greedily. Her neck was extended so far that she seemed about to jump through the window.

"The flowers are dead." He was surprised to hear himself speaking in a buoyant tone.

"It's gone, the crazy season." The woman's lips moved so slightly it was almost impossible to see she was talking.

"It was really a dreamer's life, day and night . . . but it passed by so fast. In those days, the disturbing flowers drove us mad. Have you ever dreamed . . . " He wanted to go on, but the woman disappeared.

Under the glass cover, everything was a yellow oval shape. The light from outside was dazzling. No shade could be found.

All the dreams were lost amid the flowers.

2

Hesitantly, he opened the door. She sat eating pickled cucumbers from a small dish. On the table stood the jar from which she had lifted the cucumbers with her chopsticks. She chewed softly like a rabbit, paying no attention to him. As soon as she finished the first cucumber, she began the second. Her eyelids drooping, she tasted each pickle attentively. Two trickles of juice ran from her lips. She poked out her tongue and licked them away.

"Let me mention something. Actually, it's not 'something' but a kind of sign," he began, part in inquiry, part in anger. "Frankly, have you noticed anything? Have you had a feeling of foreboding?"

Xu Ru-hua glanced at him blankly. She lowered her eyes and munched her pickles. She remembered that he was her neighbor, the sneaky man who always played some little trick in the courtyard to block her view. At lunch, when Old Kuang saw her eating cucumbers, he was startled and advised her to stop. He believed sour food would damage the nerves. She waited until he left for work, then ate to her heart's content.

"When I saw it in my dream, there seemed to be something sitting under the window. Now I remember what it was. . . . How long do you think it has been crawling in that mudhole?" He wouldn't give up, but persisted in questioning her. "That mudhole, isn't it in our yard?"

"What did the dead sparrow mean?" she asked. She didn't look at him but pulled out a handkerchief to wipe her mouth. "Lately I've been spraying insecticide in the house." Her voice was so cool he felt his head rattle as if filled with stones.

"Well, I've just been a little flustered," he admitted, embarrassed. "You know, those blossoms make everyone perplexed and uneasy. There was a time when I was all right. I even worked on a geological prospecting team. The mountain was very high. And the sun was so close you could touch it. . . . But, of course, it's meaningless to talk about that. We've been living under one roof for eight years, and you see me every day. I've always been like this when you've seen me. The night the turtle came, you were wandering in the room. I heard your bed creak under you. I thought, 'There's a person in that room suffering from nightmares just like me.' The nightmare was attacking our little house. It sneaked in through the window and pressed against your body. . . . Wait until the tree grows red berries. The scarabs will fly over and we can sleep calmly. This happens every year. I like to anchor my pillow with two bricks at night because it can flap suddenly and scare a person. You've sprayed insecticide all day and poisoned the mosquitoes. Don't you feel afraid when something attacks you in the dark? I love mosquitoes humming in my ears as if they were boosting my courage . . . " He rattled on and on and was taken aback when he lost track of what he was talking about.

"I'm going to spray insecticide now," she said, glancing at him. She stood up to get the sprayer. A few paces away, she turned around: "I'm growing a pot of datura flowers. They're said to be extremely potent. Just two blossoms are enough to kill a person. I love the idea. It rouses wild fantasies. Your wife always spies on us in the mirror, right? If you want to talk about what's in your heart, come over often, when I'm in a better mood."

He opened his mouth to say something, but she had already begun pumping the sprayer.

Looking toward the mirror, she saw her image floating in the air. She saw two big shiny grease spots on her chest. She remembered they were made at noon when she was drinking soup absentmindedly. Suddenly she felt ashamed. This was a strange feeling. Why? For something meaningless, perhaps. She couldn't remember. When the man from next door spoke, she felt she herself was talking. She didn't feel surprised by his words at all, but only listened as though to her own voice. She recalled those stormy nights when dark branches stretched in through the window with threatening gestures, jabbing directly at her face. How could the man next door resemble her so much? Perhaps everyone was like everyone else. She could never distinguish Old Kuang from his mother. In her mind she always considered them as one. When she hinted at this, Old Kuang felt uneasy. He worried about her nerves and advised her to go for some kind of therapy, and so on. The day before yesterday, he talked furtively with his mother about tricking her into seeing a doctor. Without doing that, they said, heaven knows what disaster might occur. She had chuckled at their solemn air. Her laugh made them realize she was eavesdropping. Both of them jumped on her, their shame sending them into a rage. Shaking her shoulders violently, they asked her why she was laughing.

"If you go on like this, you'll pay the consequences," her mother-in-law said, gloating over Ru-hua's possible misfortune. "We've done our duty."

Lately, Old Kuang had taken to relieving himself in the sewer at the back of the house. He closed the door tightly, thinking she wouldn't realize what he was doing. When he finished, he pretended nothing had happened. She, too, feigned ignorance, spraying insecticide according to his instructions.

When they married, he was a high school teacher. His hair was cropped, and he was always in a pair of shorts. At that time, he kept bringing home small things such as fountain pens or diary books, saying these had been confiscated from the pupils. Once he even brought home two flowery handkerchiefs that had belonged to girls.

"They're usable after washing," he said.

At first they thought they would have a child, but later she began to feel content with her misfortune. The whole family—she, Old Kuang, and the mother-in-law—always gloated over their own bad luck. Even the furtive man next door had a child. She couldn't help feeling astonished when she thought of it. Little children couldn't be as drifting as adults, could they? This morning she paced around the room naked from the waist up and patted her belly repeatedly.

Old Kuang was furious: "What are you doing?"

"Sometimes," she grinned at him derisively, "I don't think this is a woman's belly. It's nothing but a sheet of skin, some dirty intestines, and some other damnable unknown parts."

"You'd better take a sedative." Old Kuang rushed to her side, almost knocking her down.

She went out back to water the datura flowers. She was struck dumb when she glanced at the fishtank. The two goldfish were floating on their backs. The water was turbid and smelled of soap.

She pressed the fish with her finger, but they remained motionless. Then she saw the neighbor woman standing on her toes in front of the mirror watching her. Slowly she picked up the fish and threw them into the garbage can.

Next time the man came over to talk, she would tell him she used to like oleander. When the sun was so near it could be caught by stretching out the hand, the oleander blossomed with a bittersweet scent. She could dash beneath the tree as quickly as a rabbit! Thinking thus, she gave the plump back of the woman a sidelong glance, her heart full of vicious delight.

"What are you doing back there?" Shan-wu sneaked a pack of biscuits into his briefcase and snapped it shut. "I'm going to work," he called.

Mu-lan came out from the back of the house. She said absent-mindedly, "I poured out a basin of soapy water." Her face was long and blue. "I've been thinking . . . how can it be that I also . . . we still owe the rent for last month."

"You've become sentimental," he sneered as he walked away. He didn't look back until he reached the street and turned the corner. Then he took the biscuits from his briefcase and started to chew them noisily.

His daughter came out of the department store. She was strutting, putting on airs, her nearly bald head raised high. Shan-wu ducked behind a public toilet and watched her cross to the other side of the street.

"She's turned around," a voice whispered behind him. Looking back, he saw his father-in-law. The old man had a sparse goatee with wine sediment clinging to it.

"Of whom are you speaking?" Shan-wu asked stonily.

"Feng-jun, of course. Who else?" His father-in-law winked one bloodshot eye. Putting his long thin arm on Shan-wu's shoulder, he said, "Come on, let's go have a drink . . . on you!"

"Bah!" Shan-wu shook off the old man's arm in disgust. He heard the dry bones scratch and grind against each other.

"Ha-ha-ha! Hide-and-Seek! Eat steamed bread! Ha-ha-ha!" the in-law yelled, dancing and jumping in glee.

Shan-wu felt his face redden and touched his briefcase unconsciously. There were still three biscuits left.

His father-in-law, too, was a spy. Since the day Shan-wu married his daughter, the old man had been digging up information about him. He appeared like a ghost in the most unexpected places and squeezed into Shan-wu's soul. Once, Shan-wu was so angry he leaped at the old man to tie his hands behind his back. Then, just as today, he heard the man's bones creak as if they were breaking. Shan-wu had been startled and had loosened his hold without realizing it. The old man had sprung away like a grasshopper, shouting threats as he fled: "You wait! There will be a fatal revenge!"

"Hide-and-Seek! Eat steamed bread . . . . " the old man was still yelling. Stretching his arm out to the side, he let himself sprawl across a garbage can, chuckling endlessly. Finally, he rushed into a temple. The temple was run-down and no one lived there. He often climbed to the attic and threw pebbles at pedestrians through a small window. When he hit someone, he would scramble down and hide someplace to have a good laugh.

Ten years ago, Shan-wu had put on his khaki tunic and gone to his future in-laws' home to propose. Mu-lan paced heavily in the room as if bursting with youthful vigor. Her mother, farting from indigestion, said, as she faced the long moss-covered wall in the yard, "Bad fortune that I have let a ruffian like you abduct my daughter." Three years later she was lying in the mortuary at the hospital. When he went to see her, she still had her strange look, her eyes bulging out as though she would eat him.

One day after their marriage, they were strolling along the street. Mu-lan bought a bag of plums and was popping them into her mouth. The street seemed endless. Suddenly, she threw herself on him and closed her eyes. Spitting out a pit, she said, "I'm so sad!" Why she felt so sad Shan-wu never understood, even now.

Every time the father-in-law came he would circle the house like a spy. When he found a good chance to hide behind the back door, he called Feng-jun softly and persistently. The two of them talked under the eaves. The sun cast a slanting ray on his red nose. His face looked resentful, and he peered into the house the whole time, hatching some secret scheme. Finally, as he was leaving, he would dash into the room, grab something trivial and flee. When she heard his footsteps, Mu-lan would come out to demand, "Damn it! What has he taken this time?"

Shan-wu reached his office just after finishing the three biscuits. Yesterday he had fed bread crusts that he prepared to the sparrows on the balcony of his office.

An Guo-wei patted him on the rear end and asked, "What's your conclusion about the mudhole problem?" Guo-wei's triangular eyes narrowed. Spitting out his cigarette butt, he sat on the edge of the desk and crossed his legs.

Shan-wu pondered the question all day, but couldn't figure out what Guo-wei meant.

At home after work, he pretended to trim his beard at the door. With the mirror in his hand, he observed his neighbor's movements behind him. He felt a little relaxed after assuring himself nothing suspicious was going on. Maybe his erratic heartbeat gave him away? During the upsetting days of the paper mulberry blossoms, his heart had thumped so hard that it felt like a jumping fish when he put his hand on his chest. He thought everybody could hear the noise. That was why everyone at the office stared at him meaningfully and said in hypocritical tones, "Oh, these days your face . . . "

To prevent people from hearing his heartbeat, he sneaked into his corner as soon as he arrived at the office and looked out the window for hours, feeding sparrows the crusts he had prepared beforehand. Today, stretching his head out the window, he noticed heads at the other two windows. Drawing back, he realized they were his colleagues in the same room. They faced the windows with their hands folded behind their backs as if deep in thought.

Shan-wu slipped stealthily into the corridor and looked into the other offices. He found the same situation everywhere: serious-looking people standing at every window. Others paced back and forth with anxious expressions. Then his colleagues became excited as a big butterfly fluttered in. Its black wings had a dark purple sheen. It circled majestically above their heads. Everyone jumped up like marbles, closing the doors and windows. Two of them beat desperately at the butterfly with feather dusters, and the others jumped and cheered to urge them on. They were red and purple in the face and crazy as drunkards. To cover his stealth, Geng Shan-wu also started yelling and followed the others in acting like a madman.

When the butterfly was beaten down, the two who stood at the windows resumed their serious expressions and sank into their unfathomable daydreams, their heads stuck outside and their hands folded behind their backs. Suddenly it occurred to him that these two who pretended to be so serious stood at the windows every day. Because of his absentmindedness, he hadn't noticed this until now when he had joined them. They stood there like two piles of wood until the off-duty bell rang. Then they picked up their brief-cases to go home. He noticed that even their bearing on the street was rigid; they walked with heads bent low and their hands folded behind them. Their steps were both slow and steady. The sun set on their hunched backs and penetrated their fat trousers. He could glimpse their hairy legs.

"Today I've prepared some well-done bones. You can suck them clear to the marrow," Mu-lan said excitedly, licking the grease from her lips.

"I'm always afraid of spareribs. They blister my tongue." He was poking at the spider's web on the windowsill with a small stick. "Why can't you make something else?"

"I can't think of anything else. The neighbors are cleaning again. I noticed it in the mirror." She gave a snort of contempt. "Fussy every day. Spraying insecticide, cleaning, raising goldfish—nothing but neurotics! The woman has already found out I watch her in the mirror. Have you smelled their foul pee in the back sewer? Shocking! It's said there's a secret recipe for drinking chicken blood. Do you know about it? They say it can make you live forever."

"Well-stewed ribs can also make you live forever."

"You're mocking me again!" She contorted her face in surprise. "When you left this morning I was about to tell you what I was thinking. It's like this. I was sitting at the door and the wind was blowing fiercely. I was thinking—oh, yeah, I was thinking about Feng-jun. This child is very promising. Yesterday I bought her a cheap checkered blouse. Guess what she said. She said, 'Thank you. I don't think I'm a poor beggar.' I've been thinking about that, and I'm pleased. The girl was born with the good quality of being content with her lot."

"She's just like her mother, so promising as to startle others someday," he said sarcastically.

He had hardly arrived home when the dream of the turtle disturbed him again. As he paced the room, his footsteps echoed, and sun-scorched heliotropes appeared in his mind's eye. The shrill, cracked voice of his neighbor woman wafted over on a fine breeze, dry and hot.

" . . . that's right. The hot mud was bubbling like boiling porridge. When it crawled over, it had blisters on its feet, and its eyeballs protruded as if they would drop out. . . . What's the difference between the scent of oleander and that of mountain chrysanthemum? Can you distinguish them? I dare not go to sleep. When I fall asleep, those branches whip at my face so painfully I think I'll go mad. I often wonder how they can stretch in through the window. Haven't I asked Old Kuang to fix the iron bars? I told him it was to protect our house from thieves. I want to have two doors with iron bars. Then the room will be like an iron cage. Perhaps I can sleep only in an iron cage. I'm so tired!"

Mu-lan took the ribs out of the earthenware pot and tore at them with her teeth. Watching her open her huge bloodred mouth, Geng Shan-wu was bewildered and startled.

"What's making that noise . . . " he asked hesitantly.

"Rats. I shouldn't have put away the rat trap. Finally it's gone. The blossoming season is terrifying . . . I thought you might play some tricks."

"What!"

"I'm talking about the blossoms. Why are you staring at me in such a frightening way? These days you get up at midnight and open that creaky door. When you get up, the cold air sneaks in."

"So she's a spy, too . . . " he thought in a daze.

3

Leaning against the door frame, Xu Ru-hua listened intently. A plane buzzed horribly overhead. Since the death of the goldfish Old Kuang had kicked down her datura and nailed up the back door.

"The whole family is enveloped in an aura of murder," he complained to everyone he met. "I owe all this to our inability to live an independent life."

He had become hot-tempered and suspicious. He searched the house day and night in fear of being murdered. Once he jumped up at midnight. Turning on his flashlight, he bent down and peered under the bed for a long time.

The mother-in-law always came wearing a worn-out straw hat and a pair of tall rubber boots. And she always had an iron club in her hand. As soon as she arrived, she cast her eyes around the room suspiciously, even peering cautiously behind the door. When this was done, she stood there nervously, her cheeks twitching, until a rash appeared on her neck.

Once Ru-hua came home only to find the door bolted and the curtains down. She tried to break open the door, but in vain. She peeped in through a corner where the curtain was curled back. The room was filled with smoke. With their teeth clenched, the mother and son were "exorcising evil spirits" by waving the iron club. She could hear their whispers, but too faintly to tell which voice it was. A moment later, the door creaked open. The old woman came down the steps supported by Old Kuang. Both kept their heads low as if in a dream and sleepwalked past her.

Having "exorcised the spirits," Old Kuang fixed a bell on the door, saying it would ring if a thief and murderer came in. They waited and waited. No murderers came, but they shook with fright whenever they themselves set off the alarm.

When visitors came, Old Kuang lowered his voice and complained that he could no longer live in such fear. Already having an early stage of heart trouble, he might be frightened to death by one of the unexpected terrors. Since the exorcism, the mother-in-law no longer came to visit them. Instead, every two or three days she sent her nearly bald niece to deliver a note. This niece wore a round blue hat all year. Her hair looked queer, and she was always chewing something in her toothless mouth. The notes said things like, "Be on guard of the spies around you!" or "Before going to bed, remember: (1) Wash your face with cold water (not including your neck); (2) Put three pebbles under your pillow"; "Maintain proper bearing while walking. Never look around, especially toward the left"; "Take an antiphlogistic (can be replaced with sulfanilamide) before going to sleep"; "Looking into the distance can ease the fatigue of the lower limbs," and so on.

Old Kuang got so worked up when he received his mother's notes that he itched all over. He scratched here and there and twisted back and forth in the chair for a long time before he could manage to write a reply for the bald niece to take back. While writing, he hid the letter with one hand lest Ru-hua steal a glance at it. Once she did peek and saw (or guessed) on the slip of paper, "Execute immediately; the former instruction is very effective."

Then one day the bald niece stopped coming. Old Kuang restrained himself for several days, tossed in bed at night, and mumbled to himself all the time. He lost a great deal of weight. While eating, he would become startled, then put down his bowl and nestle his ear against the wall to listen to some sound.

At last, the mother-in-law came and took him away. That day she stood in the shadow at the corner with her big straw hat on and her face wrapped in a huge black scarf with only her eyes uncovered. She muttered, "Bad luck! Bad luck!" scolding her dawdling son. Stepping out the door, she grasped Old Kuang's hairy arm in fear of losing him. The two fled as though they were escaping from something.

Ru-hua heard the old woman giving advice as they walked: "It's important to maintain a good carriage. Haven't I warned you? I'm sure you were too careless. You've lacked vigilance ever since you were young."

Once Old Kuang came back from his mother's house. Ru-hua was watching the scarabs under the mulberry tree. He tapped her thin, dried-up shoulder and called, "Hey!" before he dashed into their room. She heard him rummaging through chests and cupboards for a long time, banging everything. Then he appeared with two huge bundles on his shoulders.

"These days I've been in high spirits." He wiped the sweat from his beard with a grease-stained handkerchief. "Mother was right when she said the most important thing is to pay attention to minute details. First, one should straighten out one's attitude about being a person. . . . What's your reflection on this?" He left, toting the bundles in a light spirit.

At night Ru-hua shut the iron-barred door and propped trunks against it. In the dark, innumerable tiny creatures shuttled back and forth on the ceiling above the bed. The swollen bed legs grated like clenched teeth. The blanket was so light it flapped up and down in the wind. Even when anchored with bricks, the blanket was of no use. Long-horned beetles appearing from nowhere clattered down onto her pillow and crawled toward her face. She had to keep turning on the light to drive them away.

She covered her head with the blanket but still couldn't block out the sound of the man next door tossing in bed. The painful grinding of his teeth alternated with a whistle like a wolf's howl and muttered curses. Once he even talked about the mudhole. What he said was what she saw in her dreams. Do people who sleep under one roof have the same dreams?

Ru-hua was drying up every day. In her dreams she always saw the burning sun, the sandy beach, the hot rock. All of these were boiling away the remaining water in her body. "Illusion caused by prostration," Old Kuang used to say. Every morning she got up soaked with sweat. She went to the mirror to examine her flushed face.

"Tell me, is that illusion?" The voice stopped on its flight to the sky.

Finally, the neighbor came again. His long neck stretched through the window. His eyes had an odd sparkle. His neck was red, covered with a layer of golden hair. Ru-hua was eating the half-bag of broad beans left by Old Kuang. Having regained moisture, the beans were soft and moldy. Chewing them made no sound.

"Do you eat pickles? I have made a lot. The plane has been

humming overhead all morning. I'm afraid my head will explode."
When she heard the haste in her voice, she blushed like a girl. The
hair in her armpit prickled so much that she felt pain. He was silent
for a while, and her voice froze in the air like printed words.

He paced the room, sniffing everywhere. His movements were
soft and gentle, his body resembling a rag fluttering in the wind.
At last he dropped onto the desk, his long, thin legs almost reaching the floor. The desk was covered with a thick layer of dust.
When he sat on it, dust clouds flew up in all directions and drifted
into his nostrils.

"The room has not been sprayed with insecticide for some
time," he said with confidence. "I hear mosquitoes whining every
night. I also hear you squash them on the wooden wall. There's a
lot of bloody spots."

"The mosquitoes are nothing compared to my crazy blanket. It
keeps trying to fly out the window. I have to struggle with it every
night. The effort leaves me sweating as if I had been dropped into
the mudhole." She started complaining without knowing it. Then
she felt the desire to say something nice, something intimate, to
the man who ground his teeth at night. "In the corner grows an
odd mushroom as big as a human head. Often a leg unexpectedly
stretches down from the ceiling, a leg with spiders crawling on it.
Since you sleep under the same roof, you must have got used to
things like this, eh?"

"Sure, I've seen many such things." He yawned suddenly, looking sleepy.

She immediately felt nervous. She raised her bare arm abruptly
to his nose. Pointing at the bulging blood vessels, she rattled on,
"See how thin I am. You didn't notice the sweet-scented oleander?
In the hot sun the oleander gives off a bitter smell. I was once a
sprinter. When you see me, I resemble you. We are almost twins.
Even when we talk, we sound similar. When I toss in bed, waking
from a dream, I hear you toss in bed. Maybe you've had a dream,

too. Maybe our dreams resemble one another. This morning when you came and spoke to me about the thing, I understood your meaning immediately because I was thinking about the same thing. Hey, cheer up!" She pushed him, but stopped her hand on his back. "Yesterday a dead tree in the park grew human hair . . . " She stroked his back.

Pulling his legs up to his chest, he arched his back like an old cat and remained motionless. "I'm worn out these days." His voice hummed between his knees. He yawned. "Spying everywhere. Simply no escape."

"How pitiful," she said, recalling her own shrinking belly. "The mulberry is bearing fruit. You'll be able to sleep like a log when the fruit ripens. You told me that. My mother once told me not to go out in the rain and not to get my shoes wet. She's a severe woman. She once broke a stick beating her children. She's always suffering from boils because of her bad temper. But at that time, I could still sleep soundly without any dreams."

"When I go to the toilet, someone peeks through the crack in the door. I have to stand all day in my office keeping my face toward the window. After a whole day, my legs feel as though they've been broken in a beating."

"How pitiful," she repeated, pulling his head against her dried belly. His hair was prickly, standing up like a brush. Then he got down from the table and she led him under the black mosquito net. Her hipbone bumped on the bedframe. She bent over in pain. The dust from the bed flew all over the room. She felt regret, hoping he didn't notice.

Ru-hua was still lying in bed covered with the flying blanket. But he had gone home. The desk retained the semicircular trace of his hips. Before he came, she had expected him to talk about the geological prospecting team. But he forgot and so did she.

She hadn't sprayed insecticide for a long time. As a result, insects had begun to hatch in her room. The newly born crickets had begun singing. Their song was broken, gloomy and tiring. She was always breathless with anxiety for them. Old Kuang called this room the "insect nest." Maybe he moved out because of the insects. Three years ago her mother-in-law discovered the first cricket in the house. From that time on, Old Kuang, following his mother's instructions, had brought back large quantities of insecticide. He ordered Ru-hua to spray twice every day. Despite the insecticide, the crickets had kept growing. But they were sick and their songs were pitiful. When the old woman came, her face would change color when she heard the crickets. She would pick up the broom and crawl under the bed, only her bottom sticking out. After swatting around under there for some time in hopes of driving the tiny things away, she would emerge with a dusty face and shout, "This is outrageous!"

Once in a while, Old Kuang helped his mother drive out the insects. The two of them would crawl under the bed, their two big rear ends sticking out. Then Old Kuang would exclaim, "What a place this would be if it weren't for the insecticide!"

This morning when she got up, she heard the crickets groaning. Tapping her wizened belly, she remembered not having sprayed for a long time. She couldn't hold back her grim smile. When Old Kuang came to get more things, she would ask him to fix iron bars on the back door and to bring more broad beans. She had started chewing the beans at night. She planned to write a note and ask somebody to deliver it to him. But opening her drawer, she failed to find a pen. Finally, she abandoned the idea.

Her own mother came to see her only once after the marriage. That was the day Ru-hua had just struggled through a near-fatal attack of pneumonia. Her mother walked in wearing a black jacket and trousers. Her head was wrapped in a black scarf. It seemed she was prepared to attend Ru-hua's funeral. Staring at her daughter as she regained consciousness, the mother stretched the corners of her mouth in astonishment. She pinched the daughter's pale fingertip and said, "So isn't it great! It's just great!" In a rage she twisted about and returned home. Her expression told how regretful she was to have come in vain.

After Old Kuang left, Xu Ru-hua saw her mother near the house, again dressed in black. She was sweating profusely, and her black clothes stuck to her fat back. Even from a distance, Ru-hua could smell the familiar, nauseating odor of the toilet.

She avoided going out as much as possible so as not to meet her mother. Every day she all but ran home from work. She pulled down the dark curtain as soon as she entered her room. One day when she lifted a corner of the curtain, she saw the black figure behind a tree. As expected, not long after, her mother stuck to her door a slip of paper which said in big letters, "Lazy bones, vain hoper, it's bound to lead to deterioration of the will, and finally to end in your becoming the garbage of society!" After that, the mother continued to write notes, sometimes wrapping them around a stone and leaving them outside the door, sometimes sticking them on the trunk of the mulberry tree. Once she even hid behind the tree and threw the paper-wrapped stone into the room when her daughter opened the door.

There was no way to avoid these attacks. Ru-hua never read the notes, but kicked them far away from her. Then she would hear curses from behind the tree.

At night when the scarabs flew to the mulberry tree, Ru-hua struggled with the blanket, sweating and out of breath in the cloud of dust she raised. Suddenly she heard footsteps, gruesome and horrifying. Trembling as she arose, she opened a crack in the curtain with her finger. She saw a flickering shadow wrapped in black and seeming to grin hideously. Though both the door and the window were covered with iron bars, Ru-hua was frightened. Not daring to turn on the light, she lit her flashlight every now and then and peered under the bed, behind the door, on the ceiling, in fear her mother might hide in the most unexpected places. But the old woman was skulking outside the window, coughing mischievously. This went on until daylight. When Ru-hua opened the curtain, there was no one outside.

"It might be an illusion," Ru-hua thought doubtfully. From then on came endless spying and pursuit. When she got rid of the "tail" that followed her and returned to her room exhausted, she rubbed her ribs only to discover that her body was filled with reeds which rumbled horrifyingly whenever she exhaled.

The morning before, her mother had stuck on her door the "Final Diplomatic Note," which read, "Cling obstinately to your course; the cobra will take revenge tonight." The note ended with three ferocious exclamation marks in red. When she pulled down the note, Ru-hua noticed the woman next door was stretching her neck to look in her direction. But when Ru-hua turned around, the woman withdrew her neck in a hurry and put on some stupid expression, considering herself very clever. She went so far as to say to herself while looking toward the sky, "The tree sounds disturbed." Later Ru-hua heard quiet talking from the other side of the wall.

"I feel so s-a-a-d," the neighbor drawled.

"The whole matter is driving me frantic as an ant in a hot pot," an unfamiliar voice answered. "You can never tell about your life. . . . Please move the mirror outside. It's convenient to hang it on the tree. We must keep on spying, and be on guard against a last-ditch struggle. A cornered dog can do something desperate."

The sound was so strange that Ru-hua's hair stood on end.

"I roam around here, and somebody else is roaming in my courtyard. It's pitch-dark everywhere . . . It's been like this for days," the odd voice continued.

The door creaked. Ru-hua lifted the curtain quickly and saw her mother rush out like a black leopard and disappear. So it was she who had spoken next door!

"The mother's having heart failure. She's unyielding." Mu-lan wiped the grease from her mouth with her finger. Chewing loudly, she continued, "Someone's disturbing all the neighbors. Pretending to be mysterious to show off her lofty character. Just think about it, and you'll see there's nothing but emptiness in her mind."

"The sparerib bones in the garbage will attract ants. See, there are ants all over the table." Geng Shan-wu glared at his wife as he concentrated on picking the gristle from his bone. "My stomach is full of these splinters of bones that prick me at the slightest movement."

"The weather is getting hot." Mu-lan wiped the sweat from her armpit. "My hair turns sour if I don't wash it every day. I can't even stand the smell myself."

TWO

1

When the first juicy red fruit dropped to the windowsill, the doors and windows cracked and sputtered in the heat. The long-horned beetles groaned; the scarabs hummed; the stagnant air in the room turned pink. Xu Ru-hua, wiping the dripping sweat from her body, ate two pickles to keep awake.

"Once I smell pickles, I can't stay away from them."

The door opened, and a man's long shadow stretched into the room.

"Don't you plan to hang a mirror on the tree?" she asked grudgingly. "You want to spy on me."

He grinned. His teeth were snow-white. His two canines protruded.

For eating spareribs, maybe? She frowned at the idea that he might have leftover pork between his teeth. The smell of stewed ribs from next door always made her sick.

"Every night, I cook in boiling sweat." She went on with her complaint like a spoiled child. Her voice raised goosebumps on her skin. Pointing at her belly, she said, "My body is filled with reeds.

Look here, pat it if you don't believe me. The echo is hollow, right? Once I actually thought about having a child. How silly. I often feel I will float up to the sky if I stand on tiptoe. That's why I never sleep. The wind in this room keeps me awake. People say I'm in a trance all the time."

In bed his ribs poked her for a short, uncomfortable moment. At her insistence, he told her a story about the geological prospecting team in a hot, savage wilderness. The ground crawled with lizards and locusts, and the sun rumbled overhead all day, giving off red sparks. The team's sweat streamed like a brook from their pores and condensed into a salty frost.

"The geological team, what happened to it then?" she urged him.

"Then? That's it. Only a brief instant, completely meaningless. Sometimes I can't keep myself from saying, 'I once worked on a geological prospecting team.' But it's nothing more than a remark, nothing serious. I am what I am when you see me."

"Maybe that's a lie! Isn't there a marriage, also?" She became indignant.

"Right, marriage. It came about through a basket of plums. We ate and ate, endlessly. I got so impatient that we finally married."

"You're pitiful." She stroked his back with compassion. "I know what you're going to say before you open your mouth. You resemble me so much. Wait, someday I'll tell you about the oleander. But not now. I still have a bag of broad beans. Old Kuang asked somebody to bring it to me."

They chewed the beans in darkness, cracking away as if they were happy.

A rat rustled beneath the bed, giving birth in a bundle of rags. The beans were all gone, and both of them felt uneasy.

"There are so many rats in the house," he said, trying to provoke her.

"You're right. My whole body feels sticky from the dust," she said in shame, secretly hoping he would leave soon. Gazing down at her body, she thought it looked more wrinkled and shrunken. She remembered putting on makeup in the morning for his sake. Even facing the wall, she could sense the sweat pouring from his armpits. His long back was sweaty. His wet hair clumped together. It seemed that after what they had just done his bones vanished, and he became like a finless eel or a carp. His body was soft and smooth with a sticky fluid. She smelled a faint sour odor.

"Lately, I've wanted to raise cats," he said. It seemed he wasn't about to leave. "I've already caught a scrawny black one with green eyes. It always watches me viciously. How did your goldfish die?"

"Old Kuang believes he smells murder in this room. The goldfish were frightened to death. I've been clipping and pasting up pictures. I even get up at midnight to do it. I make all kinds of patterns. I plan to tear off the wallpaper and put up pictures that will arouse you as soon as you step into the room, and you will never feel nervous again. Don't you feel bored sleeping here?"

Silence. Both of them regretted their nonsense.

Geng Shan-wu had just left the room when he stepped on a piece of watermelon rind and fell flat on his back. Rubbing his butt, he looked around and discovered several chunks of watermelon rind scattered in front of the doorway. Then he found a big pyramid of them stacked in the kitchen. While collecting the rinds for the garbage can, he saw his father-in-law digging at the front wall, his rolled-up trousers revealing thin, hairy legs. Two pieces of brick had already been broken off.

"Get out of here!" Shan-wu knocked him down.

Getting to his feet, the father-in-law shouldered his spade and shook the dust from his clothes. He walked away spitting and waving his fist.

"Dad took your porcelain teapot," Mu-lan said, frowning. The teapot was Shan-wu's favorite.

"Is everybody helpless here?" he roared.

"I tried to stop him, but he threatened to do something murderous. Who can tell? He might really do it. I once saw him kill a child . . . he's half mad because you upset him so badly. You've turned out to be talentless. You gained the trust of my entire family by cheating. My mother was annoyed to death. . . . Why?" She started to cry.

"Shit runs from your mouth!" he cursed, stomping his feet. Entering the room, he threw himself on the bamboo sleeping chair and stared blankly at the spiderweb on the ceiling. He was listening. Hearing the chatter of birds in the tree pecking at the red fruit one by one, he recalled the talk about the cricket that died of heart failure. What was its last song like? It would have been worth hearing. For a long time he'd waited for the fruit to turn red because he'd told her everyone could sleep in peace when the juicy red fruit appeared on the tree. So when the first fruit dropped on the windowsill, he was wild with joy! But he still couldn't sleep well. On the contrary, he'd had no sleep at all that night.

Tortured by the heat, he paced back and forth beneath the tree, using his flashlight to find the red fruit, which he then trampled flat. The big moon cast his puny shadow on the ground. The woman's groans came to him through her closed windows. Under one window a cricket suffered from heart failure. The woman was fighting weakly against a nightmare. No wonder she was always soaking wet.

Some people never dream. Are their nights pitch-black? Once he couldn't resist asking Mu-lan. She stared at him for a long time before clapping her hands and wailing, quite beyond his expectations. His hair stood on end at her outburst. Then she sneaked an alarm clock under her pillow. When it went off at midnight, she jumped up, poured a glass of water, and forced him to swallow a yellow and black pill which smelled like chicken droppings. He wondered if it was made of chicken droppings. This went on until he finally smashed the alarm clock with a carving knife. Mu-lan, ghostly pale, hid behind a chest. After that, she, too, suffered from insomnia. She had no dreams, and she tossed and turned in bed, passing smelly farts and chattering sadly, "Ever since the discovery of the range of his talent, his digestive system has gone wrong."

The black cat howled hungrily and gloomily. The cat was the dreaded enemy of his daughter, Feng-jun. One day when he came back from work, he saw his daughter holding the cat's tail, her knife raised to cut it off. When he shouted, she dropped the knife.

"I just wanted to scare it." She gave a false smile. The expression resembled her grandpa's.

Once when he was sleeping with the woman next door, he found himself killing a bug. Wiping the blood on the bedside, he made up his mind never to sleep there again.

"Don't you have any insecticide in the house?" their neighbor Ma Lao-wu asked, popping his smiling head in the door. He had a large tumor on his chin.

Shan-wu's heart sank. He answered coldly, "Ran out of it."

The old man wouldn't give up. He sneaked into the room and searched around with his eyes.

"This will do." He picked up a bottle and walked away.

"That's insect repellent! We need that ourselves!" Shan-wu shouted.

"OK, OK." The old man pretended not to understand and fled with the medicine.

"Why let him in?" Mu-lan prowled behind Shan-wu like a cat. "He's a thief! He pretends to want to borrow something, but he comes to look the place over so he can rob us at night. You're an idiot!"

"I want him to steal something. Nothing important. Your father steals something every day, and you're secretly happy about it. Be fair! Treat this old man equally! At least he makes some noise so we don't feel scared. Your father hides in our kitchen at night . . . I simply don't understand," he said in a vague tone.

"That Old Lin, this is the third time he's shit in his trousers."

Forgetting the current argument, Mu-lan started chatting in high spirits.

"Old Lin? You two are the same person," he said unconsciously while thinking about something else.

"Sinful!"

"I do think of you two as one." He was serious. "Don't you think about his shitting all the time? It sounds like remembering yourself. You probably keep a diary of the things you think about. I'm all for it. This way . . . " He was still staring out the window and mentally lending his strength to the red fruit which was about to drop.

"What are you for?" Observing his expression intently, she became more and more baffled.

"I'm for your things. Every problem is caused by the tree. You certainly know it. At first it was the blossoms. Their stink filled the room. Now it's the red fruit. There's no end to it all. I haven't had a decent sleep for a long time. Sometimes I feel so worn out I'm afraid I might commit suicide."

The drifting expression on his face stopped her rage. He must be possessed to talk so crazily.

"Old Lin and you are in reality one person." Puzzled for a while, he continued, "When you think of something, go ask him. He must be thinking about the same thing. Just try it. You shouldn't feel funny about it. The people living under this roof are always talking about the same thing and having the same dreams . . . "

He stopped abruptly, realizing he was repeating Xu Ru-hua's clichés. Could she be listening at the other side of the wall?

"How could Old Lin and I be the same person? That's outrageous! You know he shits in his trousers and has become a laughingstock." She defended herself without confidence.

"All the same, when you laugh at him, you yourself are a laughingstock. The way you talk about him sounds like talk about yourself. I can see you're scared. You're indulging in wild fantasies, like a child, but what's the use?"

His wife was trying hard to distinguish herself from Old Lin. They always tried to laugh at others out of their inner fear of exposing themselves. They acted as though they had discovered something surprisingly funny. Take Mu-lan, for example. She jotted down things like "shitting" in her notebook, considering it her own discovery, because she could only act surprised when she herself discovered something. She started this trick when they first began to know each other. There used to be an old man who fried cakes. One day she called Shan-wu to the old man's door in a mysterious way. She invited him to peek in through a crack to see an "excellent performance." He bent over and peeked in for a long time but saw nothing. Standing aside, she bent over with laughter. "I could die laughing!" she had said. So she was laughing at him? He only realized that a long time afterward.

"Why did you laugh at me?" he asked later.

"Because you're a fool."

"And you?"

"How can I be a fool? I couldn't discover your foolishness if I were a fool."

"I see."

He'd seen through her, but she didn't know it. She still played the old tricks. He felt delighted to have laid her bare.

"Drinking three mouthfuls of water before a meal is an effective measure for keeping emotional balance," his wife was chattering. "It's important to keep a realistic attitude and to avoid trances. The couple next door is a warning. I observed them in the past but could never understand them. What can their odd, senseless actions lead to? Isn't that a meaningful lesson? If . . . "

Yesterday the head of the institution gave him a long talk about raising parrots. In a roundabout way, he said Geng Shan-wu could gain favor with him by locating a good species. He should know that raising parrots is an elegant hobby. While talking, the chief's smiling eyes sparkled with wicked light. But Geng appeared puzzled, and his mind wandered during the talk. What was more, he even interrupted irrelevantly at the end: "Do you also raise cats?" The head, slapping Shan-wu's thin back, laughed at a fearful volume until two tiny tears fell.

Ma Lao-wu must have sprayed the insect repellent in his room. The evil old dog never tied his trousers properly, so they fell down every now and then, revealing his "horrible thing." He had a bald white rooster, which he often pelted with stones until it developed welts. The old man despised Geng Shan-wu bitterly. When he saw Shan-wu's wretched figure on the street clutching his briefcase, he gave a snort of contempt, saying, "Idiot!" Sometimes he spoke loudly enough for Shan-wu to hear.

Shan-wu was greatly disturbed by the old man's disdain because he had to pass his door every day going to and from work. He tried all kinds of ways to escape. For example, he would hide in a toilet opposite the door, then dash out when he saw the old man go inside. Or sometimes he dragged a colleague along, chatting all the way, pretending not to notice the old man.

But Ma Lao-wu was so determined that he became yet more diligent when he saw through Shan-wu's evasions. He calculated the younger man's office hours and waited patiently on the street. As soon as Shan-wu approached, the old man would come forward to greet him, and after Shan-wu passed he would utter the curse that made the son-in-law so angry. This had become Ma's greatest enjoyment. Even in snow or rain, he would stand at the door under an oilskin umbrella waiting for Shan-wu's arrival.

One day Shan-wu didn't go to work because of a cold. Lying in bed, he felt lucky for being able to escape the humiliation of the old man. But raising his eyes he saw a figure in a straw hat, very familiar, outside his window. The figure flashed past. It took him a long time to realize that it was Ma Lao-wu who had come in disguise to check up on his illness.

"The room is damp," the section chief of his wife's factory complained loudly in the front room.

"The man is a fool," the wife sighed, as if she were worried.

"So he is." The section chief belched loudly.

"And stubborn, too."

"True, and stubborn, too."

"I'll cut off two locks of hair near your ear and put them in a box."

"What! That scares me!"

"For a souvenir, you little monkey."

"Don't call me a little monkey. I'm a little cock."

"Little spider, little louse, little locust, little . . . "

The chief suddenly cackled like a hen laying eggs. He laughed and laughed, shaking the whole house. The floor trembled, the dishes in the cupboard rattled, the air rang. Geng Shan-wu covered his ears in terror before he opened the back door and fled. The odd laughter continued for about ten minutes. Then there was a muffled bang in the room. Peeping through a crack in the wall, Shan-wu saw his wife and the chief rolling under the bed, clinging to each other.

"Oh, they're fighting," he breathed out in relief. "There must be a scorpion under the bed."

After the chief left, Shan-wu fought with his wife again. They were joking at first. He pushed her onto the bed, tickling her. Suddenly he couldn't refrain from giving her a kick. Screaming, she jumped on him and bit him. Gripping him by the neck, she banged his head against the wall. Feeling suffocated, he shuddered with hatred. Finally he struggled loose and kicked the vital part of her body fiercely. His daughter came in and watched coolly for a long time. Suddenly she threw the black cat at him. They were startled and stopped fighting at the same time. The daughter smiled maliciously before she fled the room. The black cat used Shan-wu's grease-spotted trousers as a post for practicing Kung Fu, exercising its paws happily.

"It's hard for me to go on living," he said to Mu-lan. "This is all caused by my insomnia."

"We should increase our surveillance of the neighbor woman. Lately she keeps her light on all night. I can see it through the crack in the wall. Once I spied her collecting pictures of female buttocks. Her wall is covered with them, really intolerable to look at. Do you think she sells obscene pictures in secret?"

Mu-lan left. Picking up one of her shoes, Shan-wu threw it into the sewer at the back of the house. He had a good laugh. Ma Lao-wu's invasion had become intolerable. Today the old man had grabbed his arm in public and squeezed a bug into his palm. Then he jumped away and declared to the onlookers that he would announce Shan-wu's personal secret to the public. Shan-wu was humiliated and sneaked away like a rat.

"I'm going to live a hundred years!" Ma Lao-wu proclaimed to his back.

2

Xu Ru-hua found a pile of newspapers and cut them into pieces. Climbing a ladder, she carefully sealed every crack in the wall. She kept herself busy until midnight, the pouring stinking sweat painting lines of dark stain on her dusty body.

She was sitting in her room when the fight started. Her worn-out curtain had a big hole where an ugly spotted moth crawled in and made a puddle of yellow water before laying a thick mass of eggs. The scene was disgusting. The heat intensified every day. As soon as she entered the room, she took off all her clothes. Looking at her familiar wrinkled body in the mirror, she vaguely recalled the long, thin figure of the man. In her memory his image was too elusive to catch.

She tried to remember the time they were sleeping on the bed, but only caught some scattered, obscure episodes. The dust on the desk had been wiped off, so not even the semicircles of his hip marks remained. Might she be completely wrong? At the very beginning she really had something like desire. But since the last time, when she finished the broad beans with him and he told her the story about the geological team, she could feel her desire fade. Maybe it had been nonexistent from the beginning, only some idea to deceive herself?

For many days her heart was in her throat. She feared he might force his way into her room. Bolting her door, she hid in the mosquito net, sweating all over and regretting bitterly. She could hear their argument next door clearly. But she was not really paying attention; instead, she was watching the moth nervously, fearing it might fly to her bed to lay its eggs.

"The man is only a sneaky monster," she thought calmly. She had already forgotten that she had once remarked the close resemblance between the two of them. Inside the net it was suffocating. Two big flies buzzed above her and rolled together to mate. The sun was burning down. In her memory the day was forever murky, and the mulberry tree and the little room were sunk in this murkiness. The mosquitoes sang their stuffy song in the sealed room. The glittering days existed only in the past. It came with the bitterness of the oleander. At that time, the leaves on the tree were burning and the ground was covered with tiny circles, as if someone had dropped a whole collection of silver coins. No sick groan of the crickets was heard; only two turtledoves sang softly as in dreams from morning to night.

Ru-hua's father used to be an engineer. "She is going to take over her father's career," her mother often boasted to others when Ru-hua was young. She failed to do so, however, but became a candy seller. For that her mother hated her bitterly, swearing, "I'll never give her peace. The villain has ruined me." She complained to everyone, crying, "A really poisonous snake. Why?" Ru-hua's mother was always brooding about something. This might have been the reason her husband couldn't stand her and moved in with an old woman who sold cigarettes on the street. Every day when her mother went to the vegetable market, she saw him sneaking out from beneath the narrow eaves of the old woman's house. But being too proud to get down from her high horse, she had to pretend that nothing had happened.

Yesterday Old Kuang asked someone to deliver another packet of beans. This time the fried beans were even harder than before. She felt uncomfortable after chewing them for a while. Her temples swelled. Going home from work, she saw Old Kuang strolling along the street, his mother clutching his arm. The mother wore a bright crepe jacket and her shabby straw hat. Her flat, dried-up body looked as if it had been cut out by an ax. Old Kuang's shiny, greasy face had a new confident expression, so different from before. Full of energy, he kicked a broken brick far down the street.

"You should have an obvious goal to struggle for in your life," she heard her mother-in-law say with curt finality. With confidence she took off her worn-out hat to shake off the dust.

When Xu Ru-hua passed her husband, the mother-in-law saw her. Nodding coolly, she held Old Kuang's arm and passed swiftly.

"The straw hat has special meaning to me . . . " Her enthusiastic tone was only a cover for her spiritual emptiness.

"So she even puts on perfume." Ru-hua could scarcely hold back her laughter when she saw the serious manner in which they carried on together. But she dared not laugh this time, for she noticed a curtain was shaking. Someone must be watching her from behind the curtain. The person opened the window and cleared his throat conspicuously before spitting. The man showed the whites of his eyes, glanced at her, and closed the window again. He must be hiding behind the curtain again.

The mother and son were far away by now, their voices carried back to her by the wind. "Keep sharp-eyed and clear-headed and you will have boundless energy . . . "

The day was murky. Even in the daytime rats scuttled across the table, jumping about heavily and rhythmically. When she closed her eyes, she saw the discs of the sunflowers one after another, burning hot, golden . . .

"I can't live on." His voice had a plaintive tone. She saw that his shoulder was whitened by dandruff.

"You're not at all excited. Don't play games." Opening the door, she stared at him arrogantly, her arms folded across her chest. "It's funny to see you like that. Here's an odd moth sticking to one place and refusing to go. Kill it for me." She pointed at the broom.

Bending from his long waist, he moved toward the moth. The broom swiped suddenly and the moth dropped to the ground.

"Perhaps I'm not strong enough." He felt embarrassed. "Of course, you've heard everything. Nothing serious, is it? I behave like an old woman selling rat poison."

"Narcissist." She breathed out, relaxed, and killed the moth with her foot. "You've changed. You begin to resemble my mother. People like her have an uneasy life. From morning to night she's aggrieved, busy running around. Really hard work. Sometimes I can hardly imagine she will live another day. Maybe she'll die of cancer sooner or later."

"I haven't had any dreams lately," he told her haltingly, retreating to the door as if he were going to open it.

"Of course, you're too busy," she said with understanding. "You've been thinking of trying to change. I think you might achieve something. You've been trying all along. It's hard, unimaginable . . . "

"Too hard! I'm almost an idiot." He stopped, worried and indignant. "Everyone, every word they say, everything they do, is fixed. But I, I'm nothing. I can't change into them, no matter how I rack my brains to imitate another's walk, no matter how I pretend to be thinking as I stand at the office window until my legs break. In fact,

I, too, am fixed. I can only be nothing." Pausing for a moment, he went on, "For decades, I've been like this. How about you?"

"Me? Oh, I can never remember you. To me you're like a shadow. You are indeed nothing. In fact, I'm the same. But I'm not troubled by this, nor do I think of changing. I'm dried up. I told you long ago that I'm full of reeds. Just one thing worries me, the flying blanket. I intend to nail it to the bedside, lest it fly again. Among people like us some want to change and succeed, resulting in ordinary people. But some can't succeed, yet can't stand being nothing. They want to find a clear-cut rule for themselves, but only struggle in vain all their lives. I don't believe you'll succeed. Your bones are too heavy, you suffer from arthritis. You find it difficult to move your body in front of people. You see, I'm what I am, eating pickles and living relaxed."

"My neighbor pretended to borrow insecticide in order to steal the repellent right before my eyes. My wife said it was a great insult."

"It was not at all insulting. In fact, you didn't really feel insulted, right? Why should you come here and put on this act? It's no good. You shouldn't be afraid of him, I mean the neighbor. In darkness can't you hear the tree creak? The tree is furious. I see all the leaves on the tree explode in a shower of sparks . . . "

"I haven't had any dreams lately. I must go now." He went out without leaving his semicircular hip marks on the table.

His guilty conscience when he said "I must go now" made her happy. She noticed that his T-shirt was very dirty, very greasy. A seam near the armpit was unraveled. He looked pitiful in it. His wife must have been on such bad terms with him that she refused to mend his clothes. But he still pretended, saying something like "I don't have any dreams." It was odd.

In fact, he had heard the explosion of the tree trunk and had seen the sparks of leaves. He said that he had no dreams because he felt ashamed. At that moment, he had jumped up to close the window when he saw a cloud of moths fly into the room like sparks. Outside in the pale moonlight stood a motionless naked woman with her hair let down. The silhouette of her body startled him. His own body was covered with a rash. Later on, he tried to sleep. As soon as the back of his head touched the pillow, something sharp pinched him. Patting the pillow and turning it upside down, he got pricked more severely. "Ouch!" she cried out. The woman was standing outside the window, her shriveled breasts hanging down, her body covered with sparks. She moved her mouth silently.

"What are you tossing about for?" His wife gave him a hard kick.

"The red fruit is dropping incessantly on the tiles. Can't you hear anything? Look outside. Something strange is standing there."

"Nonsense!" She walked to the window, dragging her heels. Opening the window, she stuck her head out, saying, "Pah! Don't scare me. It might be the reflection in the mirror I hung up today. Does it bother your sleep? You're too nervous. How can you be so fragile? Let me take it down." She clattered out and clattered in again. "Tomorrow should we invite the Master to drive out the evil? Someone told me privately that our little room has been haunted for a long time. Why do you think I watch our neighbors' movements in the mirror? I have constant suspicions. They've tried to drive out evil, but with no luck. That's why the man left. Haven't you noticed? The woman must have been tied up by some evil spirit. One midnight I heard her wrestling with something in her room making all kinds of noise! You should never even glance at her. In her eyes is a steel needle more than two inches long. I saw her shoot it at a child who cried out painfully!"

Because of his talk with the director of the institution, he had become a laughingstock. One day An Guo-wei yelled to him in the office, "Hey, do you have cats of good breeding? Donate one!" Everyone whispered to one another and made faces. One of them wet his fingers with saliva and drew a cat on the dusty window. He stood there stunned, but the others started chasing a rat, screaming and staggering around. They seized the chance to push him and bump him. He was butted against the wall one minute and shoved against the table another.

"I—I don't raise cats . . . " he stammered, rubbing his painful back.

"What did he say?" Everybody stopped, forgetting all about the rat and surrounding him. They stared at him intently.

"I—I'm saying . . . I mean to say—I'm extremely self-conscious." He looked at the mob timidly, not daring to continue.

"Good heavens!" All the people around him jumped high, laughing themselves to death. "He said he had superfine sensitivities, Comrades! Isn't the guy bragging? Ha-ha-ha-ha!"

"Ha-ha-ha-ha," he also laughed, but hesitantly. He felt he had to express something.

The rat rushed out from under the table, so the mob swarmed after it. All of a sudden, he felt he had become one of them, and he joined in the chase.

"Wait a minute." An Guo-wei grabbed him by the neck. "I'll report to the director that you don't raise cats," he said smilingly.

Entertaining dark schemes, he held out for several days, but the head of the institution never came to him. Instead, he circled to avoid him whenever they saw each other at a distance. But once, outside the office, Shan-wu overhead the director call him a "funny old parrot" and burst into loud laughter. "Why should my toes be so itchy, eh?" He could hardly catch his breath in his laughter. "Whenever I laugh my toes itch, damn it!"

One drizzly morning Ma Lao-wu again stopped Shan-wu on the street, only to throw greenish snot on his trousers. Shan-wu made up his mind to remold himself completely. Gathering his courage, he walked toward the director's house.

The mess in the house startled him. He felt he was in a salvage yard. All kinds of things were piled up to the ceiling. Two huge storage lofts were on the verge of collapsing under the weight. Blinking hard, Shan-wu recognized among the countless dusty objects a wine bottle, a shovel without a handle, a string of beads, a pile of plain porcelain bowls, a birdcage with two half-alive parrots perched inside, a long tress of woman's hair (hanging down from the loft in a frightening way), an antique bed with only three legs, a heap of plaster models of genitals, a set of sharks' skeletons, a broken walking stick, and so on. In one corner, the director was having a meal with his wife. The rice and dishes were set on a bamboo chicken crate in which there was a yellow hen. The wife looked like a dark mud figure. Her eyes never moved.

"I may be . . . " Shan-wu started slowly, while moving carefully to avoid the sundry goods. "I've thought about it. I can find a way to get the good breed."

"Hey, hey?" Stopping chewing, the director turned his eyes upward. He dilated his red nostrils to sniff Shan-wu's jacket. "What's your impression? I've only opened your eyes. Have you seen the sharks' skeletons? What do you think? Now you can boast in the institute. You lucky dog! But the two I've got can't be worse. They're not parrots, but crows! I tell you, don't sit on that bed. It has only three legs. You'd better sit on the birdcage. We often use it as our stool when we have guests. Wait till you get me the good breed. Then I'll let you see my treasure in the two back rooms. But now it's too soon. You've got to hand me the good breed. I don't want to let you see for free or just for boasting's sake. Don't dare get that tricky idea. Brother, you're said to be tricky, right? Maybe you're involved in collecting stamps in order to become famous overnight? Bah! You need to learn from me."

"In fact, I have a serious intention. I'm trying to remold . . . "

"Hush! Shut up! Lately my heart isn't beating normally. That's right, that's right." He patted Shan-wu's back magnanimously.

Suddenly something came to him. "You can't be later than the day after tomorrow, otherwise I won't allow you to explore the treasure in my back room. Do you hear? Then you'll regret it to your grave!" Extending one fat finger, he slapped Shan-wu's face as a warning. "First class! Unrivaled in this world! Understand?"

These days Shan-wu could feel he was getting on in years. Though occasionally he could recall the geological team, those memories retreated so far that they shrank into a vague spot of light. During the day, he sometimes discovered himself doing something unreasonable: once he tried to saw the legs off the bed; another time he peed on his wife's socks. Yet the woman next door could still eat her pickles casually. He felt terribly vexed at the faintest thought of this. He could hear mosquitoes swarming in her room as if they were holding a sports meet. Despite the paper sealing the cracks, he could still hear the rubbing of her hipbones against the wooden bed, and her weak panting. Why were his ears becoming sharper with age? Mu-lan never heard anything. She couldn't hear the red fruit dropping on the tiles or the cracking of the tree trunk or the noisy mosquitoes next door or the tossing of the neighbor woman. Every night she only passed indigestive farts, a bad heritage from her mother. When he occasionally asked her abjectly if she had heard anything, she flew into a rage, accusing him of being like people "born with an appearance petty and low" and "always nursing shameful and evil ulterior motives."

His black cat had run away. Once in a while, it came back sniffing here and there like an intriguer, meowing to him ingratiatingly before it fled again. He noticed the cat had only half a tail. Had his daughter cut off the other half? It seemed she was doing well with her plot. When he bantered with her about this pretending to be joking, she started to wail in an eccentric way, threatening to drown herself in the well at the back of the house because she was fed up with this family. She had long acted bored, as if she were much superior to the rest of them.

The day finally came when the last red fruit plopped between the tiles amid the delirious gabble of the heat-ridden people from the dark windows.

3

"The distracting thoughts in one's soul are the blasting fuse leading to detonation." This was the fifth time Old Kuang's mother had quoted the sentence. She gulped her saliva. Every night since moving back, he had seen her sitting in the shadow behind the cabinet spitting into a carton. She never went anywhere, and nobody came to see her. At first, Old Kuang was surprised, but his mother told him, "I'm undergoing a thorough cleansing of the soul."

From that day on he devoted himself to collecting famous quotations. In two months, he accumulated two thick books of them and became more and more addicted to it. "There is boundless subtlety in the thoughts of famous people." He began to use such tones when talking to others. "The mere thought of it induces reverence and awe and heartfelt admiration. My heart was in utter darkness before I found the purpose of my life. I can't recall how I survived. But now everything looks different, and the meaning of my life is clear . . . " He had changed unexpectedly from a quiet man into a womanish old gossip, chattering about everything in his heart to whomever he met.

"His new life has inspired him," he heard his mother tell the old woman at the cigarette stand. (She lived with a skinny, bald engineer who, according to her, was the most intriguing man in the world, "possessing a style so elegant it can't be described in words.") "He has a whole new attitude. Just think, after more than thirty years, the whole meaning of life suddenly unfolds before your eyes!"

At dusk every day Old Kuang took a walk arm in arm with his

mother, swollen with arrogance, his heart filled with a curiosity and pride he had never before experienced. When his spirit surged high in his chest, he itched to kick the cobblestones on the street or to drum on the electric pole at the roadside, then to laugh until he trembled.

Once in a while, he recalled his life in the small room under the paper mulberry tree. It seemed like a dream: the sleepless nights chewing broad beans, the inescapable terror. At the mere thought of it his face turned blue and broke out in beads of sweat. "Everything was caused by the pickles," he complained to his mother. "Unusual habits often lead to criminal desire. One of my colleagues has a wife who is fond of eating strong-smelling preserved bean curd. One winter, when the supply of bean curd ran out, she became so greedy that she bumped off her husband. What a painful lesson!"

"Your wife does not exist," his mother said slowly between her teeth. Her front tooth showed two cavities. "She will finally wither away of her own doing."

But Ru-hua hadn't vanished yet. She lived like a rodent in the dark, moldy room, chewing pickles and broad beans quietly, her behavior becoming more and more clandestine. Old Kuang sent broad beans to her every week. His guilt resembled that of someone who feeds a rat.

"How do you feel after our separation?" Ru-hua asked him one day, casually spitting out a shell as if she were chatting with a neighbor.

"Maybe I feel healthier both physically and spiritually," he replied, his face glowing with vigor. At the same time, however, his guilt surged up and he blurted, "You could move over there, too!"

She grinned at him queerly, saying, "The mosquitoes in this room are like athletes at a sports meet. Can't you hear them at night? When the wind blows to the south, the noise might even reach your pillow."

Old Kuang's mother later called his guilty conscience "remaining dirty thoughts." Long after moving out of the room, he heard people talking about its being haunted. That night he tossed from side to side but couldn't go to sleep. As a result, for several days he felt dizzy, and his back was damp with cold sweat. Sometimes while lying by the window he saw floating clouds vanish from the sky. He felt deeply touched, even moved to tears. "Keep on learning as long as you live," he muttered to himself, happy to be able to use this set phrase to describe his feelings.

"You should try eating silkworm pupa," his mother said. Her small eyes were ringed like a chicken's. "An acquaintance of mine tried them. They work so well they can bring the dying back to life."

Two days before, on his way back from the school, Old Kuang had seen his mother-in-law stealthily stick her head from behind the door of a bar waiting for him to go in. Turning around, he had made off at once. She had chased him, yelling all the way, "Swindler! Degenerate scoundrel! I'll send you to jail!" She had even thrown cobblestones at him.

She had not been to their small room since their marriage, nor had she ever acknowledged him as her son-in-law. However, she had become extremely interested in their private life since he moved out on his family. She hung around his building day after day, and even stopped him on the street, shaking her fist and warning him that she would report his mean trickery in detail to the authorities of the school. He was digging a grave for himself if he didn't wake up to reality. She stomped her feet while raving on. The pained expression on her face puzzled him.

"She's been waiting for this day," Ru-hua told him smilingly when he brought her beans. "Her hair has turned white from waiting. Don't you know? She's popped up now because she believes her time has come. For years, day and night, she's been cursing and cursing. She's too stubborn and takes everything to heart. I hold my breath for her, considering her tough life. She's dying, and this may be her deathbed struggle. I can see she's badly off-color these days."

As soon as he got back, he started his complaint: "The mosquitoes in her room jump on you like a robber, stinging and biting at will. The sprays and insecticides are nowhere to be found. I don't understand what she's thinking. This is outrageous! It's all because of the pickles. I shouldn't have let her eat them in the first place . . . "

His mother snorted in contempt. "I'm told that wolflike howling comes from her room at night, and that it's ghastly and blood-curdling."

"You're right." He was flipping through a book of quotations by a famous leader, his eyebrows furrowed. "First the tragic death of the goldfish; then the disappearance of the thermos bottle. Why couldn't I add it all up? I've observed her for so long; now I see she's beyond caring. It's all a cheat. I'm completely wrong. She's been trying to bite me to death . . . "

"Such a woman will finally wither away of her own doing," his mother emphasized each word, "because she has never really existed."

When the matchmaker introduced them to each other, Ru-hua was already an old maid, past marriageable age. Her short hair was a mess because she never combed it but only ran her fingers through it. But she was not obstinate. On the contrary, like a child she had no definite views of her own. This had won his heart. In her presence, he felt like a man. He took her to the small room under the paper mulberry tree with his mind full of big, vague plans, like setting up a grape trellis in front of the house or building a shed at the back. But none of these plans had been realized because the invasion of crickets drove him to distraction.

As time flew by, he realized in horror that his wife was in reality a rat: she was quiet but always chewing something. All the furniture in the house had her teeth marks on it. One midnight he felt a stinging on the back of his head. He woke up and touched his head. His hand was bloodstained. Enraged, he shook her awake, screaming, "What are you doing?"

"Me?" She rubbed her swollen eyes till her hands were covered with the excrescence of sleep. "I caught a tiny rat trying to escape. It startled me so much that I bit it."

"Ah! So you want to bite me to death!"

"Bite you to death? Why should I?" she muttered indifferently to the air before yawning and dropping into another dream.

Turning off the light, Old Kuang listened closely. He discovered her snoring was false and saw that she shivered with nervousness. From that day on, he couldn't sleep, and this soon developed into a neurosis. Later on she bit him several times. Thanks to his vigilance, he was never seriously wounded. Once she bit him on the shoulder and refused to let go after he woke up. He had to slap her and knock her off the bed. He forced her mouth open and saw the old blood on her teeth. She bit him so hard because she really wanted to suck his blood! Sometimes he felt so demoralized that he suspected she was a vampire. But he gave up the idea lest people laugh at him.

Getting up his courage, he had forced her to search for crickets. She was as obedient as a robot, three times a day spraying insecticide, relentlessly smashing cricket nests with a stick, limbering up her muscles and joints hundreds of times (this on the advice of a doctor he knew), carrying out broad bean therapy, sleeping with her face to the east, and so on. However, none of these measures worked. He could see her gradually shrivel up, turning into a dried-up lemon. Her teeth became loose.

After she stopped biting things she started chewing pickles, of which she made jar after jar. She would interrupt her sleep to have a pickle. From morning to night she was chewing constantly. When he was in the room he could hear "smack smack." Even with his eyes closed he knew what she was doing. Though she often chewed quietly, the sound made him furious. Once he broke five jars of pickles. The smell filled the house and left him sleepless the whole night. It was extremely painful for him. Meanwhile, she was watching, deep in thought, looking gloomy and sad. But one day he discovered another five jars lined up under the bed.

Several day before he left, she got him to put iron bars on all the windows under the pretext that a thief roamed nearby and might one day break in. But while he was working he wondered if she was playing the fool and feigning madness in order to attack him when he was asleep. Otherwise, why should her eyes give out evil sparks while she talked? Those days he never closed his eyes in sleep. By the time his mother came to fetch him, he was on the verge of a mental breakdown.

"Hey!" His mother came out of the shadow behind the cabinet with her carton. She was spitting as she talked. "I've finished my cleansing of the soul. Let me tell you something strange. I heard it from the old lady at the cigarette stand." (She never mentioned the cigarette seller's name. Maybe she didn't know it herself.) "She said that every night after twelve the fragrance of osmanthus spreads into the whole street from shoemaker Wang's house. Yesterday at twelve I sniffed hard and actually smelled it. I was still pondering this at noon and became so upset that I skipped my nap. I'm determined to get to the bottom of this matter tonight. It may turn out to be some plot. Don't lock the door after supper. I intend to wait outside his door till midnight. If necessary, I'll check his ears to see if they are the source of this odor. Haven't the newspapers reported supernatural doings? That will set my mind at rest."

"Mother, can you see what Xu Ru-hua has changed into recently?"

"That woman?" She moved her chicken eyes closer to look him up and down.

"Haven't you noticed she changed into a rat long ago? A person will change into anything he imitates too often. She used to imitate rats and bit everything in the house. Now she's actually turned into a rat, a rat with loose teeth. Sometimes I think about mixing arsenic with the broad beans to poison her quietly like killing a rat. Isn't this mean?" He hesitated and added shyly, "If I could divorce her, I would be quite attractive to women."

"You've never had a mean idea, and you won't do this either. How can you have such an idea? You can never learn to act on your own. The woman has already outlived her time. Sooner or later she will vanish completely from this world. Sometimes you're so weak you lose your confidence. You'll grow strong gradually if you mind everything you're doing. Never neglect the antiphlogistic before sleep, and persist in doing your soul-cleansing. Stop mentioning this foolish thing. Do you want us to become a public joke? You were very weak when you were young, very dull, and you tended to daydream. You were overly emotional and lost your head in excitement. People like you shouldn't get married. Why didn't you recognize this at the start? Because of me . . . "

She suddenly stopped her lecture and frowned. At that moment, she hated his foolishness. She cleared her throat loudly and spat with force into the carton. Then she glanced at him with a white eye.

"Mother's right. I'm beside myself." Under her glare he shrank into a heap like a trembling meatball.

"That's better," she said softly, her eyes turning muddy and dull as frosted glass.

He was always frightened by his mother's anger. When she took offense, he panicked so badly that he felt too pained to go on living. That night he had a nightmare in which somebody took his bed out from under him, leaving him suspended in air, unable to get down.

"What are you flopping around for?" his mother asked from the next room.

"There's a wildcat crouching behind my bed trying to climb up. I'm scaring it."

"Recite some quotations to yourself."

The moonlight spread across the yard like a winding sheet.

"Have you ever met a wildcat?" he asked, trying hard to look hideous. "You should know a wildcat is ferocious. It might scratch your face in your sleep."

Ru-hua turned blue. Looking toward the ceiling, she said quickly, "What are you looking for? When you were gone, I threw your sprayer and insecticide in the garbage can because they looked so unpleasant. It's better to be rid of them. I'm used to life among the mosquitoes. They fly around me without biting. I feel at home listening to the crickets. Since you left, the crickets have sung more and more confidently and powerfully. Now I can sleep soundly. No need to worry about their heart failure."

"How can it be that so many moths land on the wall?"

"They're here to lay eggs. Pitiful, aren't they?"

"You should chew the broad beans I bring you thoroughly. People say this house is haunted."

"It may be haunted by me. I always get up at midnight and shake out the blanket. You might have been scared to death if you hadn't moved out. You're too weak."

"Maybe so," he sighed sadly. "You were trying to bite me to death."

" . . . "

"You've been crazy for a long time. Why didn't I realize it?"

" . . . "

"Your mother's mad, too. It's hereditary. Once I planned to raise grapes. Those crickets almost robbed me of my life. Cold sweat pours out when I recall the past, and I even sleepwalk. My mother says I'm suffering from a persecution complex."

" . . . "

"Chew your broad beans well."

"Next time you don't need to come in person. Our neighbors have put up a mirror on the tree. Did you see it on your way in? They're watching your movements. I really don't know what their intention is. It's frightening, isn't it? They might be planning a murder."

4

While Ru-hua's mother was chewing the salted beans with her eyes closed, another chunk of plaster fell from the ceiling. This time the lathes were exposed. For eight years she had lingered on in steadily worsening conditions. Strangely enough, she hadn't died. After every illness, her shaky, skinny legs somehow supported her heavy body as she moved about the house, bracing herself against the wall.

As soon as she got better, she waited in the yard day after day trying to capture sparrows under a basket. On the wall surrounding the yard hung dozens of dead sparrows, all nailed through the eyes. Outsiders were stunned and got goosebumps when they saw this sight. Not long ago, her appetite had suddenly returned, and as a result she was getting healthier daily. Someone told her what was happening in her daughter's small room. She grew full of vigor and armed herself for spying.

"So that's it!" Ru-hua's mother shouted at the old woman selling fried cakes. "Just imagine, eight years of pain! Miserable old age! Bug bites every night! Who else has suffered like that? Now at long last he has seen through the poisonous snake! Once I saw him on the street. What a character! Half of his face was twitching oddly, his neck was covered with scars, and his body was stinking. Poor thing, how did he fall into her hands? Just as the fly drops into the net of the poisonous spider. She has drunk his blood dry! This is a mystery. Is he an idiot? I believe the way he walks is peculiar. According to his neighbor, he put up a grape trellis in the bedroom. My god!"

She had had expectations when her daughter was young. But the girl was born with a bad personality and was dishonest in her deeds.

"Ru-hua, you've spilled vegetable soup on the front of your blouse again. It's disgusting! You stomp so hard I think you must have horseshoes on!"

Ru-hua's mother was continually upset and shouting. And the daughter, though she heard it, refused to respond and continued to bend her head down looking for ants' nests along the foot of the wall. She took no care when eating and chewed her food noisily. She resembled her crazy father to a tee.

One day her mother beat her with a club, and Ru-hua turned on her to bite her. She set her teeth between her mother's thumb and index finger, lightly, like a bird pecking. But the wound was swollen for more than a month. Later on, the mother checked Ru-hua's teeth and found them to be odd—sharp and extremely small, unlike any ordinary human teeth. The mother tried several times to knock out some of her teeth while the daughter was asleep. Once she had even raised the hammer, but Ru-hua had opened her eyes and stared at her sneeringly. So, she had pretended to be asleep all the time, laughing at her in private?

When her husband had started living with the cigarette seller, the mother had pretended to ignore them to prevent her daughter from finding out. One day when she passed by the cigarette seller's house, she heard laughing and merry talk. Peeping through a crack in the door, she saw the father and daughter having tea. But in her family, no one had ever drunk tea. Several dishes stood on the table, and a huge mirror reflected the terrifying light.

The man laughed so hard that saliva dribbled from his mouth. His two thin hemplike legs rubbed against the old cigarette seller's strong hairy ones. The daughter was also laughing like a fool, holding her belly in an affected way. The cigarette seller was as old and wrinkled as a dead tree. Her teeth were black from heavy smoking. Only a lunatic would take a fancy to some rubbish like this. But her husband was an out-and-out madman, and now he had passed his madness on to his daughter.

"A couple of buffoons," she muttered between her teeth, feeling as if she had swallowed maggots.

Hardly had the daughter grown up when she started to treat her mother like a deadly enemy. The girl committed all kinds of outrages trying to get on her mother's nerves. At the same time, she put on an apathetic air to hide her own happiness. She was once attacked by pneumonia. Believing that the girl would no doubt meet her doom, the mother considered this a good chance for revenge. But she had rejoiced too soon.

"Oh, Mom," the daughter said, affecting sweetness. "Why should you bother to come to see me? I'm OK, far from death. Set your mind at rest. Just think, how can people like me die so easily?"

Not long ago it came to her that she should make an alliance with the son-in-law to deal with her daughter. With her plan in mind, she waited and waited at the wall of the public toilet until he came, still looking idiotic. Rushing forward, she grabbed his sleeve and started her tirade with something like, "Fellow sufferers should commiserate with each other"; "friendless and wretched" she declared herself; "needed drastic measures for self-defense," and so on. "In my heart I've always considered you my own son, and I worry about your life even in my dreams," she flattered him. And he, rolling his dull and heavy eyeballs, couldn't understand a word she was saying. "A real idiot," she thought.

At last, he seemed to have made up his mind. Scowling, he jerked himself from her clutches and asked in a hoarse voice, "Hey, who're you? I don't remember seeing you before. You want to murder me for my money? You've made a big mistake then. My mother is really something. I'll call her here to teach you a lesson!"

"But you're my son-in-law!"

"You can't trick me! I'm not your so-called son-in-law. You've stopped me on the street and glared at me maliciously. What do you want? If you go on with your bullying, I'll tell my mother and let her show you something new!" As he spoke he fled so fast that no one could have caught him.

Her husband's legs became as thin as hemp. Long ago, he was a tall man with a ruddy face. However, he had a dream one day in which the canna outside the window blossomed crazily, and the sun was both high and remote. Suddenly, he was stung by something and awoke in pain. He saw his wife sucking at his leg like a cat eating meat. Her tongue was covered with thorns, which had stung him painfully in his dream. He tried to withdraw his leg, but she held it with sheer animal strength. She was biting with force, as though she wanted to tear off the whole muscle and swallow it. In despair, he tried to relax, closing his eyes and putting up with the nausea. He didn't expect that the attack would be further intensified. Every morning he found his body black and blue, sometimes even badly swollen. He got thinner day by day, his muscles vanishing and his lymph nodes swelling into lumps the size of pigeon eggs. He suspected she had been devouring his muscles while he slept because she was getting heavier.

"You, why should you eat my flesh?" he asked.

"Bah!" she yelled. "Snob! Schemer! Good heavens!"

She never washed her hair. He was revolted by the stink. But one day when she finally did wash it, clumps of filth and hair fell into the basin. All of her hair peeled off. She asked him to pour water over her head, but his hands shook so badly that the ladle dropped to the ground. Jumping up, she cursed him with all her vulgar language. With her head red and bald, she chased him and poured a whole pail of cold water over him. The following week he lay in bed with a high fever. Holding his head, he screamed that someone would peel off his scalp and his brains would show if the scalp were gone. After his recovery, he escaped to the old woman at the cigarette stand. She smelled like sunflower seeds. In her huge dark bedroom he felt secure. At the start his wife came to look for him, peeping in through the window lattice and banging loudly at the door.

"Has your mom's hair grown out?" he used to ask Ru-hua when she was young.

"No. Haven't you seen her in her scarf? Every night I see her massage her scalp. She's forever scared of catching a cold. She might die." Thus Ru-hua gave her childish analysis.

"Poor thing." After some thought, he said in a frightened tone, "She might be plotting revenge?"

"Yesterday I bit her lightly."

He gave a shocked exclamation. Stretching out his hand, he stroked her hair like a sleepwalker. "Your hair is firmly rooted. You should wash it regularly," he said. "Have you ever seen the ceiling open up in your sleep?"

"The ceiling?"

"Yeah, ceiling. The house is huge and old. The wall often echoes with the noise of people fighting. When you're asleep, the ceiling might break open unexpectedly and human heads as tiny as snake heads come down. . . . Of course, I'm teasing you. Are you scared? I love to tell you thrilling stories."

Later he didn't recognize Ru-hua when they met in the street, but walked right past her. When his colleagues told him that, he felt baffled. Ru-hua was going to get married. He thought she must be crazy or must have been taken in by vicious people. The child had been weak-willed from birth. Like her father, she had always been sluggish. The prospective son-in-law was a hooligan and an idiot. The first day of the relationship he came, driven by his own fantasy, to blackmail his father-in-law by asking him to bear all the costs.

"So you're a big turtle," Ru-hua's father said in a slow, dignified way.

"What did you say?" The idiot was scratching his head.

"I said you're a big turtle! My daughter has affairs with every man! Do you understand?" He pressed toward him. "Beat it!"

The son-in-law was frightened out of his wits, and his mind went blank. Still, with his eyes rolling, he threatened to break the engagement if he had to pay all the expenses. Ru-hua's father could hardly wait until he left to start laughing. He rolled on the bed three times in his mad laughter.

He met this son-in-law every now and then. Each meeting started with the young man demanding money and ended with him leaving empty-handed after the ridicule of the older man. However, the fellow was foolish enough to keep his fantasy alive, and his attitude was always unaccountably bold and assured.

"You have to give me some money." The old trick started again.

"I won't." The father cast him a sidelong glance.

"You're behaving like a hoodlum."

"What? You beg money from a hoodlum?"

"You're her father. You have to give me money."

"I'm nothing but a hoodlum, so I simply refuse."

"I curse you to die immediately."

Every time, the son-in-law was beside himself with rage. It seemed he had a violent personality.

As soon as the son-in-law abandoned his family, the father ran to his daughter and asked her, "Why do you think he married you?"

"I don't know." She gazed at him cautiously. "According to him, he wanted to set up a grape trellis. I'm afraid he was tricking me."

"Pah! He married you to murder me! The one he settled on is me, the old man, not you, definitely not you! He mistook me for a boss with hidden treasure. He circled around my house, stamping his feet restlessly even after I was asleep. I know he lied to you about getting up in the night to pee. How could you be so self-confident as to get married? He waited for eight years, but never had a chance. He's left because he ran out of patience."

"You could be mistaken, too," she jeered at him. "I don't think he had any illusions about your money. But your present wife—I've seen her flirting with him. Is this beyond your expectations?"

"Mere rubbish!" Feeling taken in, he turned red in the face. "You jump to conclusions. I was thinking about your mother on my way here. She's said to have dug a hole in the wall to stuff dead sparrows in every day! Something sobs all the time in her yard. I hear the crying every time I pass by. She's evil." He was always ready to gossip about his ex-wife and felt refreshed by doing so.

"You used to say you were taken in by my mother. But how can I believe it? It's too ridiculous. People say you want to cheat her out of her private savings. Nasty, isn't it? I don't believe such slander at all. It's an interesting question, why you married her." She behaved like an outsider, making him feel as if a worm were gnawing at his gums.

He was vexed. He had meant to provoke his daughter into talking about the son-in-law so he could feel the intoxication of self-satisfaction for a while. But now he was being slandered to his face, and the talk had run out of control. Recently she had become swift as a snake. An old man with slow wits like his had no hope to win.

"He often comes to spy on me, hoping to sniff out my hidden treasure." He refused to give up.

"I dreamed of you turning into a sparrow, twittering endlessly. Why should he talk about the grape trellis all the time? It's only a monstrous lie, and so is what you're telling me. You two must get along well."

The room was dim. Some tiny creature rustled at the foot of the wall and on the beams overhead. Five or six moths on the wall flew up suddenly, circling around, scattering their poisonous powder, making him shiver all over. The daughter wrapped the naked upper part of her body in a ragged blanket and paced the room quickly. The blanket flapped up and down. She looked frightened.

Suddenly he felt at his wit's end. Murmuring "I must be going," he flung himself out the door and ran all the way to the wall at the corner. Turning his head, he saw the door again shut tight. A black figure sneaked out from behind the house and hid behind the tree. He saw it was his ex-wife. The window curtain shook a bit, then everything was quiet.

Ru-hua heard somebody moving the tiles of the roof—"creak, creak"–a ghostly, terrifying sound. Peeking out through a crack in her curtains, she saw her mother's short, heavy figure, standing on tiptoe playing this trick with a bamboo pole.

"Toot your own horn?" Her mother gave a contemptuous snort. "Answer me clearly, understand?" she wheezed, puffing with exertion.

The daughter paced back and forth in the room, checking every iron bar. The clanging became louder and sharper. Several tiles fell and shattered. Lately the mother had thrown all restraint to the winds. The night before she had dug a hole in the roof. She threatened to peel off the tiles and freeze her daughter to death in order to slake her own hearty hatred. She stuffed anything she picked up—from worms to stale fish to rotten shrimp—into the cracks in the wall.

When the father came, he examined the roof and said maliciously, "Can the big tree crash down on the house when it's windy? Yesterday your hooligan came to me again telling me he couldn't wait for your death so he might get rich. He has often come for heart-to-heart talks with me, from the very beginning. You don't believe me, thinking I'm tricking you. You're too conceited. He has even offered to make friends with me, of course hoping to get money by using me as a go-between to deal with you. After serious consideration, I have decided to agree. But he can't expect to get anything from me. He's no rival of mine. Just like you, your hooligan is utterly aloof and conceited. But he's so foolish, almost an idiot. He keeps slandering you. . . . "

Once he started there was no end to his rattling on, standing up, sitting down, standing up, sitting down, scratching his butt, scratching his back, as if numerous flies were biting him.

She stopped him short by teasing him, "So you know the old woman who sells rat poison?"

"Why should I?" He was distracted again.

"Nothing, I'm just joking." She fixed her eyes on the ceiling, pretending to observe the spiderwebs.

"Oh!" It suddenly dawned on him. "The big tree at the doorway will crash down on your house. Everybody says so."

THREE

1

She heard the dry leaves rustle and drop to the roof and then to the ground. She heard the reeds in her body crackle and explode. She hadn't moved her bowels for a week. Everything she had eaten seemed to have changed into sticks and straw, making lumps and protrusions in the skin of her belly. She poured some water from the glass jar on the table. She had to drink enough to keep the reeds from bursting into flames and burning her alive. As she opened her mouth, a burning smell poured forth. As she exhaled, she gave out smoke and sparks.

"Drink some water," the dark shadow said outside her window.

She gulped down the whole jar of water before she opened the door. The shadow drifted in with the fragrance of sunflowers.

"You smell of sunflowers." She had her back to him.

"That's right. I was just now thinking about something far away. On the long stretch of hill murmurs a stream. My body smells of sunflowers only because I've been thinking of these things. Your smelling it is also a fantasy. It's not real."

"I have to keep drinking, otherwise I'll be burned to death." She filled the glass jar and put it on the table again. "There must be something wrong inside my body."

"I've given up." He felt embarrassed. "You guessed right. I'm nothing after all. I sneak here and there along the wall peeing in my pants. Sometimes when it's getting dark and my shadow stretches longer and longer on the ground, I cry out."

"That's better." She looked at him intently and tenderly. His image blurred in her eyes. "See how cool I am. I never get worked up by the outside world. My annoyance is different. My body's not functioning properly. I have to drink constantly. It's annoying. In the sun outside, there's a place where cicadas sing on the tree, dull and peaceful. It's autumn already. Can the forest get so dry that it burns?"

"Even though you sealed the wall with strips of paper, I can still hear the weeds crackling in your body. You said you haven't had a bowel movement for a week. Is that true?"

"Not only that. I no longer sweat either. I used to get up from the bed soaking with sweat. The little cricket I raised in the tile jar died yesterday. It hadn't even grown up yet. Perhaps none of the crickets in this house can grow up. I didn't notice that in the past. It's really a pity. You have a daughter. How can that be?"

"I'm surprised, too. Sitting here with my eyes closed, I can't even recall her face. You're suggesting that she can't possibly exist because I myself am so empty and adrift, right?"

"Over the forest hangs a bloodred sun, horribly red. I happened to be there and looked until my temples throbbed. Sparrows darted above me; leaves dropped constantly on my head and shoulders. Someone walked past me on the road. He spat at me in anger, his steps rumbling on the concrete."

"I was there at the same time. I was at the other side of the forest. I stood there until the sun set. Crickets were singing energetically. The grass and weeds were waving as if they were alive. My whole body was glowing. Those crickets may be the last batch."

Lying there, they heard the autumn wind skim over the roof. A child shot stones onto the tiles with a slingshot. When they heard the last tiny cricket groaning in the tile jar, they hugged each other in terror, then separated in disgust.

"Your T-shirt smells sweaty around your armpits."

"I changed it this morning."

"Maybe, but I smell it. You told me it was a sweet odor, but you were wrong. It's a sour smell. There can't be a mountain so tall that you could catch the sun even if you were at the peak. Can you be wrong about everything?"

"But I just want to tell about these things. I have to find something to say."

"True. I love talking, too. Maybe we're both wrong. Maybe we're doing it on purpose, so we have something to talk about. For instance, you came just now smelling of sunflowers. Then we talked about sunflowers which do not exist in reality. You know that."

"My father-in-law incites his daughter to steal things for his home. They think I don't know it. They just like to put on a show."

"But you don't care at all?"

"I pretend not to have seen through their tricks and act greatly annoyed. And sometimes the funny way the old man eggs my daughter on, too, makes me feel like holing up and having a good laugh. Yesterday my daughter came and said she hates her mother bitterly and could no longer tolerate her. She claimed her mother constantly put pressure on her, hid rats under her pillow, stole and burned her letters to her friends, and forced her to dress like a beggar. When she leaves the house, she said, her mother follows her, spying to see if she flirts with anybody. While my daughter feels so humiliated, the mother boasts to her colleagues that her daughter is striving for perfection and will have a bright future. My daughter also told me that all the things that disappeared from my home were stolen by her mother and her grandpa in collaboration."

"What did you say then?"

"Me? Definitely I won't be taken in! I gave her an angry stare and yelled, 'Beat it!' I scared the wits out of her. Only after a long time did she state her grievance: 'I've come to inform against others only to get shouted at.' 'Who asked you to inform against others?' I said fiercely. 'Spying on people! Learning such tricks at your young age!' She looked at me with terror, and ran away. As I expected, my wife flew into a rage that night, saying I suspected her of being a thief! I dashed into my daughter's room and searched her bed. I found a paper box containing half of the cat's tail. I threw the tail at my daughter, and she started to twitch immediately. These people are crazy."

"You make such a great show of being in earnest. Did you tell me you were standing at the other end of the forest at the same time? And you saw something?"

"When I was standing there, I saw long columns of smoke. The whole city was trembling in the red light. The sky was crackling. Something was crawling haltingly in the mud. Its back was cracked. Dark red bloodstains crimsoned the long path."

"The sky full of red light?"

"It made me dizzy. I regretted that the thing could never crawl to its destination. The smallest stones tipped it over. Where did it intend to go?"

"Where did it intend to go?" she echoed.

The wind blew open the curtain, scattering the layer of fine white dust on the table. The cold water rippled in the jar. They clung to the blanket with all their might to prevent its flying into the sky. A plane flew over, humming heavily as if it were fixed forever overhead. The wind carried the talk of two men to their ears, the voices remote at one moment and close in another.

"Everything of value is in the well at the back of the house, dear friend." A sweet voice urged, "You'll get rich overnight if you can borrow a pump. You've been waiting so long. I was scared sometimes that you might sneak in and cut off my head."

"You're completely wrong. I don't have the faintest intention of getting rich. What I want is only the part belonging to me. You're always creating purely fictitious stories for others," another voice said stiffly.

"Why not get rich? People should have ambition. When I was young, the idea of finding a gold brick lured me. Later, I was involved in grave robbing. On those nights little fir trees shouted angrily in hoarse voices, will-o'-the-wisps floated around, dark shadows haunted the graveyard. I saw the gold brick. It was shining underground. . . . All these years, every night, you drew marrow from my daughter with an injector and put it in a glass bottle full of centipedes by the bed. When my daughter took a bath, you poured the bottle into the tub. You've ruined her completely. Then you made friends with me, thinking I didn't know what was going on. In fact, she came to me every day in tears telling me your tricks. You did all that because you couldn't get money from me, right?"

"I'm going to tell my mother your slanders against me and let her teach you a lesson. She's not a woman to be trifled with. The water she spits out every night could drown you. Your whole family are conspirators. Your daughter was mad long before the marriage. I was too honest to see through it. Bah! Just think, for eight years she's been secretly raising crickets and centipedes in the house. How disgusting! For eight years I lived day and night in horror, buying insecticide constantly to fight these poisonous insects. I was on the verge of a mental breakdown. Eight years of youth! The best time in one's life! My god! Now you can go and see for yourself. It's nothing but an insect nest. Just stay there overnight—the insects will eat you to the bone."

"Don't make me laugh! 'Eight years of youth'? 'The best time'? . . . Who are you putting on these scenes for? Aren't you ashamed? My daughter exposes you every night. She even wakes up at midnight complaining of your crimes. You'd be scared to death by nightmares if I told you what she's told me."

The footsteps of the two men receded and finally died out. Two big flies zoomed into the mosquito net, circling around, trying to sting their faces. All efforts to drive them away were in vain. He stood up, depressed, with his sweaty back toward her, and started to pull on his T-shirt. It was wrinkled, and a spotted moth was stuck to it. In fear he shook it with force, and the moth dropped to the floor. Fixing her eyes on his narrow, sweaty back, she imagined her own glance as a moth. She hiccuped twice in discomfort, picked up the jar, and drank her fill. When she put it down, she heard his footsteps already on the doorsteps. The pillow he slept on had a semicircular hollow. She sniffed it. It smelled of sweat. Tossing the pillow into the corner of the room, she lay down to sleep again.

Someone peed in the sewer at the back of the house. The water splashed down noisily, long and brazen. She went to the window and looked out. She saw the T-shirt. He was buttoning his trousers as though nothing had happened. He blew his nose. Jumping aside, she hid. She could hear him yawning, and saw that the threads in his T-shirt were broken, exposing the black hair in his armpits. Then she closed her eyes, trying to sink deep into a warm reverie. In all of her mind-pictures, there was always a mature man in a tweed overcoat who made touching remarks, generously and tenderly, until her ears hummed.

It was dusk. The setting sun shone weakly on the windowpane where many tiny insects were crawling as though assembling for a meeting. Far away a funeral procession marched on; an old woman howled oddly in prolonged tones, a bad imitation of sorrow. In the dusk, numerous tiny voices resounded, disturbing, upsetting. Following all this, there was the coming of the gigantic, irresistible destruction. Once in the past at dusk she had tried to hum a tune, but it froze on her lips like icicles.

She opened her eyes, glanced over the room, and felt the firmness of the iron bars. She called "Hey!" to the neighbor. He turned around and observed the woman behind the dusty window for a long time. The hint of a confident sneer flowed over her lips. Moths fluttered down from the ceiling in terror, only to be struck to the floor by the blanket putting up its deathbed struggle. Stopping to gasp for breath, she noticed many ulcerated tongues in the mirror on the wardrobe. She was almost afraid of the dim light of the setting sun on the windowpane, the yellow strip, provoking to her eyes. She covered the glass with a dark blanket, but scattered light still penetrated.

"Today I don't have any appetite for stewed ribs. Can't you find something new? For example, fried turnips with peppers or something else?" the man next door said.

"You can never get enough stewed ribs," the woman replied in a sarcastic tone. "It'll be delicious if more meat is added. I just can't imagine how you can dislike stewed ribs. Only crazy people think like that. You poor thing, you might be delirious."

2

She lifted a corner of the curtain and peeped gloomily at the people outside. Then she felt the iron bars and made a face at them before letting down the curtain. "Only when the sun rises in the west!" she shouted in provocation from her room.

The four outside were stunned. They leaped to bang on the door, shaking the whole room. As if by agreement they stopped at the same time and looked at each other.

"We can't contend with her." After a long silence, Old Kuang said dispiritedly, "All the doors and windows are iron-barred. She urged me to do that. So she had her mean intentions long ago. She was tricking me all the time."

She hobbled ahead of him. Because of her trouble with eliminating water, her body had become extremely heavy; her skin was stretched so tight that it was difficult for her to move her hands or legs. She kept taking diuretics despite the doctor's constant warning about taking them too often. She took some pills even this morning because she felt uncomfortable.

He tried to catch up with her, his stemlike legs trembling. His slight shadow first overlapped with, then separated from her huge, dark shadow. He could tell what pain her dropsy caused her. She was so overcome with emotion that her aged, pale face quivered.

"So she has tricked us all," he started to say when they were walking abreast. "What a historical misunderstanding. She's certainly given us a head-on blow."

Surprised, she was about to stop, but then she changed her mind and continued walking silently with him.

"What do you think? Isn't it humiliating? What would others think? What would become of our reputation? I've never dreamed of that. Now everything's gone, eh?" He rubbed his chest with malicious delight.

"I'm going to destroy that little house." She spoke each word through clenched teeth. He could smell the peculiar odor of her decrepit body.

"We must stick together," he declared without hesitation. Stealing a glance around, he chattered in a mysterious tone. "First of all, make clear her intention. What causes her to shut herself in the room, cut off from the outside world? This is a subtle matter. I have some clues pointing toward the hooligan son-in-law. You might also have noticed that every night he wanders along the street, collecting sputum left by passersby into a briefcase he has with him. One day in an argument with me he threatened to drown me with the sputum he had collected! I could never sleep well after that. My legs felt cramped all the time."

She glanced at him with a touch of warmth, yet every wrinkle in her face embodied gloom. Panting, she raised her stone-heavy legs with difficulty, her lips twisted with pain. "I resemble a piece of rotten meat steeped in dirty water."

Stepping into the dusty old house, they heard chunks of lime drop in every room. Rats scuttled about as if in a race. He sat down in the cane chair as he used to do. Hardly had he touched the chair when the alarm clock jangled twelve times with a prolonged and empty sound.

"The clock is cheating all the time now," she said, grinning grimly. "Everything in this house is against me. One day I opened the window only to have the wind bring in the smell of moss from the wall. Now every piece of furniture smells of moss. When the setting sun shines in the yard, I nail sparrows to the wall. The job is far from easy: feathers fly everywhere. What did you say just now? What's her trick for? Let me tell you, her target is only me. She intends to destroy my reputation exactly the way she dreamed, day and night. Nobody can guess her intentions except me. When I stood outside the window, she was inside her mosquito net grinding her teeth in hatred. Once she bit me, you remember? I almost died. If you're thinking of eating with me, I've stopped cooking for a long time now. I just eat instant noodles. They say my dropsy is caused by lack of vitamins. I used to be strong and healthy enough to compete with her to the end. But now I've collapsed because of her new trick. Have you noticed the black spots on my face? I can't live much longer. If there's thunder tonight, I'll go look at the tree . . . "

A heavy, muffled roar from beneath the rotten floor shook the dust. He jumped from his chair. His face turned pale, his voice choked in his throat.

"Wh . . . what sound was that?"

"The millstone," she replied in a low voice. "A huge, ghastly monster, grinding day and night, milling everything to pieces. Don't be afraid. You'll get used to it. See these rats? They've become accustomed to it."

It was already afternoon. The room was getting dim. Their

voices were hoarse from talking so much. Their faces were also becoming dim, as if cut off at the neck and floating in the air. The clock on the wall chimed every half hour. Their thought was disrupted by the sound and only restarted with great effort. At last, they became silent within their disturbed minds. Their heads hung down, heavy as rocks. Just at that moment, a sparrow shot in through a hole in the rotted window screen. It made a half circle in the room before gliding under the bed with a furtive sound.

"Every day sparrows squeeze in through that hole. My mother's crematory jar is under the bed." Her voice quivered, and she breathed out in relief as if she were about to stand up and look for something.

"Sparrows sneaking into the room! How can you tolerate such preposterous things? You have horrifying things everywhere! Millstones! Sparrows! Is there a wandering corpse? And you've survived until now? It all gives me goosebumps."

"Yesterday I peed in an old wineglass, then threw in two bugs. As a result, I hiccuped all night." Smiling, she sank into reminiscence.

He jumped up like a dog bitten by fleas and ran away with faltering steps. "You should die!" he shouted back.

The huge millstones started to turn. A frozen smile came to the old woman's face.

"Mother, great misfortune is coming to us!"

She fixed her eyes on him. Her glance thrust through him like a pair of awls. The doves were cooing. Bits of cotton from the cotton-fluffing factory flew past the window like swarms of moths. In scorn, she picked up the sputum box and spat into it with force. "I used to be a little girl."

"Yes, Mother."

"I had a tumor in my chest for ten years. Recently an abscess has developed in the tumor, giving me fits of pain. I feel so sick when you talk to me because my nerves lose balance. Don't speak to me rashly; it's very harmful to my health. I suggest that we nail up the middle door and use separate exits. What do you think? That way we can avoid disturbing each other and keep our inner peace."

"Yes, Mother."

He left, his shoulders hunched. She saw the end of his belt droop from under his jacket.

One night not long before, she was dreaming of catching locusts when she was awakened by a sudden thunder in her dreams. Turning on the lamp, she heard the second, then the third. With a padded jacket draped over her shoulders, she headed to her son's room. He was curled up like a meatball, and the thunder came from the trembling meatball itself: rumbling, rumbling.

All night, she paced to and fro on the cinder path outside the window. Under her feet the cinders crunched; in her chest something groaned with anger.

"Who's that?" A blind fortuneteller raised her hollow dark eyes.

"A spirit," she said in anger.

The thunder didn't die down until dawn.

However, the whole thing continued the second night, starting with the dream of locusts, followed by the awakening . . .

She swept into her son's room with long strides and poked him awake violently.

"What a heavy rain, Mother," he said half awake. "I was catching locusts in the fields when thunder came and then the heavy rain."

Dumbstruck, she listened to his dream-talk. Glancing at the door joining the two rooms, she suddenly realized that the dream had entered her room, then her body, through that door.

From that day on, the door became her secret anxiety.

Putting his ear to the crack in the door, he listened carefully to what was going on in the next room.

The evening after the door was nailed up, the white-haired beggar came. He stuck one hand into his bosom to catch lice and shouted, "Why is this room so stifling?" Then he glared at the son, made three deep bows, and sat down at the bedside. "Tonight I'll sleep here," he said, taking off his shoes at the same time. His body smelled of rats.

"Mother! Mother!" the son called in a low voice, seized with fear. He circled around and around in the room, but the door had been nailed shut. He muttered complaints the whole night. Since the bed was so narrow, the smelly feet of the old man often reached to his mouth. Lice attacked him ceaselessly.

"Why don't you turn off the light?" His mother cleared her throat magisterially next door.

"Mother, there's a man . . . "

The old man suddenly gave him such a kick in his vitals that he almost passed out from the pain.

He heard his mother curse venomously, then snore loudly. That night she must have slept deeply. She didn't make a sound when the blind fortuneteller came and knocked at the window.

But the son didn't manage to have any dreams at all. The yellow light shone on the old man's face. His long white hair stuck out like arrows. His face was ferocious and savage. He crowded the son to the edge of the bed and gripped him with his thin, withered legs. Gray scales from the old man's body could be found everywhere. The room contained a secret evil under the yellow light. Before dawn, the old man got up and hobbled out.

"Mother! Mother!" The son drummed on the door, his voice as weak and soft as an infant's.

When the sun sank below the tile roof, the wind carried disturbing funeral music, and the old man came again. He still had his long ragged bag. He sat on the bed and took off his shoes as soon as he entered the room.

The bag was moving mysteriously.

"What's inside?"

"A cobra."

All the crazy, horrifying night, the cobra popped its head out of the bag.

Wrapping himself with a blanket, the son waited all night by the door leading to the other room. Boils as big as rice grains erupted in his nostrils.

"We can't fight her." Circling to the other side of the door, he pulled at his mother's sleeve and begged, "She'll work miracles. All the doors are iron barred. I put them up myself."

"Bah!" His mother spat into the sputum box and banged the door shut in his face.

Now she could sleep deeply every night, leaving her son alone catching locusts on the other side of the wall.

The night when the thunder came, he was standing outside the little house under the paper mulberry tree, his old cloth umbrella in hand. It was dead dark inside, but heavy panting could be heard from outside the window. The panting reminded him of the smoking chimney. He climbed up to the window and peeped in. In a flash of lightning, he saw her drinking water from the glass jar, her face upturned, two columns of dense smoke spinning out from her flared nostrils.

"Is that a huge spider on the window?" she asked in a mocking tone. Then she started to hum a strange tune, again and again, prolonged and dull, always about a blind white cat without whiskers who bit the thumb off a baby, blood dripping down too horrible to look at.

"Why don't you turn off the light?"

"I'm frightened, Mother."

"I thought the room was on fire when I saw light leaking through the crack. Pay attention to your soul."

"Don't abandon me, Mother. I'm crawling and crawling in the field. Locusts bite me so hard that my legs are full of holes."

3

He threw the whole pot of stewed spareribs on the entrance steps. Mu-lan had set the table and called him for lunch. He went over in silence, picked up the earthenware pot, and threw the ribs on the steps with a splat. The whole action was neat and tidy.

He sat down and stared back at the sneering glance of his wife, feeling sick to his stomach.

"A dead sparrow dropped onto the ceiling from the hole in the roof next door. How can a sparrow die without anyone shooting it?" she said absentmindedly.

She left the room just before Ma Lao-wu came in smiling.

"No more insecticide," Shan-wu said in a hurry.

"Is it true?" Ma glanced at him in disbelief. Then he sat down with him on the bedside as if they were on intimate terms. Ma Lao-wu whispered into his ear, "All morning I was thinking in the armchair in my room. I don't understand our relationship. You're my neighbor, friend, right? I often feel we have a kind of ancient relationship. Even before we were born it had been decided that we should be as close as lips and teeth. The first day you moved in, you looked familiar to me. That day there was a burning red cloud in the sky. When you showed up, I was chasing the ten cocks I had raised. You were in a jacket neither gray nor blue, pitiful looking. A touch of cordial feeling emerged inside me. It was as sweet as sweet paste. But you, you don't have any understanding. You think I'm bothering you? I have a tumor growing on my hipbone. Look, it's here. I know you'll gloat over my misfortune. But the doctor has told me it's harmless. I'm here to inform you lest you feel relieved. I'll be cured. The doctor has assured me. You and I are as close as lips and teeth. That was decided in my mother's belly."

Ma Lao-wu stood up and looked around distractedly, again and again, as if something were missing. Finally, he went away in a huff. As he was stepping out the door, his trousers dropped again.

His recent attacks on Shan-wu were more and more unbearable. The day before, he hugged him tightly in the street and kissed him several times with his stinking mouth. Jumping away, Ma then roared with laughter. Again he declared to the surrounding audience that he would let the cat out of the bag by telling everyone Shan-wu's personal secret.

Shan-wu was scared out of his wits, and his face turned pale. However, at this moment, Shan-wu did not feel relieved. Staring at Ma's back, he saw his trousers fall, exposing the old man's thin spindly thighs and the black hair on his ass. He was dropping his trousers on purpose. Shan-wu's stomach churned as if he'd swallowed rat poison. Instead of taking pleasure in Ma Lao-wu's misfortune, he had a fit of convulsions like a thin poisoned cat.

"Where are your glasses?" The head of the institution patted him on the shoulder and said, "Oh, so you're only killing time here! Well done, cleverly done! Comrades, just look, this is a queer social phenomenon! This guy sits here every day. How can it be? I once had a colleague who sat in the office during the day and robbed graves at night in great secrecy . . . ha!"

Old Liu sniffed at him and grumbled, shaking his head in suspicion. "Something's wrong, extremely wrong. What's the matter with this guy? Can he be suffering from epilepsy?"

Shan-wu could hear the tinkling of water poured by the woman next door and the gulping from her throat. Recalling what she'd told him about the thing she saw in the forest, he felt hot and pained all over his body. He tried hard to forget everything. He wished he could rid himself of the memory. Ma Lao-wu had beaten him down completely. When Ma's trousers dropped, Shan-wu's body twisted like an earthworm. He had heard of a disease called intestinal perforation. Could he be suffering from it?

"The old man has been sent to the hospital." Mu-lan fixed her eyes on his face and passed several muffled farts.

"Who?"

"Who else can it be? He even left word to his neighbors not to let you know about his hospitalization at any cost. They're going to cut off his leg. What's the trouble between you two? His neighbors are gossiping about how you fear him like a rat fears a cat. They're even suspicious about whether you're male. Since no eyewitness is available, there's no proof."

"I'm ill with an intestinal perforation," he said and fell to the ground in convulsions.

"How time has flown since then!" the woman's voice whispered through the crevice in the wall. "Have you noticed that all the leaves are dried up? Step on them and they crumble into powder. One rainy day, I dreamed that the tree roots were swelling and cracking. Why should it drink so hysterically? But now all the water has evaporated. The fire starts from inside. So many days without rain. Its roots have turned into red charcoal. This morning I raised the window curtain only to see blue smoke curling upward from the top of the tree. The branches were stretching wider and wider in pain. The fire was a feeble one, a negative fire which could never give off bright sparks. Yesterday Old Kuang dreamed about the grape trellis under the tree. I smell his odor when he comes, and I can guess his dreams. He's so annoyed by this."

"If only we wait some more, what's going to happen?" He refuted her in his mind.

"Ma Lao-wu is going to become a meatball." His wife's voice buzzed like a fly. "Just imagine that lump rolling on the ground, here and there, up and down. Why should you be afraid of him?"

"See how tight my doors and windows are shut! I'm safe now! They've come every night, but what can they do? They can only pace back and forth outside the window in vain, planning evil schemes which can never come to anything. My heart starts to thump in my chest when the sun comes up. I cover the room tightly with a curtain. They say I'm a rat and so I am. I love to hide in a dark corner chewing the furniture. My teeth have been ground sharp by doing so. Old Kuang once confessed that he planned to kill me with rat poison. He could only think about it, but could never gather enough strength to do it. He's nothing but a fat roundworm. I see him sneak into his mother's intestine and hold on there comfortably. Some day she might shit him out. It's hideous to think of him being squeezed out through his mother's anus."

Her voice got weaker day by day, but the ragged blanket screamed more and more ferociously.

Raising her head, Mu-lan pretended to listen. Then she puffed out a breath and said, "The woman is done for. It's surprising that she can manage not to give out any sound from morning till night. Even by putting my ear to the wall I can't hear the faintest sound. It's been like this for a long time. Several times I thought she was finished, but the light came on at midnight. But did you notice that the light didn't shine last night?"

"You should put this down in your notebook."

"What do you mean?"

"What do I mean? I can't remember the meaning of what I intended to say. As a result, I said something I don't understand myself. I'm always thinking of something irrelevant. Take just now. I was wondering if we should build a cistern at the back of the house to raise some fish in. I was also wondering if the wall would crack open and some snake heads pop out. I get so entangled in all these thoughts that I'm worn out with neurosis. When you're deep in sleep, I still listen to the chewing sound of the worms in the closet. The sound never stops, day or night."

As soon as the wife was out of sight, the red nose of the father-in-law poked in the window. Of course, they had ganged up.

"You think I'm acting in collaboration with her?" He wrinkled his nose in a funny way. "You're wrong, my son-in-law. I hate her to death. Whenever you argue, I wish you would kill her. I lie behind the door secretly cheering for you. But you never dare. You're a coward. When I come back to get something, she yells at me. She calls me a thief. You don't see the reality. She always stands in my way when I take something from here, forcing me to go fifty-fifty with her and pay her in cash according to the price. We once argued, and she pushed my head into the mud. She has many lovers, whom she takes to my home to sleep with her. She forces me, an old man, to stand guard for her, in rain or snow. She never has any pity on me when I'm soaked with rain. And talking about you, I've seen everything from upstairs in the temple. Nothing can escape my seasoned old eyes. For example, I know your rankling anxiety like the back of my hand. The most fearful figure to you is Ma Lao-wu. He always makes a scene with you on the street . . ."

"I want to kill you!" He suddenly jumped up and grabbed the old man's collar, his eyes in a fixed stare.

"Hush. What's the matter? Eh?" The old man shook off the son-in-law's grip. "Excuse me, but I must be moving on. What am I chattering for? What can you expect from an idiot?"

At midnight the two spirits returned, pacing up and down in the moonlight, cracking the dried leaves under foot. Shan-wu could hear their tired whispers from inside the window.

"On my way here, one of my legs sank into a deep muddy pit. I pulled hard but in vain. Something bit me right on the calf like a needle prick. The nest of new rats has grown up. Can you hear them scurrying around? We're just like two wolves in the wilderness, aren't we?"

"Just now, I could hardly get out of bed. Couldn't raise my legs. The diuretic makes me suffer so much. These days and nights I can hear the mad striking of the clock on the wall every half hour. Now its wheels are rusted and will lock up. But its last struggle is frightening."

"The same with me. I didn't go to sleep yesterday either. I've been waiting for something to happen. I saw icicles hanging in the night air. A cat sighed like a human being at the corner. Numerous thieves were sneaking around outside the window. Strange, how can I live so long? Didn't we collapse long ago?"

"Do you know how my hair fell out? That autumn it was so rainy, so wet everywhere. I was reading newspapers in the rocking chair when my daughter sneaked in like a cat. I shivered with cold as if I had an ominous presentiment. At that moment, she jumped up and pecked on my head as fast as lightning before she fled. From that day on, my hair dropped out in bunches, the whole scalp died. Touch the tree. It's hot as fire . . . right. The whole disaster started that fall. The paint on all the chairs melted. Whenever we sat down, our clothes stuck to them. Our feet are always sweaty. Our shoes are cold and damp. My whole body shivers when I put them on."

The two were groaning, tramping the ground in pain.

Shan-wu was having convulsions in bed, the bed sheet whipping his bare back. He had learned to wriggle like a snake.

In the morning, his whole body was tight and swollen, stiff and uncomfortable.

4

Ru-hua's mother found that one of her legs refused to move, as if it were nailed to the bed. The day before, when she went for a bath with a bottle of boiling water, she fell on the cement floor as soon as she entered the bathroom. The floor was slippery from not being cleaned for years. Immediately she heard a cracking sound in her left leg like breaking porcelain. It was a faint sound, but she heard it. Pulling herself up with her hands, she crawled back to her bedroom and collapsed on the bed in her sticky rotten-smelling clothes. Now death had started from her wounded leg. She was waiting, watching it extend upward in her body. Sparrows were sneaking in one after another through the hole in the window screen and flying about wildly in the dim light. She searched for the pillows on the bed with her hands, which were still movable, to throw at those bewitched little things. It might be sunny outside. Weren't the tiles on the roof snapping in the heat? The millstones gave out hollow dry noises from underneath. She would die on a sunny day and her death would be as dark as this ghastly old house. She would finally melt into the old house. The old wall clock had chimed for the final time the night before. It was such a crazy, chaotic sound. The inner parts of the clock exploded so unimaginably that the glass in the clock face shattered. Now it hung in eternal silence, glaring indifferently at her in bed with its ruined dead face.

Her body rotted from the wounded leg. The odor was exactly the same as the smell of the bathroom years ago. It dawned on her that death had come long ago. She tried to peel off the dirty clothes she wore when falling in the bathroom, but failed. The clothes stuck to her body, to her skin. The odor permeated her organs. The clothes would die with her. The ashjar from under the bed, cold as an icicle, propped up her back. Her mother had also died in this room. In her last days, her body had melted away gradually on this very bed. She remembered her mother's complaining about the noise of the clock, how each tick struck into her heart. Everyone had thought she was out of her mind and nobody paid any attention to what she was saying. She died of a broken heart. The grudging expression on her face stuck in her mind.

She wanted to cry, but her tear glands were blocked. As a result, an odd sound resembling a kitten's mew came from her throat. She had long ago forgotten how to cry. The previous night, she and her ex-husband had suddenly jumped up and butted their heads against the trunk of the tree. They both fell to the ground. The light in their daughter's room went on. It was a queer soy sauce color. From the crack in the dark curtain, they saw her naked, mummy-like body. Her grayish white skin bore green splotches from which long hairs grew.

"Two hungry wolves outside," Ru-hua said in scorn. "The child is done for. The blind cat finally broke his neck."

> That was a sad, sad day.
> Fragile honeysuckles floated to the ground
> thick and fast . . .

As soon as Ru-hua stopped, her lips froze, white frost grew in her eyebrows. She lit a match and kissed the flame; her mouth puffed out cold white vapor. Then the flame died out; she felt colder, her whole body stiff. She found a bunch of papers, piled them on the floor and set fire to them with a match. The flame licked her chest and back. As the flame lept higher and higher, her body grew soft and flexible, her skin turned rosy red, and her nostrils gave out smoke and sparks. Her eyes burned with fire, wide open in terror.

When the flame almost touched the ceiling, the mother saw in the swaying light her ex-husband melt like wax, becoming shorter and shorter, his head strained in spasms and hiccuping miserably. His eyeballs shrank into two tiny white spots.

"My brain vessel is breaking . . . " he groaned pitifully, vomiting something black.

The mother's bald scalp was itching. She scratched it with force until it bled. She couldn't forget how she had lost her hair. That wet autumn, the dried leaves in the trees were as red as blood. Black water oozed out of the walls. She was sitting in the rocking chair in a constant state of anxiety . . . but the millstones rolled again, dry and irritating. The plaster was shaken from the walls. Two terrified sparrows crashed against the ceiling and fell down like rage. The ashjar under the bed trembled. The troubled dead tossed inside. Something dropped between the grinding stones with a weak cracking sound like a faint sob swallowed quickly by a ruthless voice.

On the street, her ex-husband followed her closely and watched her repeatedly with his tricky eyes. He said heavily, "See how we've gotten on in years."

She struggled to focus on his punctured hat from behind her swollen, narrowed eyelids and replied, "Do you remember how long we've been living?" She shivered all over.

"I remember nothing. My brain stopped working long ago. These days the dried leaves outside the window simply refuse to let me go. They rustle, rustle. How long have we been living?"

"I dreamed something. Something to do with that rainy day . . . I slipped as soon as I stepped down the stairs."

Her glances swung back and forth like a kite drifting over his face. The sun was high in the sky. The light was so strong that she lost her last strength and the kite returned to her eye socket.

"I see only darkness," she complained, holding to the electric pole. "I will go blind soon. I truly regret having used them too much."

"Who?" He was stunned.

"My eyes."

"Maybe the day will come when you can go out into the yard. It will be a drizzling day. A cat will be sobbing sadly, crouching at the corner. You'll say, 'That's enough.' OK, everything will end. You'll return to your room and go to sleep immediately."

A train sped past in the distance, giving a prolonged whistle. Then came the scratching sound of the wheels on the rails, one car after another, one car after another . . .

"How can you be so confident?" She was annoyed. "On the contrary, there will never be any ending. They're right in my nerves, packed together tightly. They only leak out a little in nightmares. I can't remember how long it's been, but nothing will end. X rays show my kidneys full of pebbles. Whenever I bend over, there's a crashing sound."

He puckered his mouth as if he were going to cry. "Oh, till the death! Till the death!" He sighed in despair. "Rustling, rustling . . . my dream is full of that voice. In the past, I used to hear a person pacing on the cinder road at dawn. So the man was also suffering from that fearful torture. He had to pace on till he could no longer move his legs. That will be the end. What if we live for very long?"

She hurried forward, but he was tugging at her sleeves and begging in pain, "Please say something more, say something more. My heard is aching with anxiety."

Fluid oozed from his finger joints, sticking to her sleeves like glue. More yellow mucus streamed from his nose and eyes. He sobbed and rattled on. The sun was setting from the roof of the temple; ominous winds blew in the air She could see that he didn't want to die at all, and he chattered on because of fear of death. She was surprised that he treasured his worthless life so much. His fingers twitched on her sleeves like ugly leeches.

"I can't see your face," she started.

"Go ahead, go ahead!"

"I've told you about my hair. There's one more thing that you don't know."

"Go ahead."

"About the sparrows I nailed to the wall."

"Excellent."

"In the darkness, sparrows chattered on the wall and flapped their wings. Black blood dripped from their mouths. I stretched my head out of the quilt and started throwing up. What I vomited smelled like my toilet. The moon lit the window screen. The window frames moaned in pain. Something that looked like a dog roamed the yard. All the sparrows shut up at once. In the small storeroom in the west another big piece of plaster peeled off the ceiling. A rat dashed through the house and into the kitchen."

"One night I opened your gate with a key and paced in the yard till dawn. I didn't see the sparrows because there was no moon that night. Pitch-black everywhere."

"But I was throwing up. Moonlight was shining on the screen window." She shook her head fiercely. "Did you smell something irritating?"

"It was so dark I felt as if I were being dropped into the bottom of a narrow-necked porcelain bottle. I couldn't get enough oxygen. I had to open my mouth wide like a suffocating fish."

The millstones were turning slowly, more and more ghastly, more and more murderously. The scream of the sparrows just before being ground up was concealed by the fierce, muffled, rumbling thunder.

The whole ceiling in the next room collapsed. She could smell an irritating odor of lime. A sparrow dropped onto her quilt and flopped about for some time before it died.

She could hear the crash of thunder as lightning shattered a big tree somewhere.

CONCLUSION

Even in her dreams Ru-hua smelled burning wood. She dreamed that all the cream cakes in the drawer melted into shining greasy bugs. She propped herself up to feed the female rat with the last bit of preserved meat. She threw the meat under the bed and listened to the rat chew it. Her parents hadn't come yesterday. Maybe that's why her decayed teeth ached. She threw a small piece of preserved meat under the bed every hour. The scratching sound of the rat relieved her severe nervous pain. Toward dawn, she had used up all the meat and her toothache had also quieted down. Then she remembered they hadn't come last night and was quite surprised.

At dawn lightning struck the tree. Dense smoke streamed toward the sky; red sparks glowed in the smoke. Now it lay on the ground, its trunk gutted by fire. The neighbor couple came out together, looking among the scattered branches for the mirror they used to hang on the tree. Both of them poked their rear ends toward the sky and kept their swollen faces toward the ground. They gathered up the pieces of broken mercury glass with trembling fingers.

She watched the couple from behind the curtain, hearing their stiff toes tramp the ground, seeing them hold their purple swollen fingers in their mouths, their eyes full of painful tears. Overnight the man's hair had disappeared. His pale scalp looked sickening. Even from indoors, she could still faintly smell his familiar sweaty odor, the "sweet odor," as he called it.

After she burned all the papers, there was nothing left to burn. Though there was a hot sun outside, her bones felt ice-cold. When she got up in the morning, she was frozen stiff. She had to rub her body vigorously with a towel in order to get her leg to bend. Otherwise, her body would crack like dried bamboo at every movement. She dared not exhale with force lest sharp hexagonal ice crystals form on the tip of her nose and cut her lips. The mirror at the top of the closet had been covered with a piece of black cloth because she hated to look into it.

But one day she suddenly felt that the clothes on her body were too big. Taking them off, she discovered she had become as thin as a dried fish. Her chest and belly were almost transparent. Facing the light, she saw rows of dense, fine reeds. She tapped her body with her finger. An empty "ping" resounded. Picking up the glass jar, she ladled out the remaining black water from the vat and drank it down in one gulp. She could see clearly how the fine stream of water ran from chest to abdomen and disappeared unaccountably. She hadn't urinated for more than a month.

The rat had finally abandoned the meat and dragged its heavy body to its hole. Ru-hua was trembling under the blanket like a piece of dried fish, scratching coarsely against the wool. The south wind flooded in through the crevice in the tiles. The blanket, full of wind, carried her up from the bed. They drifted on the air for a moment before banging down on the bed again. The southern wind smelled fishy, which reminded her of the image of the rabbit. They always hid deep in the bushes.

Atrophy spread through her limbs. Soon she wouldn't be able to get up at all. She realized she hadn't taken any food for two months and twenty days. Because of this, her digestive organs were disappearing. Tapping her belly, she found it was only hard and thin and transparent, containing nothing but the shadows of the reeds.

For a long time, she lost track of day and night. Instead, she divided time according to her feelings. According to her calculations, she had shut herself up in the room for three years and four months, during which time termites had eaten a whole cane chair, leaving a bunch of veins at the corners; crickets had frozen to death even without insecticide. The floor was littered with stiff corpses. Some kind of green insect had grown in the vat, and she had drunk it down with the water.

One morning, she woke up only to discover her blanket had changed into a bundle of rags. One press of her fingers turned it into ashes. For a long time, the roof had been leaking. Pretty soon a small pool formed in the middle of the room. One fine day, several small toads hopped out of the pool. Dragging her legs, which were cracking like bamboo, she circled the room observing everything carefully. Then she tied her long rat-gray hair high with a string of hemp. Opening the drawer, she found a bottle of glycerine that she had used before, and immersed each of her cracked fingers in turn till the cuts healed. Finally she got on the bed carefully and covered herself with the blanket, making up her mind never to move again. Her eyes penetrated the wall to see the man in an extremely awkward posture. Slippery green moss grew in his high overshoes. His bony toes were blue with cold and quivered madly. He was trying hard to stand steadily, but his feet slipped up and down in the huge shoes.

"Every piece is burnt . . . its patterned back gives out a peculiar sunflower smell. The sandy mud scratches its protruding eyeball. Suddenly a sky full of red light. The mud bubbles. That looks like a real ending. . . . Oh, oh, what's the matter?" Spitting blood, he toppled and fell toward the rotten leaf-covered ground.

Her vision became so profound that she saw her mother's old

dwelling. It was covered with green caterpillars. In one window screen was a big hole. Sparrows trooped in through it. A gust of south wind came. Caterpillars fell off the wall and were attacked by numerous ants on the ground. Under a worn-out bucket, there was a pair of cracked wooden slippers. On the slippers, which she had worn as a little girl, grew a row of fungus. Her father was circling in the yard, fumbling at the slippery wall, his fingers digging deep into the moss. He was suffering from cataracts. From his facial expression, she could tell he didn't know he was circling, but believed he was advancing along a straight dark path. He had been walking in the yard for three days and nights. She couldn't see her mother, but she could hear her faint sounds from beneath the ragged cotton fibers. It sounded as if her mother was chewing her own tongue and shivering with pain. When her father heard the other's groans, a smile appeared in his deep wrinkles. He walked more briskly by the wall, almost breaking into a run. His fingers bleeding, his soles were full of corns.

"Mother might die." She could hear her own voice coming from the crevice in the wall. The voice was childish, full of anxiety. "If she dies, the yard will be full of caterpillars."

But her father couldn't hear her. His ears were bewitched. He was listening to the groaning of the mother. Some remote, vague call resounded in his ears. His face lightened and the nerves of his whole body itched for something new. His white hair flew up backward in a funny way. The moss peeled off and dropped to the ground. He was still running toward the path in his imagination.

She heard the millstone grind her mother's body. Her horrifying screams split into broken pieces. The cracking sound may have been her mother's skull. The millstones turned; the corpse became a thin layer of paste, oozing slowly down the edge. When the south wind carried the bloody smell to the little room, Ru-hua could see death approaching.

"Mother . . . " She suddenly had a strange feeling in her throat and had a fantasy of calling out. She held her breath and gave out a funny, clumsy imitation.

In the yard, her father was still running while vomiting leeches.

That evening, on his way back from work, Geng Shan-wu saw the amputated Ma Lao-wu sitting on the worn-out cane chair, yelling at him with clenched fists. At night he dreamed of thistles and thorns. He fell on the thorns without a stitch of clothing on. Shivering all over, he passed into sleep.